POWERLESS

TERA LYNN CHILDS
AND TRACY DEEBS

sourcebooks
fire

For our moms,
who teach us every day
what it means to be
powerful.
And also for Cory Doctorow,
a brilliant writer who taught us
not just how to tell an exciting story,
but how to tell an important one.

Published by Sourcebooks Fire, an imprint of Sourcebooks, Inc.
P.O. Box 4410, Naperville, Illinois 60567-4410
(630) 961-3900
Fax: (630) 961-2168
www.sourcebooks.com

Library of Congress Cataloging-in-Publication data is on file with the publisher.
2014046128

Printed and bound in the United States of America.
VP 10 9 8 7 6 5 4 3 2 1

PRAISE FOR *POWERLESS*

"Childs's and Deebs's first collaboration starts out with a BANG, literally. This action-packed novel...is patently just the beginning of Kenna and gang's journey, and teens will be chomping at the bit for the next installment."

—Ingram's Youth Librarian newsletter

"Romance buffs who like star-crossed lovers will find more than one satisfying pairing to swoon over amidst the good guy/bad guy entanglements, and they'll happily return to see what Kenna does next."

—*The Bulletin of the Center for Children's Books*

"No shortage of action."

—*School Library Journal*

"This book has all the power, romance, chocolate, and plot you crave."

—Sam G., *School Library Journal* teen reviewer

ALSO BY TERA LYNN CHILDS
AND TRACY DEEBS

RELENTLESS

March 20, 1950
To: Director of Operations, Neuroscience Task Force
From: Dr. Martin Price
Subject: Early Experimental Success

Neurological capacity experiments have proven more successful than initially anticipated. Out of twenty original subjects, results are as follows:

7 fatalities
4 severe mental damage
3 seemingly unaffected
6 show signs of advanced neurological capabilities, including: telekinesis, electromagnetic charge, superior vision and hearing, psychic ability, and self-healing

Considering the breadth of powers developed within such a small test group, it is my recommendation that testing be expanded to a greater number of subjects, which would be expected to result in an even greater variety of abilities.

Ready to proceed to access phase of testing. Please advise whether experiments should continue at current or accelerated scale.

CHAPTER 1

I f I could have any superpower, right now, I'd choose the ability to reach through glass. One thin, little pane is all that separates me from bliss…of the midnight-snack variety, to be exact. The chocolate bar hangs halfway to freedom but refuses to take the plunge, as if the vending machine is mocking me, taunting me.

As if it knows I'm powerless.

Annoyed, I slam my palms against the glass. Everything inside shudders. My chocolate bar—pure Swiss milk chocolate dotted with toasted hazelnuts—doesn't budge.

"Come on," I beg as if the candy can hear me. "Just a little farther."

No such luck.

Then again, when have I ever been lucky? I'm just glad no heroes are around to see me lose a battle with a vending machine. I would be the punch line to every joke for a year.

Thankfully, the lab is pretty much empty at this time of night. Even Mom went home two hours ago, leaving me to transcribe the notes from today's sessions. I prefer to work when no one is around. My experiments fall into a gray area in the Superhero Code of Conduct, and even though I'm not technically a superhero—yet—I try not to piss off the powers-that-be. The last thing I need is to lose my lab privileges before I've perfected my formula.

Copying down Mom's scribblings is like deciphering some previously unknown ancient language. It isn't exactly the most glamorous summer job ever, but it pays okay and gives me access to the facility.

I'm almost done with tonight's transcription from the digital white board Mom and her team spent all day filling with chemical equations for her newest power-enhancing formula. Maybe twenty more minutes, and then I can get back to my test samples.

My stomach rumbles in protest, reminding me that I skipped dinner. I really want that stupid chocolate bar. But since I just used my last quarters, my only hope is that one of the security guards upstairs has change for a ten.

I turn away from the vending machine alcove and start back around the corner to grab my wallet from the lab.

Right before I make the turn, I hear hurried footsteps. Not wanting a repeat of last week's collision with Dr. Harwood—my favorite jeans still smell like sulfur—I hang back a step.

But the boy who rushes around the corner looks nothing like the balding, old scientist who works nearly as many late nights as I do.

No, this guy is tall and lean, but not too skinny. He's got major biceps and I can see the outline of some pretty impressive muscles beneath his shirt. Yum. He's probably about my age or a little older, eighteen or nineteen maybe. And everything about him is shrouded in black—his tee and jeans, his heavy-duty boots, his shoulder-length hair—everything but his eyes.

If we weren't in superhero central, I'd say he looks like a stereotypical villain.

You'd think with all that darkness, he'd be nothing more than shadow. But he's all angles: his cheekbones, his jaw, even the collarbones I can see peeking out from the low neckline of his tee. Light seems to reflect off him like moon glow at midnight. Surrounded by all that sculpted darkness, his icy blue irises burn like the hottest flames.

Our gazes collide, and though I know it's vain, I instantly wish my hair wasn't pulled back in a messy braid and that I was wearing something—*anything*—more appealing than my dad's ratty old 1996 Stanley Cup Champions tee.

Hot guys in the underground lab are few and far between— Who am I kidding? Hot guys in my *life* are few and far between—so most of my wardrobe choices involve comfort and whether I mind if the garment gets ruined by acid, dye, or any of a million other compounds we work with every day.

If my best friend, Rebel, were here, she'd be doing an I-told-you-so dance because she's been wanting to give me a makeover forever. That, and she'd already have his number and email address, and they'd be making plans for their date this weekend. Me, I can't even manage a simple "hello."

The fact that he's scowling at me, those dark brows slashing low over those bright eyes, isn't helping anything.

"The lab is supposed to be empty," he says.

His voice is flat, but his comment almost feels like an accusation.

"I'm working late," I answer, trying not to sound defensive. "What are you doing here?"

He lifts an eyebrow. "You're working in the hall?"

"I needed a break to come get chocolate," I say, gesturing at the vending machine behind me.

He nods down at my empty hands. "You don't have any chocolate."

"That thing hates me. Took my money *and* kept the candy bar."

In a graceful movement that looks almost choreographed, Dark-and-Scowly steps around me and up to the greedy machine. He presses his palms to the glass, just like I did. Hey, maybe *he* has the power to reach through glass. After all, around here pretty much everyone but me has some kind of super ability.

When his hands don't immediately sink through the surface, I say, "I tried smacking it already. Didn't work."

Moving his hands closer to the edge, he curls his fingers around the frame. Then, with his boots braced on the floor, he gives the whole machine a solid shove. The heavy hunk of metal rocks back once, then comes forward, its front legs hitting the tile floor with a sharp thud. On impact, the chocolate bar sails against the glass before falling into the trough below.

He turns to face me, a cocky smile twisting one side of his mouth. "Takes a special touch."

I duck down and reach through the hinged door to grab the candy bar.

"You're my hero," I joke.

He snorts. "Right."

I stand up, chocolate clutched safely in my hand. There's an awkward silence that stretches into uncomfortable territory. When I can't take it anymore, I wag the candy and say, "Well, thanks."

I start to walk around him, to head back to the lab, when he steps into my path.

"So, what boring work do you have to take breaks from?"

I try to sound casual, like I'm not eager to keep talking to him. "I'm transcribing notes in the manipulation lab."

As I point down the same hall he came from, he turns his head to follow the direction of my gesture. I automatically check for the mark of the League beneath his right ear. If it's there, I can't see it behind his hair. He could be a hero. Or he could be an ordinary, just like me.

Suddenly self-conscious, I tug a piece of hair forward to cover my unmarked skin.

When he looks at me again, his scowl is back in place and even deeper.

He asks, "You're working in Dr. Swift's lab?"

"She's my mom. I'm helping her out." I shrug. "There are worse summer jobs."

He gaze skims over me. "You're Kenna Swift?"

And that's the end of that.

My mom is famous in hero circles. She's developed more than a dozen different formulas for the superhero world, from sprays that thaw victims of freeze rays to supplements that keep thought-readers out of someone's mind. She's earned the League Medal of Valor three times. And those were just for the inventions they know about. She's their very own Einstein, Edison, and Jobs rolled into one.

The only thing I'm famous for is being the powerless daughter of a superhero. My dad was one of the best of the best. And I'm...nothing.

I shift my weight, wanting to redirect the conversation away from me. "You never answered my question. What are *you* doing down here so late?"

5

Those bright-blue eyes sear into me as he takes a step back. "I have to go."

His sudden evasiveness makes me suspicious, so when he starts to move past me, *I* sidestep into *his* path. "Excuse me," I say, "but this is a secure level. Are you even authorized to be down here?"

"My dad," he says, scowling at me. "He's a security guard."

A security guard? The facility might be so big that I can't keep track of everyone who works in every lab, but I know all the guards by name. Especially the night guards, since I'm usually the last one here.

Travis and Luther are on duty tonight. Travis and his wife just had their first baby, a girl named Tia. Luther is old enough to be my great-grandfather and he never married.

I take half a step back as my suspicions turn to concern. "Who's your dad?" I demand.

This guy definitely has the *look* of a villain.

What if he really *is* one?

He glances nervously over his shoulder. "He's—"

I shake my head and start to walk away before he can finish the lie.

He reaches for me, but I shrug him off. My heart is beating way too fast. This could go way bad, way quick.

"Please, just listen." He waits until I'm looking him in the eye before he continues. "You know me," he says, his voice taking on this weird, hypnotic tone. "We've met before."

His eyes start to burn brighter and brighter. *Oh crap.* He *must* be a villain, and one with a psy power. The vilest kind. Fear and anger collide inside me as I wonder what to do about him trying to mess with my head. How to play this? I can't exactly tell him I'm—

Suddenly, the floor beneath my feet shudders violently, knocking me off balance. I lurch forward into Dark-and-Scowly's arms. He catches me, grabs my upper arms, just as a concussion wave of air and sound hits us.

That sounded—and felt—like a bomb went off in the lab. If we weren't a hundred feet underground and shielded by every protection science and superheroes can create, I'd think the supervillain Quake had struck. But that's impossible.

Then again, impossible doesn't always apply in the super-hero world. After all, impossible didn't keep Dark-and-Scowly from being where he doesn't belong.

Suddenly, every alarm in the facility blares. I freak. *The lab!* All that research—Mom's and mine—is priceless. The super-hero blood samples alone are more valuable than anything else in the building.

Panic overrides judgment and I push away, but his grip only tightens. The jerk. A little super strength would be really useful right now.

"You can't go in there."

"Who are you?" I demand, struggling to get out of his grasp. If he really is a villain, I don't want him near me or this lab. Not with what villains are capable of. "What have you done?"

He doesn't answer. More pissed than ever, I fake left and pull right. He follows my fake-out, and as his hair swings with the momentum, I see the mark I'd been looking for earlier. Not under his right ear like the superheroes. Under his left.

Shit.

"You're a villain." It's not a question. I struggle harder. "What did you do? Let me go!"

"Don't!" he shouts above the roaring sirens. "If you go in there, you could get hurt. They're upset—"

I might not have superpowers, but I know how to knee a guy in the nuts. Before he can finish his sentence, he's doubled over, gasping for breath. I dash for the corner, but I don't get two steps before his hand clamps around my elbow.

"No, Kenna, you can't!" he shouts. "Trust me. If you—"

Anger overwhelms me. I've spent my whole life running from villains—from what they've done to my family. From what they *might* do to me. And I'm sick of it. I'm fed up with the whole steer-clear-of-anything-remotely-dangerous thing my mom's had me doing for so long.

Just because I don't have a power doesn't mean I'm powerless.

I turn on him with a furious growl and, using the karate-chop technique Rebel taught me, land a solid hit to the side of his neck. He releases me and I wrench open the door to the janitor's closet, use my entire body weight to shove him inside, then slam the door in his stunned face.

Holding the door handle with one hand, I use my other to dig out my security badge. I run it over the reader pad until I hear the lock engage. I leave him pounding against the door.

Who's the helpless ordinary now?

I sprint down the hall and around the corner to find the area outside the lab full of smoke. I hold my arm up to my face, covering my mouth with my sleeve as I look around.

The windows that line the wall between the lab and the hall have shattered, covering the floor with a million shards of safety glass. No ordinary bomb could have done that. Whoever that v-bag in the closet is, he obviously has help. There's another villain here. One with some kind of explosive power.

For a moment, fear paralyzes me. A villain like that killed my father, used his evil power to blow Dad up right in front of me. That same villain would have killed me if the heroes hadn't come along and stopped him. I was only four, but I remember watching my dad die. One moment he was yelling for me to run. And the next he was gone, nothing more than scorch marks on the tile.

Rage rips through me at the memory, burning away the last of my fear and sending me careening straight toward the lab. Villains have already taken my father from me. No way are they getting their disgusting paws on my mother's lab—and my research—too. Between the smoke and the strobe lights from the fire alarms, the lab looks like a better-lit version of the club Rebel always wants to go to. Or a designated disaster area.

Through the haze, I pull open the door. I know every inch of the lab by heart. Even smoke-blind, I can find my way to the emergency ventilation button.

Weaving around stools and counters, I hurry along the front edge of the room. Seconds later, my stomach connects with the counter that lines the far wall. I lean forward, tracing my fingers up the tile until I feel the big, red button.

I smack my palm against the plastic. A whooshing sound fills the lab, so powerful it almost drowns out the alarm sirens. Faster than I expect, smoke gets sucked up and out of the room through the massive vent in the middle of the ceiling. As the haze dissipates, the shadow of a figure emerges. A man stands in the back corner of the lab, facing the vault.

And the door is wide open.

I'm too late. I've failed.

"No," I whisper, terrified at what the villains might get their hands on.

I have to find a way to warn the League. Right now. The system automatically sends alerts, but there have been a number of false alarms lately. I don't want them to dismiss this as another one.

I glance around wildly and see my cell phone charging on the other side of the lab.

Using the counter to push off, I launch myself into a sprint. Only I don't take into account the stool I had pulled into the center of the room while working on the transcription earlier. I crash into it and send myself stumbling into the nearest lab table.

"What have we here?" a sneering voice asks with a crisp British accent.

I turn to the guy standing in front of the vault. Like Dark-and-Scowly, he's dressed in all black. Must be the standard-issue villain uniform these days. Except that his shock of red hair—which is currently standing on end—and the look of surprise on his face make him seem more startled-matchstick than villain-capable-of-blowing-up-the-vault.

That is, until he narrows his eyes at Dark-and-Scowly, who has somehow appeared in the blown-out doorway. I have a moment to wonder how the hell he got out of the janitor's closet before Matchstick hisses, "I thought you were supposed to take care of problems like this."

"I am," Dark-and-Scowly answers. "I've got everything under control."

The other guy snorts. "Don't look like it to me."

"You'd better go," I tell them, disappointed by the unsteady tremble in my voice. I'm still angry, but the fear is creeping back in. I'm trapped down here in this lab with two *villains*. The last time I was this close to the bad guys, my father was murdered and I…I was—

I cut off that train of thought before it can go anywhere. I'm not that helpless little girl anymore, and anyone who thinks otherwise is going to be in for a big shock.

"Leave now," I tell them. "Before it's too late."

Matchstick starts toward me. "Why is that, sweetheart?"

"The guards are coming." I steel myself for whatever comes next. "Their response time is less than thirty seconds."

He starts laughing before I finish. Smirking, he says, "Your guards aren't coming. Aren't even in the building." He steps into the center aisle. "They took an unexpected vacation."

I don't want to believe him—he's a villain, after all—but the cockiness in his tone tells me that, at the very least, *he* believes the guards are gone. Besides, it's been at least thirty seconds since the alarms started blaring. Help should be here by now.

Which means I'm on my own.

Calling the League is the only option.

I try not to think just how badly a confrontation with two villains can go as I glance at my phone, still twenty feet away, and then back at the redheaded villain. His eyes flick to the counter, and when his gaze returns to me, he's shaking his head. He can't have missed my hot-pink case against the stainless steel countertop.

Matchstick spreads his arms wide, his fingers stretched to maximum breadth, and his palms begin to glow. And I stop breathing.

This isn't going to be good.

CHAPTER 2

I freeze as the ball of energy, or whatever he's building between his hands, gets larger and brace myself for impact. There's nowhere to run. Nowhere to hide. But just as Matchstick lets loose with whatever badass concoction he's cooked up, Dark-and-Scowly hurls himself at me, full force. We go down in a tangle of limbs as a firebomb blasts right past where I'd been standing.

"Hey! Get off me!" I shove at him as hard as I can, but he's immovable. Maybe because he's about six inches taller and fifty pounds heavier than me. But, again, that's never stopped me before. I stand up to heroes twice his size all the time. Supers might think I'm weak, but I'm not.

Sometimes, being underestimated can be a real advantage.

I start to knee him in the nuts for the second time tonight, but he's ready for me. His hand clamps above my knee and holds me in place.

"Will you relax?" he demands, his voice a lot darker and surlier than it was before I took my shot at the family jewels. "I'm trying to protect you here."

Wrong thing to say, dude.

"As if I need a *villain* to take care of me? I don't think

so." I buck and roll against him, all to no avail. This guy is strong, really strong. I'm not getting up until he decides to *let* me up.

Which just pisses me off more. Everyone around me is always insisting I'm helpless, telling me that being powerless makes me vulnerable. The last thing I need is a *villain* providing a real-life demonstration.

I think about biting him, but decide against it. He is a villain after all. And a hot-looking one at that. God only knows where he's been.

Still, I need him off me. *Now.* I can't think, can't breathe. Long-buried memories well up inside me, making me panic. Making me want to scream.

I fight the anxiety, bury the dread. I can freak out later. Right now, I need to focus on how the hell I'm going to get out of this.

"Draven, what the hell is going on here?" A third guy comes careening around the corner and into the lab.

Great. *Three* vile scumbags in the lab. This night is only getting better.

Like the other two, this one is dressed all in black, but somehow he doesn't look nearly as menacing as they do. Maybe it's the look of abject horror on his face. Or maybe it's the way his dark-brown hair is molded into a fairly spectacular fauxhawk. It's hard to take a guy seriously when he looks like a punk-rock rooster—even if he is a villain.

"Nitro's lost his mind, obviously," Draven, a.k.a. Dark-and-Scowly, answers. "He started firing energy balls at innocent people."

Holy shit. This is Nitro? Badass *super*villain and second

only to his brother, Quake, in the destruction he causes? *Nitro* is in my mother's lab?

What am I going to do? He's deadly. He could level this whole building with a single blast. No wonder the lab looks like a nuclear bomb just went off. In a way, it did.

I can't suppress a little shudder. Dark-and-Scowly, otherwise known as Draven, looks down with blue eyes that seem way too steady and way too knowledgeable, and for the first time since he tackled me, his grip loosens a little bit. He pushes up to his knees and drags his hands through his hair.

Air flows into my lungs a little more easily.

"Oi, that was just a wee blast," Nitro answers. "It wouldn't have killed her. Just stunned her."

"And that makes it okay?" I snap.

Draven reaches for me like he wants to clamp his palm over my mouth, but I shoot him a glance that says I'm rethinking my decision about biting him, and he just shakes his head.

"Are you serious?" Fauxhawk demands. "You really think this is what we need to be doing right now? When my brother has been missing for three days?"

"She was going for her cell phone." Nitro looks thoroughly disgruntled now. "Deacon obviously isn't in this lab, and we need time to search the rest of the building. What was I supposed to do?"

"Oh, I don't know. Maybe let me take care of her?" Draven says. "I had it handled."

Nitro's yellow eyes narrow. "Did you? 'Cuz it looked to me like you were just making a bigger mess."

"I'll take care of her," Draven reiterates. "Wasn't that

what we agreed on?" He climbs to his feet and I start to follow, but he puts his hand on the top of my head and shoves me back down. Which only makes me angrier. I'm not big on being manhandled.

In fact, I'm not big on being any kind of handled.

"Hey!" I complain, pushing against him as hard as I can. He doesn't budge.

"If you want to get out of this without being roasted alive, you need to stay down," he growls at me. "His control's never the best when he's this upset."

Draven's gaze is trained on Nitro, so I can't really gauge if he's telling the truth, but he seems to be trying to protect me. That must be another trick though. Villains don't help people like that.

Ignoring his dubious warning, I twist out of Draven's grip and scramble to my knees. At least now I can see what's going on. And maybe I can formulate a plan.

"Well, that's a little rude," Nitro interjects, obviously offended. "I never talk shit about your powers."

"Because Draven never loses control of *his* powers," Fauxhawk tells him, as he gestures to the burned and broken lab. "Do I need to remind you of what happened two weeks ago?"

"Wow. Set a few things on fire and suddenly everyone's a critic."

"*Me!*" Fauxhawk shouts. "You set *me* on fire!"

"I said I was sorry!"

"Like that makes it better? You burned off half my hair."

"Stop being such a drama queen, Dante." Nitro rolls his eyes. "It's growing back, isn't it?"

"Jesus," Draven says, looking like he's one step away from

pulling out his *own* hair. "Can we focus, please? We don't have long before someone finds out about this mess."

"That's what I'm saying." Nitro raises his hands and starts to build another energy ball. "I was taking care of things, until you went all hero on us."

"Screw you!" Draven lunges at Nitro.

I seize the opportunity and jump to my feet. But the villains weren't as distracted as I thought. Before I can make a dash for my phone, Dante intercepts me, wrapping a hand around my wrist in an iron grip.

He raises his other hand in the air, like someone who's refereed a lot of arguments between these two. "Can we just do something with her so we can keep looking?"

Pulling me behind him, Dante drags me toward the vault. But once he gets there, he freezes, and for a long moment, I can't figure out what's come over him. But then I see it—a shiny titanium watch with a bright-red face lying on the floor. He drops my wrist and bends to pick up the watch. Then he squeezes it tight in his hand.

"Deacon was here." His voice breaks as he shows the watch to his friends. "We need to find him before it's too late."

The bickering stops instantly. Rage vibrates in the air.

"What if it's already too late?" Nitro snarls. "What if—"

"It's not. It can't be." But Draven sounds more angry than comforting as he voices the reassurances.

"So where do we start looking for a secret level?" Dante demands. "This place is huge."

"Why don't we ask her?" Nitro nods at me with narrowed eyes, like he wouldn't mind trying to set *me* on fire this time.

"She seems to know her way around pretty well. Tell us how to get to the secret level, little bird."

"Are you insane? We don't need a secret level," I retort. "We're not *villains*."

Besides, like I would help them find it if it *did* exist.

"Didn't expect her to tell the truth, did you?" Dante glares at me. "She's a hero-worshipper."

Now, it's my turn to glare. "Hero-worshipper" is really vile, *really* insulting slang in the super world, so bad that few people even say it. As an ordinary living among superheroes, I hear it more than most, and the fact that this obnoxious, fauxhawk-sporting villain is the one lobbing it at me pisses me off more than I can say.

My heel connects with his instep before I can think better of it.

While Dante howls in pain, I back away. There are too many villains between me and the exit, but even a little distance makes me feel safer.

"I'll make her talk," Nitro says, and this time the energy ball he's building between his hands glows an icy blue. I don't know why, but it looks a million times scarier than the red-hot one he lobbed at me earlier. And when he pulls his hand back as if to throw it at me, I duck behind the nearest lab table.

Sometimes discretion really is the better part of valor.

Still, I'm not backing down. Not this time. Not to these guys.

I glance around frantically for something I can use as a weapon. I'm in a bioengineering lab, for God's sake. Just about everything in here can maim, poison, or kill. Surely, I can find something within reach that will take these jerks down. Or at least incapacitate them long enough for me to call for help.

"Stop, Nitro." Draven's voice is low and urgent, with an unmistakable note of command. "Torturing her won't do any good."

He moves deliberately, self-assured as he places himself between his buddies and me.

"It's what heroes do to us," Nitro argues. "Torture us, experiment on us. Kill us. They have Deacon. Why the hell should we care what happens to one little hero-worshipper?"

Is he serious? Heroes aren't the ones with a history of torture and murder. He should take a closer look in the mirror.

"Let me talk to her, see what she knows," Draven says. "You guys look for clues about the secret level before the cavalry arrives."

Nitro's sneer turns cocky. "Thanks to you, the cavalry's not coming. You made the guards believe they're on vacation."

"Someone's going to hear the alarms eventually," Dante says. "This place is wired into the SHPD precinct. Once they figure out there's a problem, they'll be here in less than ten minutes."

How does he know that? How does he know *any* of that?

How did they even get in here? And, for that matter, how did they even know this place existed?

The Elite Superhero Lab is a top secret facility. Our existence isn't known to most heroes, let alone villains. And our police protocols aren't exactly common knowledge. So how can these guys have so much inside information?

This is much bigger than just a simple break-in.

As the three of them argue about the best course of action, I inch toward the nearest lab table. They're so absorbed in their discussion that they don't even notice me scooting that way.

Finally. A weapon. I grab the fire extinguisher with both hands, pull the pin, and leap into the aisle, brandishing it in front of me. Dante yells in alarm, but it's too late. I depress the lever and watch as it shoots white goo all over Nitro and his energy ball.

One problem solved, at least for now.

For a second, no one moves. Then Draven turns to stare at me, his eyes wide and incredulous. Nitro takes a little longer to recover—probably because he has to take time to spit potassium bicarbonate out of his mouth. Then he lets out a roar that shakes everything that's not nailed down and fires a small and lethal-looking fireball straight at me.

"*No! Don't!*" Draven yells, diving in front of me and knocking me to the ground again. Only this time I feel him tense against me as the fireball rips along his back, setting his black T-shirt on fire and burning the skin beneath it.

To his credit, he doesn't make a sound. But his eyes clench shut and it's clear he's in a lot of pain.

Since Draven's in no position to argue, I wiggle my way out from under him and give him a good blast with the fire extinguisher as well. The fire dies out immediately, but blisters are already rising on his back and arm.

Guilt tears through me. I try to tell myself that it's all his fault. He's a villain, after all. But I know the truth. Draven might be ill-equipped to play hero, but he did his best to save me. The thought boggles my mind—a villain trying to save anyone but himself?—though I have no time to worry about it. Not with Nitro and Dante screaming at each other like crazy people.

"*Shit!*" Dante yells. "Now you're setting Draven on fire?"

"I'm sorry! I can barely see. She got that crap all over me."
Nitro lets out another yell, and a second fireball comes whizzing past us. "Shite, watch out!"

"Get down!" Draven snaps, uses his uninjured arm to tug me back to the floor.

But I'm done hiding.

"Hey, dragon breath!" I shout as I shake off Draven's grip. Leaping to my feet, I shoot another blast of potassium bicarbonate straight at Nitro's face. This time I keep my finger on the lever, covering his eyes, nose, and mouth with the nasty stuff. Then, while he's trying to wipe it away, I chuck the fire extinguisher at his head as hard as I can.

I've got great aim—it's the closest thing I can claim to a superpower—and I hit him square in the forehead with the butt of the red canister. He stumbles for a second, banging into lab tables, then lands flat on his face. If he weren't a villain, he'd be out cold. Even so, I can practically see the little birdies circling his head.

Dante's laughing his ass off at this point, which is totally not what I'd expect from a guy like him. Plus there's something that looks an awful lot like respect in his eyes as he looks back and forth between Nitro and me. The same can't be said of Draven, who's back on his feet despite his injury.

"Do you ever listen?" he demands.

"Only if a person actually has something useful to say."

Draven shakes his head but doesn't reply as he crouches next to Nitro. I get my first good look at his back and I wince. Whatever Nitro fired at him must have burned like hell. His skin is a mess.

I'm still stunned that he intercepted the fireball that was

meant for me. No one's ever done anything like that for me before. I'm grateful, even if it's just part of some weird villain plot to get me to trust him. As if that's even a possibility.

Draven wipes the potassium bicarbonate off Nitro's face, then slaps at his cheeks. Nitro's out cold; Draven's distracted; and Dante's laughing too hard to put up much of a fight. I make a beeline for the phone. One call, and every hero in the vicinity will descend on the lab in a flash.

For once, *I* can save the day.

Dante plants himself in my path. "Don't get any ideas."

I pretend not to know what he's talking about as I change course and circle the table to stand next to Draven, as if that was my intention all along.

"You need a doctor," I say, crouching to get a better look at Draven's back. Not that I would normally care about a villain one way or another, but he did save my life tonight. Twice.

"Do you have a death wish?" Draven demands, his intense gaze seeming to look right through me. "When he wakes up, he's not going to be in control."

I blink, breaking the connection between us. Gorgeous or not, protector or not, I have to remember that those bright, arctic-blue eyes belong to a villain.

"Like he was before?" I ask with a snort.

"She's got you there," Dante says, but he isn't paying much attention to us. Instead, he's examining the watch in his hand. If I didn't know better, I'd think the sheen in his eyes was from tears, not the strobe lights of the lab's alarm system. I close my eyes, shake my head. Who are these guys? They seem more helpless than heartless, more Three Stooges than criminal masterminds.

But villains killed my dad.

Villains hurt me.

They aren't supposed to protect ordinaries. They aren't supposed to care about me. They aren't supposed to care about anything but themselves. Where are the bad-to-the-bone, hell-bent-on-destruction anarchists the League is always talking about?

Nitro finally stirs and groans, but before anyone can say anything, the alarm cuts off abruptly. A loud, digital voice blasts through the intercom above us. "This is the Superhero Police Department. An alarm is going off in your laboratory and we have been unable to reach security. Is there a problem?"

For a second, all of us freeze. Then Draven turns to me with wide, warning eyes. "Don't you dare—"

I don't give myself a chance to think. These guys are villains, and I can't—I won't—have any sympathy for them.

"*Yes!*" I scream. "Send help! There are villains in the lab!"

"*Damn it!*" Dante lunges for me. "Shut up."

But it's too late. The computerized voice says, "The police have been dispatched. Help is on its way."

"*Damn it!*" Dante yells again. He bends down and pulls a still-groggy Nitro to his feet. "We have to go."

"Get him out of here!" Draven tells him. "I'll deal with her."

"We should take her with us. Use her as leverage to get Deacon back."

A shiver of terror runs down my spine. Heroes don't negotiate with villains. I can't let them kidnap me, can't let them—

"No." Draven's voice, clear and calm and cold, cuts through my panic. "That would make us no better than them. We don't do that."

"Maybe we should start. The heroes—"

"We don't have time for this," Draven says. "Take Nitro and get the hell out of here. I'll make sure she can't say anything about us."

Dante looks like he wants to argue, but time is ticking away and he knows it. With one last angry scowl at me, one I return with more than a little fury of my own, he throws Nitro over his shoulder in a fireman's carry and makes a run for the exit.

The door bangs shut behind him, and I brace myself for the worst. This is it. This is the moment when Draven proves he's a true villain.

But all he does is look straight into my eyes and say, "I'm sorry."

At first I think he's talking about the break-in, the mess, Nitro's attempted murder of me. All things he should apologize for. But his eyes have gone as cold and empty as the shards of glass that litter the floor. And I know.

He's about to wipe every trace of him and his friends from my memory.

Well, he can try.

I don't fight him. Instead, I ask the question that's been burning inside me. "You're a villain. Why stop Nitro from hurting me? Why not let Dante kidnap me?"

Long seconds tick away as silence stretches between us, taut as a circus high wire. But I want to know the answers. I want to know what would make a villain risk himself to save me. I can't remember anyone outside of family ever putting me first. I can't believe it was a villain who did.

I've decided he's not going to reply when he finally whispers, "Can't a bad guy do a good thing?"

I pause for a moment. "I've never seen it happen."

"Yeah." He looks away and swallows. "Me neither."

When he turns back to me, his eyes glow laser bright and I know this is it, the moment when he's going to try to make me forget everything that's happened. Nitro. Dante. The lab explosion. Him.

For a moment, just a moment, I think about asking him not to. But I know how futile that would be, and how stupid. "Villain" and "criminal" are pretty much synonymous. He can't leave a witness who can identify him and his buddies. And I can't reveal my greatest secret, not when it's the only protection I have. So I keep my eyes open and let him do his thing.

He takes both of my hands in one of his, and I let him. Force myself to do nothing as he pulls out a bandana—black, of course—and wraps it around my clasped hands before winding it around the faucet on the nearest lab table. He does this twice, pulling it as tightly as he can before tying it off.

"I'm sorry," he says again. "Someone will find you soon."

I manage a blank stare.

"You went to the vending machine to get your chocolate. You heard an explosion. When you came back, a masked burglar was in the lab. He tied you up, then ran."

He steps back, places my long-forgotten chocolate bar on the table, and then walks out without a backward glance as the alarm, sirens and all, starts back up again. He's got every confidence that I won't remember a thing about tonight. About him and his friends and what they were looking for.

But that's not how it works. Not with me. As I watch him turn the corner, it's not remembering him that I'm worried about.

It's forgetting him.

CHAPTER 3

K enna, my God," Mom says, rushing into the lab and wrapping me in a hug. "Are you okay?"

I sink into her, taking the comfort while I can get it. It will only be a few minutes before she notices the state of her lab, and my bruised wrists and even more bruised ego will be forgotten. "I'm o—"

"My lab," she interrupts with a gasp.

Or a few seconds…that's my mom for you.

She pulls away and looks around her, jaw dropped and eyes wide. I have to admit, it's pretty bad. A lot of the damage is superficial though. Broken glass and spilled chemicals. All things that can be easily replaced.

I rub at my wrists. Draven clearly overestimated SHPD's response. Maybe they assumed I was a hero who would be able to take on the intruders. Even after the computer response system knew there were villains in the lab, it took a solid twenty-five minutes before a human showed up. That's twenty-five minutes I spent tied to a lab table with sirens blaring and emergency lights flashing. It would test anyone's endurance.

By minute ten I was regretting my decision to help Draven when Nitro set him on fire.

By fifteen I was wishing Nitro's blast had hit Draven harder.

By twenty I regretted not beaning him with the extinguisher too.

Now…now I just hope I never see any of them again.

"What happened here?" Mom asks.

"Nitro happened," I answer.

"Nitro?" she echoes. "We're lucky there's anything left. He has a reputation for being ruthless."

Normally I'd agree with her. But while the guy I met was a total jerk, he wasn't ruthless. He wasn't…*evil.*

"Did he touch any of the research?" she asks.

I shrug. "No, he just blew the vault."

"Thank God you didn't get hurt!" She pauses but is awfully calm, considering. Then again, if any of her important research had been ruined—if my transcriptions weren't automatically backed up to the server—she'd be in a way bigger panic.

She walks through the mess, studies the destruction. Then turns to me, frowning. "Was he alone?"

This is the part where I have to decide how much to say. Do I tell her about the villain who protected me? Do I tell her that he tried to wipe my mind? Draven's not on the superhero radar yet or I would have heard of him. If I tell Mom, she'll tell the League, and he'll be on the most-wanted list by morning. Memory wipe is a big deal on both sides of the superpower fence.

But in the end, I decide I owe them no loyalty. Just because these three villains didn't hurt or kill me doesn't mean I need to protect them, protect *him.* God only knows how many people they've hurt in the past, or *will* hurt in the future if the heroes don't catch them.

"No, there were three of them," I say.

Mom gasps again. "They could have killed you."

Way to have faith, Mom.

"Yeah, well, it's not like their powers actually work on me. There wasn't much they *could* do."

I might be powerless, but I do have one secret weapon. Mom does anyway.

After the way my dad died—and what happened to me—my mom dedicated her research to developing a serum that makes whoever takes it immune to superpowers. Impervious. She perfected the serum when I was eight and has been giving it to me once a week ever since. I'm her long-term test subject. Her guinea pig.

So far it seems to be working. I haven't grown a second head or anything, and superpowers don't affect me anymore. But she isn't ready to share the serum with the heroes yet. They might be the good guys, but they're very fond of their abilities. And since her serum makes me immune to all superpowers—hero or villain—she figures they aren't going to take the news very well. At least not until she can refine the formula to only work against villain powers.

Until then, this research is our little secret. One that could get her in major trouble, since it's a totally unsanctioned experiment.

And it's a secret that makes Mom feel a little better since I'm slightly less likely to get maimed or killed because I can't defend myself.

"Ssssh." My mom glances around to make sure no one is listening. "You know you're not supposed to talk about that. Besides, just because Nitro's blast couldn't hurt you doesn't mean he couldn't slit your throat or break your neck."

The image makes me shudder. "Nice, Mom. Thanks for the visual."

"I'm just saying." She lowers her voice. "You act like that serum makes you invincible, but it doesn't. You could have died in the explosion or from fire or from falling debris. He could have killed you in a million different ways that didn't actually involve his powers."

It's all I can do not to roll my eyes. I know this is her way of saying she cares about me, but all she's doing is pointing out how weak she thinks I am.

It's an old fight, so I don't bother trying to explain that I'm powerless, not helpless. Or stupid. She can't seem to comprehend that I might actually be able to defend myself. Which is totally hypocritical, considering that if you take away that big brain of hers, she's just as vulnerable as I am.

It's a fight I can't win though, so I change the subject. "One of them tried to wipe my mind to make me forget I saw them."

Mom's eyes widen. "You didn't tell him?"

Does she even have to ask? "Of course not. I pretended it worked."

"Good," she says, sagging with relief. "That's good."

"What am I supposed to tell the SHPD?" I ask.

I managed to avoid talking to the officers when they arrived on the scene, insisting that I had to speak with my mom first. They gave in because I *might* have hinted that there was top secret intel at stake. And in a way, there is. Even if I never cross paths with the villain trio again, if it gets out that I spilled information that Draven supposedly erased, my secret immunity will be blown. Mom would totally flip.

"I don't want you talking to the SHPD at all, if we can avoid it," she says. "But I need you to tell me everything that happened so I know what Rex Malone needs to hear."

Mom worries constantly that I'll slip up, though I assure her I won't. I've spent more than half my life keeping this secret.

I give her the rundown, everything from when I ran into Draven at the vending machine to when he tied me to the faucet and walked out the door. Well, *almost* everything. I don't tell her what they said about a hidden level in the lab. That's too crazy to repeat if I want her to take me seriously.

Mom nods. "Okay, good. Follow my lead, and don't offer anything more than—"

"I don't care if he *is* in Tokyo," a male voice booms before Mr. Malone—my best friend's dad and president of the League—steps into the lab. "You tell him to get his ass back to Boulder before I send Dash to bring him back."

He ends the call abruptly and snaps the phone back into the holster on his belt. Even if he weren't a superhero, Mr. Malone would still command attention. He's big and tall, with short, dark, perfectly-in-place hair and piercing blue eyes. Almost like a real-life Superman. Rebel doesn't think so, but then she's his daughter. It's kind of her job to give him grief.

Tonight—or I should say *this morning*—he looks a little less-than-perfect in a wrinkled shirt and faded jeans.

Half a step behind him, as always, is Rebel's brother, Riley. He's only two years older than her, but blond hair and blue eyes are pretty much the only things the siblings have in common. Riley is tall, like their dad, and impeccably groomed. Plus he has the stiffest, straightest posture of anyone I've ever

met. I can't imagine anyone more likely to remind the teacher
when she forgets to assign homework. Or, as Rebel says, to
act like a bigger douche nozzle.

She would disown him if she could.

Riley trails Mr. Malone with his smartphone in hand, flash-
typing everything his father says. No surprise there. The boy
eats, sleeps, and breathes to be a superhero, and today he's
wearing a coat that, honestly, looks a little bit like a cape. I'm
sure, in his opinion, it's just truth in advertising.

Mom confronts Mr. Malone at the blown-out door.

"What the hell happened?" she demands. "This facility is
supposed to be secure, Rex. How did villains get in and tie up
my daughter?"

He turns his attention to me. "Kenna, sweetheart, are
you okay?"

"Yes, Mr. Malone," I answer obediently. "I'm fine."

Riley pauses typing for a split second to look up at me. I
can't tell if that's his way of saying hello or if he's evaluating
me for his report. I swear, if he tries to take a picture of me
for the files, I'll go Rebel on him with her signature karate
chop. I've taken enough crap from the male of the species
today. I'm so totally over all of them.

"Can you tell me what happened?" Mr. Malone asks, like
I'm a child.

I got used to his patronizing tone a long time ago. As an
ordinary *and* a teenager, I get a double dose of let-the-grown-
up-superheroes-take-care-of-everything. I stopped letting it
make me gag when I was twelve, but it's still frustrating.

"I'll tell you what happened," Mom says before I can
answer. "She went to get a candy bar, and next thing she

knows, she's tied to a lab table with the sirens blaring. It took the SHPD almost an hour to get here."

"Unacceptable." Mr. Malone nods to Riley, who—if possible—types even faster. "Can you describe them?"

"I—"

"She doesn't remember." Mom steps closer to my side. "Has no memory of anything after the vending machine."

"Damn it!" Mr. Malone rests his fists on his hips in a perfect superhero stance. "One of them must have had a psy power. I hate those mental freaks."

"Freaks," Riley agrees.

"And one of them must have been Nitro," Mom suggests.

Mr. Malone surveys the room. "You're right. No one else has this kind of explosive power."

I'm doing my best to keep my mouth shut. Mom's rules. Never answer when I don't have to. It reduces the odds that I'll say something that would betray my immunity.

Wouldn't want that.

I start mentally sketching the chemical structure of my latest test formula. Saves me from paying attention and wanting to answer when I shouldn't.

"We have to move the lab." Mom spins around and storms toward the back of the room. "This facility isn't secure."

I sigh.

This is how Mom always reacts to danger. She overreacts.

Don't speak.

Take immunity serum.

Move the lab.

For a woman who chooses to work in the world of heroes and villains—and who was married to one of the

31

greatest superheroes of his generation—she doesn't deal well with violence and conflict. At all. Then again, having your husband wiped off the face of the earth by villains will do that to a woman.

She crosses to the far corner, where one of Nitro's fireballs did a number on the file cabinets. There are papers strewn everywhere.

Mr. Malone goes after her and I follow.

"Jeanine, stop," he says, moving to her side as she starts grabbing folders off the floor. "You don't have to leave the lab."

She whirls around to face him. "Villains broke in here tonight," she says, her voice bordering on a shriek. "*Nitro* broke in here. He blew up my lab and tied up my daughter. Someone *mind-wiped* her. It's not safe here anymore."

"It is," he insists. When she glares at him, he amends, "It will be. I've already called the Cleaners. By morning it'll be like villains were never here."

Mom shoves the stack of folders into my hands. "The mess isn't the problem. The security breach is unacceptable."

"That will be dealt with." He takes the files from me and places them on the nearest counter. "I've called an emergency meeting of the Superhero Collective. We will institute new protections to make the facility more secure than ever."

When Mom reaches for the files Mr. Malone just put down, he gently but firmly puts his hand on hers. "I promise, Jeanine. You and Kenna will be safer here than anywhere else on the planet."

Mom looks like she's going to argue. Then she crumbles. Head in her hands, she starts sobbing.

I rush to her side and wrap my arms around her. I can't stand to see her cry. She might not be perfect, but we're a team. "It's okay, Mom," I promise. "Everything will be okay."

"I can't lose you too," she says. "I can't."

"I'm fine." I rub my hands up and down her back like she used to do for me when I was little.

I feel Mr. Malone's reassuring hand on my shoulder.

"You two go on home," he says in that authoritative tone that sounds like he was born to be in charge. "I'll coordinate the cleanup efforts and get those extra protections in place. The whole incident will be a bad memory by morning."

"No, no, I'm fine," Mom says, wiping away her tears. She straightens and I can tell that in-charge Mom is back. "Kenna, can you come with me to my office? I want to check on the damage in there."

That's Mom code for *It's time for your immunity shot*.

As I follow her out of the lab, I really hope Mr. Malone is right. Between everything that happened with Draven, Dante, and Nitro, plus being tied to a table and then lying by omission to both my mom and the president of the League, this is pretty much a night I would love to forget.

Too bad there's never a memory wipe around when you need one.

Maybe I can pretend that Draven's power worked on me. After my shot, I'll go home, get a good night's—or day's—sleep, and then come back to the lab to finish my work as if nothing happened.

Villains may have stolen one night of research time from me. I won't let them take any more.

✦ ✦ ✦

To the uninitiated, Mom's office would appear to have been hit by one of Nitro's fireballs. There are stacks of papers and boxes everywhere. It's amazing the door even opens with all the stuff packed inside.

But there's been no villain destruction in here. This is how it always looks—everyday, disaster chic. She swears she knows where everything is. I don't believe her.

I've volunteered to sort and organize everything a million times, but she loves the chaos. I, however, can barely think in here. A grizzly bear could be hiding in this clutter forest and you'd never know.

"I swear, sometimes that man just—" Mom drops into her desk chair and shakes her head.

She and Mr. Malone have had their conflicts over the years. I often wonder why she keeps working for him. Any genetics lab in the country would be thrilled to have her, even if she can't include all of her work at ESH on her resume. For whatever reason though, she stays on. Her research drives her, and I don't think she could walk away from it before she's finished.

I suppose I understand. I feel the same way about my research. It's my passion and it's personal.

I remove the half-empty box of petri dishes from the stool next to her desk and sit down.

"Do you believe him?" I ask. "Do you think the new security measures will keep the lab safe?"

Mom scoffs. "He doesn't even know how they got in. How can he know what will keep them out?"

34

I shrug as I roll up my sleeve.

Getting immunity shots is routine. Mom doesn't even use a syringe anymore. She has this futuristic injection gun that does all the hard work. She just pops in a vial, holds it up to my arm, and pulls the trigger.

But when she opens her bottom desk drawer and pulls out a vial from the box she keeps hidden in the back, she curses.

"What's wrong?" I ask.

"It's clouded." She flings herself back in her chair. "And I haven't started a new batch. I was going to do that tomorrow."

I don't know much about the immunity serum besides what it does, but I do know that when it goes cloudy, the chemical bonds have broken and it's on its way to becoming toxic.

"It's no big deal," I tell her, even though I know she thinks it is. "A couple of days won't make much of a difference."

She turns her scientist glare on me. I can already hear the speech in my head. *The dose is carefully calculated to match your metabolism. Immunity only lasts a week at full strength. After that, it gradually wears off.*

Sometimes I wonder if she even notices me—Kenna—anymore, or if all she really sees is the powerless girl she's desperate to protect.

I throw up my hands. "Hey, I'm not responsible for it going bad."

"I know." She tugs me into her lap for a hug. "I'm just shaken up after the break-in. When I first heard…"

I give her a tight squeeze before pushing back to my feet. On the one hand it's annoying how overprotective she can be. On the other…I totally understand. I already lost my dad, and now I'd do anything to keep her safe.

"What time is it?" I ask.

Mom checks the clock on her computer. "Almost two in the morning."

"No wonder I'm so beat," I say, stifling a yawn.

I'm usually good for another couple hours of my own work, but I guess the villain situation took a toll on me. Besides, it's not like I can get anything done in the lab now.

"You go on home and get some rest." She squeezes my shoulder.

"Sure you don't want to come with me?"

She shakes her head. "I need to make sure those idiots don't mess with any of my research while they're cleaning up."

"And you need to start the new batch of immunity serum."

"And that," she says with a smile.

"You're sure you don't want me to help?"

I'm always offering, but she always refuses. I'm not even allowed to observe the process.

"I just need a little catnap. I'll be good as new."

I give her a quick kiss on the cheek before heading back to the lab. I want to grab my things and then go straight home to bed. As I walk down the hall, I have a flashback to when Draven appeared around the corner. All I had seen was a gorgeous guy, tall and dark and way too hot to be hanging out at a lab.

I wasn't wrong. He *is* too hot to work in a lab. He's also too dark, too dangerous, and too twisted.

A villain.

Draven is a *villain*, and I can't afford to forget that. He didn't kill me this time, but that's no guarantee he won't if we ever run into each other again. Forgetting that, even for a second, is like signing my own death warrant.

With that thought in mind, I round the corner into a world of chaos. At least a dozen heroes—most of whom I don't even recognize—are working to restore the lab.

The Cleaners. Definitely the Cleaners.

A woman with frizzy blond hair—who looks more like an escapee from a hippie commune than a hero—waves her hand over the shards of glass littering the hallway, sending them swirling through the air toward the empty window frame. Another swish of her hand and the shards coalesce like the most complicated jigsaw puzzle ever, filling the space with a cracked version of the pre-Nitro window. A tall, skinny guy with white-blond hair and a nose like a rat flicks his fingers at the glass, and in one melty swirl, the cracks disappear. The window looks good as new.

Bet Nitro would be pissed to know how easily we fixed his handiwork.

Inside the lab proper, heroes clear scorch marks off the walls and ceilings, air-sweep spilled chemicals into a containment bin, and repair the half-melted tabletops closest to where Nitro had been standing. A telekinetic hero swoops up a stack of papers and folders from the floor, floating them into growing piles on one of the unmelted tables.

Must be nice. Seeing all these different powers at work could make a girl crazy if she was the type to dwell on what she doesn't have. Which I so totally am not.

Except…I cast another look over my shoulder. That melty-glass power is pretty cool. I've never seen that one before. Vending machines wouldn't stand a chance against that.

A team of lab assistants goes from cabinet to cabinet, making a list of all the supplies that need to be replaced.

When they head back toward my station, I'm jolted out of stunned observation.

"No," I shout, blocking the path. "This is mine. I'll handle the inventory."

They look at each other and shrug before moving on to the next cabinet. Mom may be okay with other people touching her research, but mine is off limits.

I make a quick sign that reads KENNA'S STUFF DON'T TOUCH in big red letters, and then draw a giant skull and crossbones on it before taping it to the door. With the kind of chemicals around here, the Cleaners should take the warning seriously.

"Excuse me," a woman says.

She points at the floor beneath my stool where an ooze of green liquid is seeping out in an ever-growing circle. It looks like Mom's Dissolve All—an acid formula that will liquefy any nonorganic material, so it's safe to touch but incredibly difficult to contain. My stool starts sinking as the acid melts the legs.

I move away and let the woman do her job. I watch as she uses her hands to sweep the goo into a special organic container. Gross.

"Ooof." Someone knocks into me, sending me stumbling.

"Sorry," the guy says without taking his gaze off the ceiling.

I need to grab my stuff and get out of here. I'm in the way, and if I'm not careful, I'll get hurt. Or worse, *not* hurt—as in my immunity will show, and then where will I be? Grounded for life, that's where.

Avoiding situations that might reveal my immunity is an art.

On my way out, I collide with another person. *God, could I be more useless?* I start to apologize, then realize I've crashed into Riley. *Damn.*

He clutches his smartphone to his chest. "Kenna. Hi, hello."

"Hey, Riley," I answer.

"Terrible business here tonight," he says, gesturing at the lab around us. "And you? Having to face down villains, um, face-to-face. That must have been awful."

And without a single power to help you. He doesn't have to say the words out loud for me to hear them. They're written all over his face. As if he could outfly one of Nitro's fireballs.

I've always felt like a powerless little goldfish in the big superpowers pond when I'm around him. He watches me. Studies me. I can tell he doesn't understand how Rebel and I are friends.

Then again, Rebel is pretty much beyond everyone's understanding most of the time.

"Not an experience I want to repeat, no." I cover my mouth to hide a yawn.

Riley doesn't take the hint.

"Well, it won't happen again. The new security measures will be unparalleled," he explains. "Retinal scans on the elevators. Freeze rays aimed at every entrance ready to stop any intruders in their tracks. An electromagnetic shield around the entire campus, configured to allow only authorized personnel signatures. It should all be up and operational within a week."

I nod absently, wondering how long I have to stand here listening to him. Riley has a tendency to ramble. If he goes on much longer, I might pass out right here.

"The IT crew will also be installing security cameras

in every hallway this afternoon," he continues magnani-
mously. "Dad can ask them to add a camera in the lab too,
if you'd like."

"No," I blurt out. "*That* won't be necessary."

Mom and Mr. Malone have had this argument before. Mr.
Malone thinks we need cameras—for security and so we have
a record of the research in case of an accident or another
problem. Mom doesn't want to feel like she's being watched.

"It's no problem," Riley insists. "If it will make you feel safer—"

Something connects with my head. Hard. "Ouch."

I rub at the sore spot and move out of the way of the guy
hovering five and a half feet off the ground as he works on a
sprinkler head in the ceiling above me.

Only I could get kicked in the head by a flying superhero.
I don't actually have the power of invisibility, but some days
it's hard to remember that. Especially around here. To the
superheroes of the League, an ordinary like me might as well
be nonexistent. The powerless are pretty much beneath their
notice, unless they have a useful skill like Mom's super brain.

When my research is complete, I'll be invaluable to the
heroes. They'll have to notice me.

The collision draws Mr. Malone's attention. "Kenna,
sweetheart, I thought you were heading home."

"I am, Mr. Malone." I gesture at the flurry of activity
around us. "Just wanted to see if there was anything I could
do to help."

"Our team has the cleanup under control," he says with his
standard patronizing smile. He exchanges a look with Riley,
who resumes typing on his smartphone. "You go on home.
Everything will be good as new by morning."

Before I can respond, he wraps an arm around Riley's shoulder and guides him away. And just like that, I'm dismissed. I get it. I'm not a super, so there's nothing I can do to help. I'm in the way.

That's the problem with being an ordinary in the world of heroes—it's impossible not to feel *less* all of the time.

It won't always be like this, I promise myself. Mom might be working on a way to neutralize villain powers and *amplify* hero ones, but I'm working on a way to *create* them.

If my research is successful, if I can get the chemical sequencing right, then I won't be ordinary forever. I'll be powerful, and more important, I'll matter.

To everyone.

CHAPTER 4

The elevator doors glide open and I step inside, away from the chaos of the heroes and the Cleaners and the aftermath of the security breach on sublevel one. Walking away from the lab feels strange. Everything is different now, and not because of the break-in or the explosion. It's because of him. *Draven.*

For a second the image of his face pops into my head—all high cheekbones and sculpted jaw—but I refuse to acknowledge it. Refuse to acknowledge *him.* If I don't think about what he said, what he did, what he *didn't* do, then I don't have to think about how confusing it all is.

Villains are bad. I know this. I have *always* known this. I've seen them blow shit up on the news a million times. Seen the aftermath of the earthquakes and fires and devastation they've caused around the world. One of them killed my dad in cold blood while another—

I stop myself. I've worked too hard to put that behind me. The fact that I'm even thinking these thoughts now is just more proof that Draven and his friends are bad news. Just because they didn't kill me doesn't mean they aren't bad—and bad *for* me.

After all, it's not like I ran into them while getting a milk shake at Sonic or hanging at the mall with Rebel. They were breaking into a top-secret superhero lab to steal…something. I don't know what, but they were really pissed that they couldn't find it.

Not pissed enough to take it out on me, but they were distracted. And in a hurry. Thinking, even for a minute, that they might not be evil simply because they let me live is stupid. Worse, it's suicidal.

Draven might have stuck up for me once, but I doubt he'd do it again. Besides, my wrists still hurt. Which means if I'm around the next time he catches on fire, there's no way I'm putting it out.

With that promise to myself, I turn the corner into the ESH lobby. The face we present to the public is all very normal looking. Shiny chrome, gleaming leather, and sparkling glass. Just what you would expect from a company that designs innovative technology.

There's no indication that the ESH has anything to do with superheroes, which is how they've managed to keep their power and influence out of the limelight for more than sixty years.

I'm almost to the exit when men start streaming through the front door. It's the middle of the night and even Mr. Malone, who doesn't normally have a hair out of place, was dressed down. Not these men. Each is dressed in a perfectly pressed suit in some shade of gray—heather, slate, asphalt, ash… And they're all wearing sunglasses. Aviator Ray-Bans, it looks like. They spread out in pairs, fanning across the lobby like an army. Or a plague of locusts.

"Let me see your ID," one says as he and his partner approach me.

Who are these guys? I mean, they look like top secret government agents, but that doesn't make sense. SHPD has already taken over this investigation. Besides, it's not like we have a superhero version of the CIA or FBI. We've never needed one. Superheroes take care of their own trouble.

"I'm just leaving." I try to step around the one who addressed me.

"Your ID," the second one insists, blocking my way. If possible, he sounds even more obnoxious—and determined— than his partner.

"Who are you?" I demand.

"Your ID," the first one repeats. There's no emotion behind his voice. No threat. No rage. Just the assurance that I am not getting out of here until I give them what they want.

I've had enough. I took enough crap from the villains tonight. I'm not taking it from these guys too. *Where do they get off?*

I go nose to nose with Suit 1. "Do *you* have a badge?"

He reaches into his jacket, produces a small leather wallet, and flashes a shiny gold badge and ID at me. I can only make out the initials NTF before he stuffs it back in his chest pocket.

"What did that say?" I ask. "I couldn't even—"

"If you don't produce your ID," Suit 2 says, "we will take you into custody until your identity can be confirmed."

"Are you kidding?" *I'm* not the one who doesn't belong here.

"Counterfeit IDs were used to access the facility," Suit 1 says. "All personnel IDs must be tested for authenticity."

When I don't immediately reach for my badge, he steps toward me and clamps a big, beefy hand around my forearm.

"Don't touch me!" I yank at my arm, but he won't let go.

Fine.

Annoyed all over again, I fork over my ID and watch as Suit 2 swipes it through a small, handheld machine. It beeps, long and high-pitched, and I tense despite myself. I have a reason for being here. I'm not doing anything wrong. But these guys don't look like they care one way or the other. For a moment I have visions of being swept into a nondescript vehicle and taken away to parts unknown.

If that happens though, I'm not going without a fight. I am sick and tired of being pushed around.

"Thank you, Ms. Swift." Suit 2 hands my ID back to me. "Have a safe night."

And then they're turning away, walking away, as if they didn't just threaten to physically detain me without cause. As if they didn't just grab me. I guess I should be grateful they're letting me go, but all I am is pissed.

Determined to get out of here before things get even more screwed up, I make a beeline for the door, plowing straight into my best friend who is walking in as I'm rushing out. Rebel wraps me in a vanilla-and-leather-scented hug.

"Oh, Kenna! Thank God you're okay!" She squeezes me tight enough to cut off my oxygen supply.

And for a second—just a second—I cling to her.

"I'm fine," I tell her, pulling away. "What are you doing here?" I keep my voice to a whisper, though I'm not sure why. Maybe because I still have the heebie-jeebies after my run-in with the suits.

Rebel has no such heebie-jeebies—and no such reason to keep her voice lower than a shout. "I was worried about you! My dad got the alarm that there was a break-in. Then I started thinking about how you like to work late in your mom's lab and I tried to text you, but you never answered. I drove by your house and your car wasn't there. I freaked out."

She stops to catch a breath and I take advantage of the pause to get out a few words of my own.

"I wasn't hurt," I tell her. "The villains who broke in were looking for something—I don't know what—but they didn't do much damage, at least nothing the Cleaners can't fix."

Rebel looks relieved. "So nobody was hurt?"

"Nope. Just some broken glass and scorched walls. Your dad and Riley are on it," I say. "Oh, and by the way, did you know your brother has taken to wearing a cape?"

Rebel rolls her eyes. "He swears it's just a coat. But I'm so glad you're all right!"

She throws her arms around me again, and again I put up with it, despite her studded leather belt digging into my stomach. After all, that's kind of par for the course in a Rebel hug.

My best friend is about as different from her dad and brother as she can get and still be a member of the Malone family. In fact, while there's never a doubt in anyone's mind that Mr. Malone and Riley are *heroes*—they pretty much wear it on their sleeves…or their *capes*—at first glance, most people in our world would assume Rebel is a villain. She's the sweetest person I know (to everyone except her dad, at least), but it's easy to see how someone could make that mistake.

Tonight, she's dressed in a short leather skirt with ripped-up, melting tights in black and white, a black tank that proclaims "Love is the movement," and worn combat boots that have definitely seen better days. Her razor-cut, bleached-almost-white hair is short and spiky, and she's wearing more jewelry than I even own: four earrings in her left ear, three in her right, a bunch of mismatched bracelets on both wrists, and a ring on every finger. Even her bright-blue eyes—so like her dad's and brother's—look punk with heavy, black eyeliner and fake lashes.

"Were *you* freaking out?" she asks when she finally pulls away.

"You know me," I say with a meaningful shrug. Rebel is the only person besides my mom who knows about my secret immunity and that I can't be harmed by superpowers. Who can a girl trust, if not her best friend, right? "I handled it. I even put one out with a fire extinguisher."

Rebel bursts out laughing. "You put Nitro out with a fire extinguisher? I wish I could have seen that!"

"I did. It was—" Her words suddenly register. "Hey, I never said it was Nitro."

Guilt flashes across Rebel's face, but it's gone so fast I almost think I imagined it. Almost.

"Of course you did."

"No, I didn't." No way would I make that mistake. Not when I'm pretending that I can't remember *who* broke in. "All I said is that they were villains."

"Huh. Well, I guess I just assumed. What other villain actually needs to be extinguished?"

I huff out a little laugh and shake my head. "Good point."

After all, if I hadn't been so stunned by the situation, I would have known it was Nitro just from his abilities. Why wouldn't Rebel? Especially when life at her house is a daily course in villain identification. I swear if Mrs. Malone would allow it, Mr. Malone would display photos of the twenty most-wanted villains in their house like a museum displays Picasso paintings. All in an attempt to memorize their faces so he can eradicate them from the planet.

"So, are you going home?" Rebel asks after an awkward silence.

I nod. "My mom doesn't want me here during the cleanup."

"She's right. No one wants to be here for that." Rebel slings an arm around my shoulders. "Too much time with the zeroes...oops, I mean *heroes*"—she gives me an overly dramatic eye roll—"could cause cavities."

I ignore the dig. She knows it bugs me when she calls them that.

"But seriously," she says, "you shouldn't be alone tonight. Come home with me."

Normally I would protest, out of pride if for no other reason. But the truth is that I really don't want to go home. While I'm not exactly freaking out, I think I've earned a night at my BFF's house.

"Yeah, okay. Thanks."

Rebel gives me another oxygen-depriving hug before walking me to my car. Then I follow her home.

The Malones live about ten minutes from the lab in a house that looks like a giant wedding cake. Big and white, with huge plantation shutters and trees lining a driveway that stretches a half a mile from the street to the front porch. It looks more like a vast southern estate than part of a wealthy Boulder neighborhood.

I park in my regular spot in the designated guest parking

area—yes, her parents are more than a little anal—then follow Rebel into her house. There's a light on in the foyer but the rest of the house is dark, which means her mother is still in bed. I can't help feeling relieved. I like Rebel's family, but they're all a little high strung. My half-goth, half-hipster best friend is actually the low-maintenance one in the Malone household.

Rebel and I became friends in kindergarten. On the first day of class, the teacher asked everyone to demonstrate their powers—teleporting, cloud making, even changing the color of people's hair, which Rebel totally wishes she could do. When they got to me, I had to admit that I didn't have a power. It wasn't unheard of for an ordinary to attend the school for superheroes, but it was unusual. Enough so that no one wanted to sit with me at lunch.

When she saw me sitting alone at a table, Rebel made a big production of picking up her lunch, skipping across the cafeteria, and sitting next to me. She said, "You're special. We should be friends."

We've been inseparable ever since.

Once we're in her room, Rebel loans me a pair of pajamas and it's all I can do to keep my eyes open long enough to change into them. Funny, half an hour ago I was pumped so high on adrenaline that I felt like I'd never come down, and now I'm crashing so hard all I want is to pull the covers over my head and hide for a week.

I reach instinctively for my journal. Even exhaustion can't keep me from my nightly ritual of scribbling at least a line or two about my day, about my results.

But my backpack isn't where I usually drop it in Rebel's room. It's not here at all.

"Crap," I say as I fall back into the bed. "I forgot to grab my bag."

This is all Riley's fault. If he hadn't started droning on about security systems and surveillance equipment—while wearing a freaking *cape*—I wouldn't have been in such a rush to get out of the lab.

"Get some sleep," Rebel tells me, crawling in the other side of her king-size bed and pulling out her tablet. "You can go back for it tomorrow."

I don't even argue. Instead, I close my eyes and fall into a restless, dream-filled sleep.

I'm not sure how long I'm out before the sound of an incoming text wakes me up. I'm starting to grope for my phone when I hear Rebel tapping out an answer. Seconds later, she throws back the covers and climbs stealthily out of bed, so stealthily that I simply watch her instead of saying something, like I normally would.

She walks to the French doors that lead out onto her veranda and pushes one open. Then, after flicking on the exterior light, she steps outside and softly closes the door behind her. I wait a minute, two, for her to come back in, but when she doesn't, I climb out of bed too. Through the glass, I can see her silhouette walking toward a small copse of trees at the back of her yard.

A tall guy steps out of the shadows and Rebel runs into his arms. They kiss for long, drawn-out seconds, and I can't do much more than stand there in openmouthed shock. *Rebel has a boyfriend!* Rebel has a boyfriend that she hasn't told me anything about. It doesn't make any sense.

We tell each other everything. We always have. Every crush,

every first date, every kiss. Rebel can list every guy I've ever liked, all the way back to kindergarten. And I can do the same for her. She knows about my *immunity shots*. We trust each other with our deepest secrets. Or at least I thought we did.

But now as I stand here watching her kiss this guy like they're the only two people on the planet, I can't help wondering why I don't know about him. It's not like Rebel to keep secrets, so if she's been hiding this guy, there must be a reason.

Unease crawls through my belly as they finally split apart. The guy wraps his arm around her shoulders and starts walking her back toward the house. My apprehension grows. There's something about the way he moves that is familiar. Something about the way he holds himself and his rolling, long-legged stride.

Is he someone from school? But that doesn't make sense. Why wouldn't Rebel tell me about him if that's the case?

Maybe he's an older guy and her parents wouldn't approve. But still, she could have told me. I'd never judge. Or if I did, I'd support her anyway. That's how our friendship works.

As they get closer, I crouch behind the purple love seat near the doors and peer over the back of it. It takes a couple minutes for them to reach the pool of light from the veranda, but when they do, shock ricochets through me. Because this isn't some boy from school. This isn't some guy she met at a concert or a club.

No, the guy Rebel is currently leaning in to for one last kiss, the guy whose arms are wrapped around her waist, whose body is pressed flush against her own, is a villain.

And not just any villain. Dante, the guy with the fauxhawk

who broke into my mother's lab and who wanted to kidnap me. Me. His *girlfriend's* best friend.

As I stare at them, I'm overwhelmed by a deafening noise—the sound of my mind *exploding*.

CHAPTER 5

As Rebel waves and watches Dante head back across the yard, I have about fifteen seconds to decide if I'm going to sneak back to bed to pretend to be asleep or if I'm going to confront her about the fact that she's dating a villain—one who, now that I think about it, knew an awful lot about me.

As did Draven.

You're Kenna Swift? I thought Draven had been shocked because he'd heard of my mother. But maybe that wasn't it at all. Maybe Rebel had mentioned me to Dante. Maybe that's why they knew my name—

Rebel turns back toward her room. I have to make a decision. I glance at my side of the bed. It's so inviting. So easy.

After the night I've had, it's the clear win. I need time to process all that's happened before confronting Rebel. I mean, what would I even say at this point?

I slip back into my side of the bed. I'm just easing the comforter over my head when the door whooshes open and the chilly night air forces me deeper under the covers. A moment later, Rebel slides back into the bed.

My heart pounds like a jackhammer. My mind races back through everything that happened tonight. The break-in.

The explosion. The interrogation by Mr. Malone. The guys in gray suits.

It all plays out in rapid-fire succession.

In a flash, it hits me.

I bolt upright.

"It was you!"

Rebel stretches and does a really spot-on impression of someone waking up from a deep sleep. Her voice even has that groggy, haven't-used-it-in-a-while tone. "What was me?"

"Oh. My. God." I throw off the blankets and jump out of bed. My mind reels as I pace around the room, half talking to myself. "I should have known. I should have seen it! When the gray suits said the villains had a security pass, it meant they were working with someone on the inside, someone who had access. Then you brought up Nitro when I hadn't mentioned his name. But I trusted you. I. Trusted. You. Because no way would *my best friend* send villains into the lab *I work in* when she knew I would be there. No way would *my best friend* put me in that kind of danger, right? Except you did. It was you. It was *you*."

My head really does feel like it's exploding.

Rebel is at my side in an instant. She grabs my shoulders to stop my pacing. "What on earth are you talking about?"

She's a good liar, better even than I've given her credit for. But I'm not falling for it. I level an unamused glare at her. "Don't pretend it's not true. Don't lie to me any more than you already have." I point at the door she used just minutes ago to go meet her secret boyfriend. "You're dating a villain."

"What? No, I'm—"

"Don't. Lie. You're dating the crazy villain with a fauxhawk who wanted to *kidnap* me. *Torture me!* And you were going to *let him!* What's wrong with you?"

She opens her mouth, probably to tell me I'm crazy, to spout another lie. But then she just sighs. After a heavy silence, she shakes her head. "Dante would never have hurt you. I swear. He doesn't have it in him."

I want to throw up. "You don't know that."

"I do. I know him. I love him, Kenna. I really love him. He'd never hurt anyone, certainly not you. He knows you're my best friend."

Best friend? That's a joke. "You sent them there tonight. You knew I would be there, and you sent them anyway— without even giving me a heads-up. Why? Because you knew I couldn't fight back!"

"I didn't!" she insists. "You said you were so tired last night that I thought you were going to go home early. That's the only reason I told them it was okay."

I don't know if I believe her, but I can't dwell on that right now. Not when there are more important things to talk about. Like what motivated her to help supervillains break into the superhero lab, and the fact that her father would have her arrested—would have her tried for *treason*—if he knew what she'd done.

Not to mention how my best friend, the person I trust most in the entire world, the one person who has always treated me as something more than ordinary, could betray me like this.

Rebel's the only person I've ever been able to be completely honest with, and I thought it was the same with her. It hurts to find out I was wrong. Not only has Rebel been keeping at least one major secret from me, she all but served me up on a platter to Dante and his friends.

Maybe she believes they wouldn't hurt me, but she wasn't there when Dante suggested kidnapping me like it was a perfectly reasonable idea. She wasn't there when Nitro was throwing fireballs at me. Yes, I have immunity, but only from superpowers. All three of those boys are bigger than I am, and if they'd decided to kidnap me—to hurt me—no fire extinguisher in the world would have been able to stop them.

I rub a hand across my tired eyes and take a deep breath as I try to sort out my thoughts. "How long have you been with him?" I ask.

"Six months."

I sputter. "*Six months? How could you hide this for six months?*"

"It's not like that."

"Not like what?" I spit. "Not like you're dating a *villain*? Not like you're snuggling up with our sworn enemies? Not like you've been lying to me for half a year?"

"That's the whole thing," she says. "It's not like *that*. They're not our enemies."

"Are you joking? They nearly killed me tonight." An exaggeration, but she doesn't know that.

"But they didn't," she points out, as if that makes it all okay. "They wouldn't. They aren't bad guys."

Who is this girl standing before me? She looks like my best friend. But my best friend would never knowingly consort with a villain. The daughter of the most powerful superhero would *never* date the enemy—even to get back at her father.

At least, the girl I thought was my best friend would never do that.

A night alone in my empty house is looking better and better. "I'm out of here."

"Kenna, wait." She grabs my arm before I can walk away. "You have no idea what's going on. There is next-level shit happening at the lab."

"Yeah, I know," I snap, yanking my arm out of her grasp. "My best friend is giving a team of villains complete access."

"Dante's brother is missing."

I shrug. "So? What's that have to do with the lab?" But even as I say it, I remember them talking about finding some guy named Deacon.

"He was kidnapped," she insists. "Taken by the superhero goon squad that my dad and his douche nozzle cronies work so hard to keep secret. They're best friends, closer than close. Dante's been a mess since Deacon went missing."

"And he's being held in the lab? Just where do you think they're keeping him?" I hope that injecting some logic into the conversation will make her see how crazy she sounds. "It's not like they're hiding prisoners in the janitor's closet."

"No, they're sneakier than that." She scrubs a hand over her hair. "They probably took him to the secret level."

Ugh. Again with the secret level? I work in that lab, have for years, and my mom is their top researcher, yet never before tonight have I heard about a super-secret level. The whole thing is absurd. Too many really smart people work in the lab for her dad to keep something that big a secret.

It's like she's been brainwashed.

"Seriously, Rebel? Listen to yourself. Secret goon squads? Secret lab levels?" She sounds more like my conspiracy-loving ex. And she knows better than anyone that his never-ending paranoia killed our relationship. "Have you been hanging out with Jeremy again?"

"Believe me or don't. But all those things are happening."

Before she can say another word, I grab my purse off the floor and start to storm out of her room. But she's been my friend for too long to just leave it like this, no matter how tired or angry I am.

I turn back when I hit the doorway, my eyes meeting her watery ones. Obviously, I'm not the only one affected by this fight—she looks as miserable as I feel.

"I wanted to tell you," she whispers. "So badly."

"Look, I've got to get some sleep," I tell her after a few long seconds. "Let me clear my head and I'll call you tomorrow. We can talk then."

She nods. "Yeah, okay."

"I love you, Kenna," she calls after me.

"Yeah, me too, Rebel," I murmur.

I'm halfway home when the tears start pouring down my face in a silent stream.

Stupid allergies, I tell myself as I swipe my cheek with the back of my hand.

If I was a better liar, I might even believe it.

❖ ❖ ❖

My head is whirling as I climb into my own bed. I feel like a puzzle with all the important pieces missing.

None of this makes any sense.

I expect to spend what's left of the night staring at the ceiling, but I'm out the moment my cheek hits my pillow.

Only it's not a peaceful sleep. My thoughts race through a bizarre version of the night's events. Rebel using her power to slam me into the ceiling during the break-in. Riley turning into a giant microscope so he can study me on a slide. Mom and Mr. Malone making out next to a grizzly bear in her office. I'm pretty sure that last one's going to require future therapy.

But then my dream turned to the past. Instead of Mom's office, I was in Dad's. Four-year-old me, playing under his desk at the superhero high command. He was president of the League before Mr. Malone. Before they built the Elite Superhero Lab.

The door burst open.

"Kenna?" my dad shouted. "Kenna, baby, where are you?"

I climbed out of my hiding spot. But when I saw the look of panic on his face, I wished I hadn't.

He grabbed me, clutched me to his chest, and raced into the hall. Long and gleaming white. All brightness and light. Except for the gang of villains who stood at the other end.

When they saw us, they started running.

I panicked, screamed. The light fixtures in the hallway exploded.

The villains hesitated, startled by broken glass raining down. Dad turned his back on them and set me on my feet.

"Run," he said, gently at first. The sound of footsteps echoed behind him. He shouted, "Run!"

I froze as he turned to face our enemies.

I tried to make out their faces, to see their features in the enveloping shadows. But I couldn't bring them into focus. A dozen years of trying, and their identities still remained a blurry mystery.

"You shouldn't have crossed us," one of them said.

"What you're doing is wrong," Dad countered, stepping toward them. *"You can't just—"*

The hallway exploded in a flash of light.

I wake up screaming, my body drenched in a cold sweat.

It takes me several deep breaths to remember where I am. When I finally calm down, I check the clock on my nightstand. It reads 2:43 in big, green numbers. Judging by the sun streaming through my windows, I'm guessing that's two forty-three in the afternoon.

God, I must have been tired. My body feels like I've been flattened by a steamroller.

I need caffeine. Or sugar. Or—even better—both. I drag myself out of bed and downstairs. I'm just stirring hazelnut creamer into my coffee when the front door opens.

"Kenna?" Mom calls out, her voice strained with worry.

Can I blame her?

"In the kitchen," I answer.

She drops her massive bag on the floor when she walks into the room.

Mom looks more frazzled than usual. Her messy brown bun is falling out, the circles under her eyes show through her makeup, and her cheeks are drawn like she hasn't eaten in days. Driven by her research, it's normal for her to spend twelve or even fourteen hours at a stretch at the lab searching for the key to eliminating villain powers and enhancing superhero abilities.

But today, she looks like she's taken on Nitro, Quake, and the rest of the v-bag army—all at the same time.

I don't bother asking if she wants food—she'll just say no. Setting down my coffee, I grab a carton of eggs and a container of chopped veggies out of the fridge and start fixing a scramble.

"How's the lab?" I ask.

"Almost back to normal." She shrugs out of her coat and then flings it on the counter. "The Cleaners work fast."

I turn my attention to the stove and throw some veggies into the sizzling pan. My culinary skills are limited, but I'm a scramble master.

"I've started the new batch of immunity serum." She walks to the vitamin cabinet and pulls out the bottle of aspirin. "My alarm is set for me to go back at seven tomorrow morning for the second phase."

I add the eggs to the pan, scraping and stirring to make sure it all cooks thoroughly.

Mom guards her immunity juice recipe like the password to Fort Knox. I can't even help her make the serum, and if she knew I'd told Rebel about it in fourth grade, she'd have a fit. No one else knows it exists, but I think she's still afraid someone might torture me for the information.

I don't like to think about anything happening to her, but if it did, where would I be? You'd think she'd want me to know the formula, just in case.

"If you tell me what to add," I offer, "I could go in and—"

"No." She throws back a couple aspirin and swallows them without water. "I don't want you going near the lab. The serum won't be ready for forty-eight hours, and until then, you're too vulnerable."

"What? No," I argue. "I'm in the middle of a trial. I have to go in to check the results."

She shakes her head. "Now is not the time for your impractical experiments."

"They're not impractical," I argue as I scrape the scramble onto a plate. My experiments are the only way I'm going to prove myself valuable to the superhero world. They're my only chance of feeling powerful enough to go after the monsters who killed my dad. Not that I'd tell her that. "Besides, I left my backpack there. I need my stuff."

Mom takes the plate from me. "It's not safe."

I clench my jaw, anger rolling through me. After surviving the villain attack and my fight with Rebel, I'm not in the mood for more bad news. "You can't just make decisions like that—"

"Actually, I can. I'm your mother. In fact…" She sets her plate down and walks over to my purse. I'm too stunned to react as she reaches in and pulls out my ID badge. "I'm going to make sure you stay away from the lab."

"Mom, no!" I lunge for the pass.

But I'm too late. She grabs the scissors from the junk drawer and cuts my ID into tiny plastic squares. I watch in horror as my badge—my access—falls to the tile floor in a series of little pings.

For several seconds I can't breathe. It seems like such an insignificant piece of plastic. But that ID with its magnetic strip and RFID chip represents my chance to do something that matters. My experiments matter. They make *me* matter.

And she just took it all away, like it was nothing. Like *I'm* nothing.

"I'll get another one." I cross my arms over my chest. "Heather likes me. She'll print me a new one."

Mom casually picks up her plate and forks a bite of egg. "The lab is on lockdown. No new passes are being issued until the security breach is eliminated."

The security breach—a.k.a. my supposed best friend.

Great. Just great. My life is getting better by the second. I swear I'm going to kill Rebel.

I clench my fists at my sides to keep from punching something. I might not have super strength, but I could do some serious damage to a stack of dishes right now.

"Hopefully they'll have the new security measures in place quickly. Rex is trying to sneak cameras into the lab again, but I'll tear them out if he does. That damn place already feels like NSA headquarters," she says, her voice growing distant and distracted. "We're just lucky the villains didn't get to sublevel three, or he would have the entire facility on military lockdown."

The hair on the back of my neck stands up.

"Sublevel three?" I echo.

Our lab is on sublevel one with the other neurological and bioengineering facilities. Chemical and physical labs are on sublevel two. There *is* no sublevel three.

But this is the third time in less than twenty-four hours that I've heard about a secret level. The first two I can dismiss as crazy conspiracy nonsense. My mom, however...

Her eyes widen for a split-second before she shakes her head and laughs. "Sublevel two. I meant sublevel two. It's been a long day."

Rebel's words echo in my mind. My mom is the most senior scientist at ESH Lab. If anyone had access to a secret level, she would. My chest tightens.

I must be so tired that I'm having aural hallucinations. Except…except Rebel seemed so sure. As did Draven and his friends. And even my mother said it casually at first, like its existence is obvious.

"I'm exhausted," Mom says. "I've been up for nearly thirty-six hours, and if I'm lucky, I'll sleep until morning."

I nod and manage to force out a whispered, "Good night."

She stops in the doorway and turns to me, a soft smile on her face. "In the meantime, don't go getting into fights with any villains."

I nod weakly as she walks upstairs.

They can't be right. There can't be a secret sublevel where heroes torture and experiment on kidnapped villains. Evil or not, villains are still people. They're still human and deserve basic human rights. Superheroes are the good guys. They don't hurt people. They sure as hell don't torture them.

I'm not sure how long I stand there, palms splayed on the counter to hold myself up, mind whirling while I try to make sense of it all. Finally I shake my head, knocking the crazy thoughts from my mind.

"It's not true," I tell myself again. "Like Mom said, she's exhausted. It was just a slip of the tongue."

But as I stand there, trying to convince myself of what I know to be true—what I *want* to be true—I catch sight of her coat draped across the granite. Her coat…with her security badge.

She may have cut my pass to pieces, but hers is right there. She's planning to be dead to the world for the next dozen hours. I could take her card, reassure myself that there is no secret sublevel at ESH, and get the stuff I forgot at the lab too.

She'll never even know her badge was gone.

I stand there for another minute, staring at the badge. It's the answer to all my problems. Well, at least, all my non-Rebel problems. Then, before I can talk myself out of it, I snatch my mom's pass and slide it into my pocket. In a few short hours, as soon as the sun sets and the security guards change shift, I'm going in.

I'll prove Rebel and the villains wrong.

CHAPTER 6

Sneaking out of the house isn't a problem. Once my mom falls asleep, it would take a foghorn or a full-scale villain assault on her bedroom to wake her before she's ready to get up.

Getting into the lab isn't a problem either. The night security guards haven't seen my mom yet, so they don't know that I've been banned from the facility. They don't bother to check the badge—they just let me scan my way in like I do every night.

Even packing up my research isn't a problem. There's a lot of it, and some of it is kind of hard to carry, but I find a couple boxes that will hold the fragile stuff pretty well. It's not ideal, but I'll just continue my experiments at home until Mom gets her sanity back.

Everything goes like clockwork. All that's left is to find sublevel three. The problem is that I don't have a clue how or where to look. There must be an entrance. But where?

This building is huge. There are three levels above ground and two—well, maybe three—below. Plus, the layout is down-right labyrinthine. A million different hallways crisscross each other, and each hallway leads to four or five separate labs or storage areas or offices. I explored a lot of them when I was younger. There's not much else to do when your mom is obsessed with her job and you're too young to actually touch anything in a state-of-the-art research center.

It was annoying when I was little, but now I'm glad, because I don't have to waste time wandering these halls. I already know where they lead. At the same time, if sublevel three exists, that means, even with how well I know this place, I've missed something.

Even worse, it means I've been in the dark for a very long time.

The thought doesn't sit well. But it makes me even more determined to prove these crazy suspicions wrong.

Unsure of where else to start, I search my mom's lab— back to pre-Nitro condition, thanks to the Cleaners—from top to bottom. I feel a little ridiculous pressing against walls, pushing buttons, and checking out every nook and cranny. But I don't know what a secret entrance is supposed to look like, so I'm trying to examine anything and everything that might fit that bill.

My mom's lab is clean, just like I expected it to be. But really, I consider, while one might imagine the center's top scientist would need access to the supersecret level, she wouldn't be the *only* one. I think about Mr. Malone, about the Superhero Collective—the elite group that makes all the decisions in the super world—and their immensely huge egos. They would demand access to a special level. And not just access, *easy* access.

Which means I'm totally looking in the wrong place. Although my mom is down here on sublevel one, the Superhero Collective's offices are all above ground. They have huge offices with huge windows that reflect how important they are. Of course access to supersecret sublevel three—if it exists—would be wherever *they* are.

Leaving my research in a pile near the door so I can swing by and get it later, I head for the elevators and the building's third floor.

As the elevator whooshes me upward, my stomach sinks. *What am I doing?* I almost reach for the button to take me back down. Not only is this a ridiculous wild-goose chase, but I could be in big trouble if I get caught.

I've never been good with unanswered questions though.

I have no choice. I have to follow the goose.

The good thing about my mom's pass? She has access to everything—even the inner sanctums.

I decide to search Mr. Malone's office first. I've seen my mom swipe her access card at the entrance to his suite.

It works. I'm in.

Walking into this room is like taking a step back in time to a nineteenth-century palace, complete with a king and an unlimited budget. Silk curtains, antique couches, expensive paintings.

I try to ignore the opulence, but being here makes me uncomfortable. Not because I'm spying on Rebel's dad, but because this office is all about power. It clearly belongs to someone who is impressed with himself and wants everyone else to be impressed too. Which makes me feel icky, especially given what Draven and Rebel said. A guy who turns his office into a shrine to his self-importance, who is so egotistical and power-happy that he actually named this building after himself... Suddenly, all the outlandish theories don't seem quite so far-fetched.

But taking in the view isn't going to get me anywhere, so I start looking. I'm totally lost. There's just so *much* in this room, so many places to hide a secret entrance.

I peek behind all of the paintings, then check the filing cabinet, the closet, even underneath the rugs. I don't find anything. No trapdoor, no secret panel. Nothing is even the least bit suspicious.

There is a gigantic safe on one wall, tucked behind a painting of some epic battle scene, but it's certainly not big enough for a human to fit through—especially one as tall and broad as Mr. Malone. I don't know how to break the combo, but I feel pretty confident in assuming it's not the secret door.

At the same time, I wonder why he needs a safe anyway. What kind of secrets is he hiding? The heroes are supposed to be all about transparency. *Secrets are for villains*, Mr. Malone always says.

Jeremy would laugh at how paranoid I'm being, but it's a massive safe. It could hold a lot of secrets.

Still, it's not like I have the ability to melt steel, so I move on. I've searched the office, so I head for the bathroom—yes, he has his own bathroom attached to his office, complete with shower and steam room.

I can't imagine the Superhero Collective traipsing through a bathroom to get to a secret sublevel, but maybe that makes it the perfect access point. The shower, specifically, would be a really clever place for a secret door. All that tile provides plenty of places to hide an access button. Before I can do much more than step into the shower, I hear Mr. Malone's office door opening and muffled voices.

Oh shit! He's here! I have absolutely no excuse to be in Mr. Malone's office except for the truth, and it's not like I can just blurt *that* out. *Who, me? I'm just investigating an accusation made by villains who I'm not even supposed to remember. But I believed them enough to doubt the president of the League's integrity.* Yeah. That would go over well.

I'm totally screwed.

I would trade anything for the power of invisibility right now.

I launch into full-blown panic mode. Glancing frantically around the small room, I try to find a place to hide. It's not like there are a lot of options—the shower is a glass cubicle, the cabinet under the sink is stuffed with Kleenex boxes and other stuff, and the towel closet has shelves that only leave about two inches between them and the door.

I settle on the steam room—it has a full-length door with only a small, square window. Hopefully Mr. Malone's not here for a late-night sauna session.

As the voices get closer, I slip inside and close the door carefully, holding the handle so it doesn't click into place.

"I don't know, Rex," a male voice I don't recognize says. "I'm not happy with this recent breach of security."

"I understand, but it's fine. Sit down, have a drink." There's the tinkle of what sounds like ice cubes on glass. "They didn't get anything."

I can't believe how clearly I can hear them. What if they can hear me too? I try to quiet my panicked breathing.

With all the money Mr. Malone spent on this office, you would think he'd have spent some on soundproofing. But isn't that typical? All show and no substance.

I press myself back against the wall.

"They knew to come here. To look for the missing villains—"

My heart stops. Terror rips through me and for a second I forget how to breathe.

"Again, they didn't find anything or we would have heard about it by now. And if they try to come back, they will run into deadly security measures."

"I'm not sure that's good enough," a different male voice says.

"It is, John," Mr. Malone insists. "Trust me."

The other men don't respond, or if they do, their voices are too soft for me to make out. They must be displeased though, because Mr. Malone suddenly booms, "Why don't you come down with me? You can take a look at what I've done today. I assure you, it will put your minds at ease."

"That might be best," the first man says. "I'd like to look over the new security, make sure there are no flaws."

"Absolutely, absolutely." Mr. Malone's joviality sounds forced, but that's not exactly a surprise. I've been around the Malone house enough to know he hates being questioned about anything. He gets furious every time Rebel stands up to him over something stupid. I can't imagine how angry he is right now.

He would never trip over himself to please the other members of the Collective. So who are these other men that Mr. Malone feels the need to placate them?

The voices fade a little, and I hear what I think is the office door shutting. Then I don't hear anything.

For a few seconds I just stand there, shaking, my heart in my throat. I can't believe how careless I was, how close I came to getting caught. And I really, really can't believe what I just overheard.

71

I replay the conversation, the sick feeling in my stomach getting worse. For the first time tonight, I'm not sure that I'm going to prove my doubts wrong.

The idea is devastating. Terrifying. Incomprehensible. Even though I'm almost positive Mr. Malone is gone, I open the steam-room door slowly. Creep out. Peer around the door into the office. The *empty* office. Thank God.

The best chance I have to get answers is to follow Mr. Malone and the others. But I have to be careful. Something tells me, Rebel's best friend or not, things won't go well for me if I'm caught snooping.

I cross Mr. Malone's office and peer through the interior windows. He's walking down the hall with two men, both in *slate-gray suits.*

Damn, the Ray-Ban brigade. I knew those guys were bad news.

I start to follow them, making sure to leave a good distance between us. It's not unheard of for me to be up on the third floor, even at this time of night, so if Mr. Malone sees me it won't be the end of the world. But he can't think I'm following him.

When the men reach the elevator bay, I dart into an alcove, press myself against the back of it, and hold my breath until the elevator car arrives.

The doors swoosh shut and I peer out. They're gone. The coast is clear.

I press the call button, and the second elevator starts up from the lobby. As I wait, the first elevator's indicator light stops on sublevel two. My heart beats double time as the second elevator arrives and I step inside. Clearly they're not going to my mom's lab to see the new security measures, because that's on sublevel one.

When I swipe Mom's security badge on the access panel and press sublevel two, the elevator descends quickly, bypassing all other levels. It only takes a few moments, but it feels like forever. I clench my hands into fists to keep them from shaking.

The elevator opens onto a containment hallway, a long, empty space with no labs or rooms on either side. Sublevel two is laid out differently than sublevel one. They conduct far more volatile experiments here, so additional safety precautions are in place. No one wants a nuclear blast getting out of the basement.

Mr. Malone and the gray suits are nowhere to be seen. Where could they have gone? I'm only a few seconds behind them. And since Mr. Malone doesn't have super speed, it makes no sense. They can't have made it out of the containment hallway already. They couldn't have just disappeared into thin air, right?

I step off the elevator, wondering if I made a mistake. But when I press the call button, both elevators' doors slide open. No, Mr. Malone and the Ray-Ban brigade definitely came to this level.

So where did they go?

I start running, and still it takes me a full minute to reach the end of the hallway.

No way did Mr. Malone turn the corner before my elevator arrived. No freaking way. Which means...what? I don't have a clue, but something shady is going on.

I head back and push the elevator button again. Again, the doors to both elevators slide open. I get in the one on the left this time, the one Mr. Malone and the gray suits took.

I don't press any buttons. Instead, I just stand there as the doors close in front of me.

What am I missing? They got in this elevator, descended to sublevel two, and...what? Vanished? I know I live in a world of superpowers, but that just doesn't happen. Only about one percent of superheroes have the power to go invisible, and Mr. Malone isn't one of them. Which means they are somewhere.

I tap on the floor, push on the walls. Nothing. I'm frustrated now, really frustrated. I press the button to take me back up to three. The elevator rises effortlessly. At the top level, instead of getting out, I press the button to go back down to sublevel two.

It's crazy, but I can't help thinking that the answer is here in this elevator. I just need to find it.

Come on, Kenna. Think.

The elevator goes back down, but when it stops at the second sublevel, the doors don't open. It just sits there, like it's waiting for me to do something. Too bad I don't have a clue what that something is.

I start to step forward and the door slides open.

My movement must have signaled the door sensor. Why would they need a pressure trigger in an elevator?

My jaw drops.

"Unless..."

Instead of stepping out into the hall, I swipe Mom's badge over the reader and return to the center of the elevator. When the door closes, I turn and take a step toward the back.

The rear panel of the elevator slides open, revealing a dimly lit concrete space and a winding staircase. The staircase doesn't go up, like an emergency stairwell might. It goes down. To what I can only imagine is secret sublevel three.

CHAPTER 7

My ears strain for sounds of movement or danger. I don't hear anything, so after a minute, I step out into the stairwell. It's a circular staircase—which is weird enough in a lab—so I can't see the bottom. I close my eyes, take a couple deep breaths, and start down one slow step at a time.

I can't believe this. I just can't believe this. How can there be a secret level? *Why* is there a secret level?

I'm confused, worried, more than a little scared. And annoyed, really annoyed. My mother lied to me. She looked me straight in the eye and lied. She made me doubt Rebel, made me doubt myself, and that pisses me off. It also makes me wonder what else she's lied about. And why.

At the bottom of the staircase there is a door. It's locked, requiring a security pass. I swipe my mother's badge and the light changes to green. Proof that she not only knows about this level, but she has authorization to be here.

Before I open the door, I look through the narrow, rectangular window just above the doorknob. Two cameras hang on the opposite wall, scanning the length of the hallway, one on each side. The whole thing is monitored at all times.

Which pretty much sucks for me. My mom might have

clearance, but I certainly don't. If they catch me on camera, I can't even begin to imagine how much trouble I'll be in.

But I'm close, so close, to finding out what's going on down here. I came back to the lab against my mother's specific orders because I have to know. I have to prove to myself that the crazy thoughts I've been considering for the last eighteen hours are as nuts as they seem. Villains aren't victims. They're liars. I can't walk away. Not now.

So I wait and I watch the cameras sweep the hallway again and again and again. I track the arc. I memorize the pattern, rendering the data as a 3-D image in my mind. And I notice a blind spot. A couple of them, actually.

There are exactly four seconds when neither of the cameras picks up the hallway right outside the door. Two seconds when they meet in the middle and can't see directly beneath each other, and then another four seconds when the second camera can't see the end of the hallway.

It's a long distance, but if I time it precisely right—and run like hell—I can make it. I hope.

I wait a little longer, count the seconds again as I watch the cameras run through one, two, three more sweeps. I know if I don't go now, I never will. I'll lose my nerve and I'll never know what's down here.

Taking a deep breath, I wait for the camera to get into position and launch into motion, running full-speed down the hallway. I get to the first true blind spot, where the cameras cross, and wait, breath held, always counting. Then I book it again.

I'm terrified I'm not going to make it, but I do. I turn the corner, breathing heavily and praying there aren't more cameras on this hallway.

My hope is in vain, because of course there's another camera. But thankfully only one, which gives me a lot more time to walk down the hall without getting caught.

I make it down this hallway and another using that same technique. I'm not sure where I'm going, or even what I'm looking for. But I figure I'll know it when I see it.

There are labs on either side of me, dark rooms that look empty. And while there's a part of me that wants to know what's behind every single door, there isn't time. What I'm looking for—what I need to see—will be wherever Mr. Malone and the gray suits went. Which means I need to keep moving.

I turn the corner again, expecting to have to dodge yet another camera. But in this hallway there are no cameras, at least none that I can see. This only makes me more nervous. After all that security, all that surveillance, why would this area be unwatched? Unless there's something going on here that Mr. Malone and the Superhero Collective don't want *anyone* to see.

Fear rockets down my spine. It's not fear of getting caught that paralyzes me. It's fear of what I'll find. Of what I'll see. I don't want my faith in the superheroes to be misplaced.

But I've gotten this far and I'm not going back until I know. Squaring my shoulders, I keep going. Most of the rooms are dark, but fluorescent lighting pours under one of the doorways. Someone is in there.

I drop to my knees and crawl along the wall. The window in the center of the door is covered by tightly closed blinds. I'm just inching up to peek through when I hear it. A scream so pained, so tortured, that I swear it chills the blood in my veins. Every hair on my body stands at full attention.

I freeze. Another scream rends the air, this one even worse than the first. Adrenaline pours through me. My chest tightens and it's hard to drag air into my lungs. I move to a kneeling position and search the window, desperately looking for a split in the blinds so that I can see something, anything.

There's a gap at the right side of the window where one of the blinds is bent. It's small, but it's enough.

I peer through, and my heart stops.

Rebel's boyfriend, Dante, is tied to a chair in the middle of the room. He's badly bruised, his head hanging down, shoulders slumped. I can't be sure, but it looks like the only thing keeping him upright is the strap around his torso and arms, pressing his shoulders against the back of the chair.

All kinds of cables are hooked up to him, and as I watch, his entire body jolts and shakes, almost like an electric current is running through him. My hand covers my mouth to keep me from crying out as he jerks and shudders and screams.

Oh God, does he scream.

I'm not sure how much time passes before the shaking stops and his body goes limp. But it's right after he vomits all over himself.

Somebody I don't recognize hits him hard on the side of the head. He barely reacts, his body listing to the side under the pressure of the blow. But that's it. His eyes are blank, his face slack. Then he starts to jerk again.

I can't watch anymore. I whirl around and sink my butt to the floor, my hands still clenched tightly over my mouth. Oh my God. Oh My God. OH MY GOD! What is going on? What the hell is going on?

My mind races and my eyes sting. This must be what shock feels like.

I sit there for a minute, two, trying to get my head together. Trying to make sense of what I've seen. But there's no sense to be made. What's going on in that room isn't an experiment— which would be bad enough. No, it's torture, pure and simple.

Another scream rips through the quiet. This can't be happening. This just can't be happening.

But it is.

It really is.

I take a deep breath. The hall spins around me, but I force the nausea down and climb back to my knees. I peer through the slit in the blinds again, then wish I hadn't. Huge fists rain down on Dante's shoulders, his chest, his back, his head.

A movement in the corner of the room catches my eye, and I press my cheek against the glass. Mr. Malone and the gray suits are watching, observing casually, like they're looking at a painting in a museum.

The look of *pride* on Mr. Malone's face turns my veins to ice.

I want to rewind time by ten minutes and not find the entrance to sublevel three. I want to stop this guy's pain. I want to open the door and scream at them at the top of my lungs. But I'm smart enough to know that would get both of us killed. By *heroes*.

The knowledge turns me inside out.

All my life there have only been three absolutes: ordinaries are useless, villains are evil, and heroes are good. Heroes are supposed to be the people the rest of the world looks up to, the very best examples of humanity.

I've spent my whole life distrusting villains—hating villains—and now I find out that some heroes are just as bad. Maybe worse. This kind of brutality is worse than anything I've ever heard villains accused of. This is worse than what they did to my father. Worse than murder.

Heroes are the good guys, the ones who stop things like this from happening. The heroes I know would never do this. But they are. They are. So what's going on?

Hypnosis? Mind control? I don't know. Somebody is responsible for this. There's no other explanation.

But who? What are they getting out of it?

Another scream pierces the air, and I shudder. I've never felt so useless in my life. There is nothing I can do to help him, to save him. Nothing I can do to make it stop. What I wouldn't give to have *any* superpower.

I've been powerless my whole life, but nothing prepared me for the horror that crawls through me.

I have to do something. I can't just walk away knowing what they're doing to Rebel's boyfriend. Villain or not, he's a human being and no one—*no one*—deserves to be treated like that.

With that one thought clear in my mind, I pull myself together. Crawl out from beneath the window. Race down the hall. I want out of here. Now. It takes every ounce of my self-control not to run full tilt back to the elevator. I have just enough awareness to remember the cameras. So I pause at the corner of the hallway and count. Then I run.

Pause. Count. Run.

Pause. Count. Run.

I do it again and again, until I'm at the stairwell.

I fling open the door and fall inside. I'm sobbing now, close to hysterical, but I make myself think. I drag myself up the stairs to sublevel two and press the elevator call button. When the door opens, I stumble inside. I swipe Mom's security badge and jab the button for sublevel one.

All I can think of is getting back to the safety of my mom's lab.

I need to pull myself together. Every second I waste is another second Dante will be tortured. That thought, more than any other, brings me back. My tears dry and my breathing quiets.

I'm not calm—how can I be?—but I'm functioning. And for now that's enough. I take a second to splash cold water on my face. Then I grab my research log and shove it into the back of my jeans. I leave the rest of my materials. I shove the boxes back into the cabinets at my station so it won't look suspicious. I even leave my backpack. No one will know I've been here. Then I race toward the emergency stairwell.

I spare a quick glance around to see if Mr. Malone's newly installed cameras cover this part of the hallway yet. I don't see any, so I reach over and pull the fire alarm.

I can't rescue Dante right now, but hopefully this will buy him a reprieve.

As the alarm shrieks, I book it up the stairs to the lobby. By the time I get there, one of the security guards is on the phone with the fire department while the other ushers me out of the building.

I follow his directions, but the second he turns his back on me, I sprint toward my car. I don't think I actually breathe until I'm pulling out of the parking lot. And even then, I'm only one shaky step from frantic.

I put some miles between the lab and me, then park at a drive-through custard shop. I pull out my cell phone and text Rebel.

Need to c u now v important

I wait impatiently for her answer. It only takes about thirty seconds.

U ok?

Yes but need to talk r u home? I reply.

No 4179 Valmont Ct

I don't know where that is and I don't care. I enter the address into the GPS on my phone, then dash off another text.

B there in 20

Fifteen minutes later I park in front of a large, gray house in an area of town I've never been before. An area said to be popular with villains.

If I was less desperate or upset, I'd probably turn and walk away. But I *am* desperate and I *am* upset and I have nowhere else to go. No one else to trust. Not when my own mom lied to me about the secret sublevel.

If she knows it exists, she probably knows what goes on in there. And if she does, I don't know what to think. All I know is I can't face her. Not now. Not with this.

I text Rebel to let her know I'm here, and by the time I get to the door, she's standing there waiting for me.

The instant I see her, tears burn the back of my eyes again. I blink, try to make them disappear, but they roll down my face instead.

"Kenna!" She reaches out for me, pulls me into a hug. "What's wrong?"

"I saw them. I saw—"

"What? What did you see?"

I choke up. "I found the secret level."

She stiffens against me, and before I can say anything else, the door is yanked wide open. Draven stands there, looking just as dark and scowly as he did the previous night. Just as badass. Like he can take on anything.

I never thought I'd be so relieved to see a villain.

"What did you see?" he demands, his voice hoarser, more gravelly than I remember.

I swallow and force out the words, even knowing how much they're going to hurt him and Rebel. "They have your boyfriend. They're torturing him."

For a moment, silence hangs in the air as they stare at me, wide-eyed.

Draven clears his throat, and though his face is pale, his voice is even when he says, "I think you'd better come in."

I hesitate. *These are villains,* I tell myself. *Bad guys. If I walk through this door, I'm committing treason.* But then an image of Dante comes back to me, strapped to that chair with electricity running through his body until he screams and vomits and cries.

Black and white is dissolving. So is right and wrong. If some heroes can be bad, maybe I have to trust that some villains can be…good?

I don't know if I can, but I don't have a choice. I haven't since the moment I peered in that window.

Taking a deep breath, I walk through the door. As I do, I feel the ground shift beneath my feet.

CHAPTER 8

I only thought I was mixed-up before.

Because the moment I cross the threshold and get a good look at who Rebel's hanging out with, everything I thought I knew, everything I thought I saw, gets a little more chaotic.

Dante stands there looking whole and healthy and entirely *un*tortured. His fauxhawk's perfectly groomed, though his eyes look dead and his face is completely drained of color. It's as if I had only imagined the scene back at ESH.

But I didn't imagine it. I might be confused, but I'm not crazy.

"You... Y-y-you're... I *saw* you." I shake my head. "How is this possible?"

I can't help but back away from the ghost. As I do, I collide with something. Someone.

"Deacon." Draven's voice is low and hard against my ear. "You saw his brother, Deacon. This is Dante."

"Deacon?" I echo.

"Identical twins," Rebel says as she wraps her arms, her whole body, around Dante as if she's trying to protect him. Shield him.

"I—" My voice catches in my throat. "I didn't know."

When she said they were brothers, I never imagined they might be *twins*. Does that make it worse? I look at Dante and think maybe it does.

For several long, heavy moments the room is silent except for our breathing and the soft, gentle words Rebel whispers into Dante's ear. I can't hear what she's saying, but it seems to be having some kind of soothing effect on Dante because he's clinging to her like she's the only thing keeping him standing.

Not that I blame him. Not when he just found out that his brother is being tortured as we speak.

His twin brother. Deacon. The guy they broke into the lab to find.

The puzzle pieces start assembling themselves to form a picture.

No wonder they had been so angry and frantic. No wonder Nitro nearly blew the place to bits. If they had even a clue what was happening to Deacon, then their restraint was actually pretty impressive. If something like that was happening to Rebel and I couldn't get to her, couldn't find her... Well, let's just say I'm shocked they didn't do more damage to the lab. A lot more damage.

I want to say something, to apologize for what's happening. To apologize for ratting on them to the SHPD last night, for stopping them before they found him, for not doing more for Deacon than pulling the fire alarm tonight. But before I can get out much more than "I—" Draven slams his fist into the wall. Slams it *through* the wall, to be more exact.

"Two-faced sons of bitches." He hits the wall again. And again. By the time he pulls back to smash his fist into the drywall for a fourth time, his knuckles are bruised and bleeding.

"Hey." I don't know what possesses me—or why it bothers me so much to see him hurt himself—but I wrap my palms over his fist. "Don't. That won't help anything."

I rub my thumb gently over his injured knuckles. He stiffens and glances down at where our skin touches.

His voice is rough when he says, "How do you know what will—"

"Was my dad there?" Rebel interrupts, talking over him.

I can't even form the words. How do you tell your best friend that you saw her dad standing over her boyfriend's twin, casually watching a torture session as if it were a baseball game? Tears spring to my eyes as I drop Draven's hand and shake my head helplessly. Not to say no, but because I don't know how to tell her yes.

"I knew it," she whispers, then turns back to Dante. "I'm so sorry, baby."

He doesn't answer. While Draven looks like he's ready to tear the whole world apart, Dante just looks like he's in shock.

Who could blame them?

"Of course Rex was there." Draven wipes his bloody knuckles on his jeans. "It's as bad as we feared. It goes all the way to the top. The whole damn hero world is corrupt."

"That's not true," I say. "It's not *all* heroes."

He sneers at me, his fierce eyes blazing with a rage that paradoxically sends a shiver up my spine. "Don't be naïve, hero girl."

While he didn't *say* "hero-worshiper," his tone tells me that's exactly what he means. He thinks I'm no better than the men who are torturing Deacon.

"Draven's right," Rebel says, like she's begging me to understand. "It's time you finally saw the truth."

"You're wrong." I'm not trying to be difficult, but I can't accept the idea that *all* heroes are bad. "I work in that lab. I see heroes being heroic every day. Just because a few bad apples—"

"No, Kenna," Rebel interrupts. "It's not just a few. I've been digging into this for almost a year. It's way more widespread than you think."

My mind reels at the thought. It's bad enough to think that a small group of rotten eggs have worked their way into power. What she's talking about is so extreme it's practically incomprehensible.

Some heroes, yes. Obviously. But not *all*. Not even *most*.

I can't believe the League would let that happen.

"I don't—" I shake my head. "There must be a logical explanation. Like mind control or—"

"You don't get it!" Rebel shouts.

I jerk back, stunned at her rage. This is my best friend, the girl I've known all my life, the girl I know better than anyone. How could I not realize how bad it's gotten?

"Rebel, I—"

"Of course she doesn't get it." Draven again. "She's been drinking the League Kool-Aid. Cherry-flavored, is it?"

"Hey, screw you!" I turn on him, frustrated and furious. "Just because you think you're so big and bad doesn't mean you've got all the answers. In fact, last night you seemed pretty—"

I freeze as it hits me that I'm not supposed to remember the break-in. Rebel might have told me about her boyfriend, but I'm not supposed to know who Draven is, am not supposed to remember him at all. The last thing I want is for a bunch of villains to know about my immunity, even if they are friends of Rebel's. Whatever Draven does to push my buttons almost pushed me into revealing my biggest secret. I can't lose control like that.

"Stop," Rebel says, calmer now that she's taken a few breaths. "Just…stop. You can't defend them, Kenna. You have no idea—" She closes her eyes. "This is only the tip of an iceberg of evil. Trust me when I say it's not just a few bad heroes, and it's not as simple as mind control. It's much bigger and much worse than anything you can imagine."

I open my mouth, but what can I say? I trust Rebel. The villainous identity of her secret boyfriend aside, she has never lied to me. And while she may be a bit out there, she's never been one to leap to unjustified conclusions or make unfounded accusations. Why would she start now?

Part of me refuses to accept her claims though. Part of me believes that she's wrong and there is some non-world-shattering explanation. Except right now, it doesn't matter. Right now, the only thing that matters is getting Deacon out alive.

As if reading my thoughts, Dante whispers, "Tell me."

My heart thunders.

Rebel turns to him, taking his face between her palms. "Babe, no."

Behind me, Draven says, "Don't."

I don't want to relive any of it. What I saw—I'm not sure I can put it into words. I'm not sure I should.

But when Dante pushes Rebel's hands away, his cheeks splotchy and eyes glistening, I can't look away. I try to imagine what I would want if I were in his situation, if it were my mom or Rebel in that chair on sublevel three. I can't even begin to imagine what it would be like if it were my *twin*.

Still, if it was me, I'd want to know. I would *need* to know. And as painful as it will be, Dante *deserves* to know.

I have to tell him.

"They had him strapped to a chair," I begin, and have to pause to maintain my composure. "I think they were shooting electricity through him."

Dante squeezes his eyes shut and Rebel hugs him tighter, petting him softly while she rests her head on his chest. I want to close my eyes too, to shut out the memories, but I can't take my gaze off Dante. As I replay all the horrifying details for him, for all of them, Dante's legs give out and he collapses onto the couch. Rebel goes down with him, holding him still.

"I pulled the fire alarm on my way out," I tell them, "hoping it would"—I look at Draven—"distract them, maybe."

I feel so helpless. When I stopped these villains in the lab last night, I hadn't known the truth. But tonight...I know. And I couldn't do anything to stop it. I'm not used to feeling helpless. Powerless, yes, but helpless? It's not a feeling I like.

There must have been something more I could have done for Deacon. I should have burst into that room and made them let him go. I should have threatened to expose them. I should have done something, *anything*, rather than run away.

I don't realize there are tears streaming down my cheeks too, until Draven reaches out to wipe them away. His eyes are distant, but his hands are gentle.

Rebel, the girl who never cries—not even when she broke her ankle flying off the swing set in fourth grade—sobs into Dante's shoulder.

The seconds tick by as we each dwell in our own private torment. Then Dante lets out a primal scream.

The windows rattle and a picture falls off the wall.

"Dante, no—" Rebel shouts, but she's cut off by a roar of wind.

Draven shoves me behind him as a dining room chair flies across the hall, slamming into the wall and splintering into kindling. Books fly off shelves and the TV crashes to the floor.

A mini tornado tears through the house, tossing around everything in its path. Every time Dante yells, it gets stronger, adding another gust of wind to the destruction.

Guess I know what Dante's power is.

"Baby," Rebel yells above the din. "Baby, come back to me. We'll find him."

Draven shields me against the nearest wall.

"You shouldn't have told him," he growls at me, as debris pelts him in the back.

Who is he to decide what Dante should hear? "It's his brother. He has the right to know."

I shove at his shoulders, but Draven doesn't move. He just glares at me. His obvious blame mixes with my own guilt about abandoning Deacon, leaving me angry at myself instead of him. I stop trying to push him away. Take the protection he's giving me.

"We can go get him," Rebel says, still trying to get through to Dante. "Kenna knows how to get to the secret level. We can rescue him."

In a blink, the wind is gone. Airborne objects fall to the ground and the windows stop rattling.

"Now." Dante's voice is rough and harsh. "We go now."

"Damn straight now," Draven replies, backing away now that the threat is gone. He asks me, "How do we get in?"

"*You* don't."

"The hell we don't. Either you tell us how or I *will* make you." His voice is calm, which only underscores the menace in his gaze. And the absolute confidence that he can bend me to his will.

His irises grow colder, start to crystallize, and I know that if I don't stop him, he's going to use his mind power on me. And when it doesn't work, I won't have to worry about keeping my immunity a secret anymore.

"I mean you *can't*," I hurry to explain. "No villain can."

He frowns, like he wants to argue, but his eyes go back to normal.

"She's right." Rebel squeezes Dante's hand. "The new security protocols the zeroes put in place will keep out anyone with a villain power signature."

"They can't keep me out," Draven insists.

Everything about him—his shoulder, his jaw, his voice—is tense. He might be looking for a fight, but he and Dante would be dramatically outnumbered. They would never stand a chance, and then neither would Deacon.

"Even without the new protocols," I interject, trying to be the voice of reason, "the place is swarming with guards and heroes. They're on high alert, especially since I set off the fire alarm. There's no way we'll be able to get in, get him, and get away without being caught."

Draven's eyebrow shoots up in the middle of my speech. I lift mine right back up, as if saying, *Yeah, I said we.*

"Then what do you suggest, hero girl?" he asks. "Call and ask them to release him? Politely?"

"I don't know. I haven't gotten that far." In fact, my

thinking hasn't progressed much beyond don't-get-killed. "But I know that running in, powers blazing, will only get *us* caught and you dead. Deacon too, probably." It's a low blow, but I figure even if they're willing to endanger their own lives, they won't want to do anything that might turn retribution against Deacon—especially after everything he's suffered.

They might have broken in last night with a stolen security pass and a guy who can wipe minds, but under the new protocols they wouldn't get through the front door if they had Mr. Malone's own badge.

"We go to my dad," Dante says.

"No way," Draven counters. "Telling Uncle Anton is a bad idea."

"Uncle Anton?" I echo. "As in Anton the Annihilator? As in—"

"Yes," Rebel interrupts, ending the questions.

Dante's father—Draven's uncle—is Anton Cole, the leader of the Core, the supervillain equivalent of the League? The guy is a legend, in the worst possible way. Rebel's own father—who usually only gets involved in the most heinous of cases—is the one who set the price on his head. Fifteen million dollars. No villain anywhere has ever commanded such a steep bounty.

Rebel couldn't have picked a more dangerous family to hook up with, which is why I return her look with one that says oh-boy-do-we-need-to-talk-about-this-later.

"Dad will get him out," Dante says. "No matter the cost."

"Exactly," Draven argues. "No matter the cost. We bring Uncle Anton back from the negotiations early and this will turn into all-out war."

Dante snarls. "Sounds good to me."

"Not to me," Draven counters. "You know what happens in a war? People do stupid things that get other people killed."

"As long as heroes are getting killed," Dante replies, "then what's the problem?"

"The problem is that heroes wouldn't be the only ones to die. And what if Deacon is one of the first casualties?" Draven sits next to Dante on the couch. "If we're not careful, he could get…hurt in the crossfire."

I bite my lip when he hesitates over the word "hurt." I know he almost said "killed," but that's the last thing any of us want Dante thinking about. Getting Deacon out safely has to be the number one priority, not worrying about Dante going off the rails and doing something that might get *everybody* killed.

"It has to be the two of us." I look at Rebel. "We can get him out."

"You're right," she replies.

"No way," Draven argues, at the same time as Dante says, "Absolutely not."

Rebel's jaw clenches in a stubborn gesture I am far too familiar with. Even with all this going on, it's nice not to be on the receiving end of it for once.

"There's no other choice," she says. "You guys can't get in. *We* can."

"How will you get him past the guards?" Draven asks. "How will you even carry him? If he's in as bad shape as Kenna says, he won't be able to walk."

"Carrying him out is no problem." To prove her point, Rebel channels her power to move the living room couch back to its pre-tornado position. "Telekinesis comes in really handy sometimes."

Draven looks skeptical. "But the guards—"

"I can take care of them," I insist. And I know exactly how I'm going to do it.

About a year ago, Mom developed a new knockout serum that can render someone unconscious. It's another one of her not-for-League-knowledge projects. It works so fast that when she tested it on me, I was out for two days. I woke up with the mother of all headaches and the dryness of the Sahara in my mouth. She has since refined the formula so that it only knocks out its victim for an hour. If we use it on the heroes, it'll give us more than enough time to get in, free Deacon, and get him out.

Mom has a whole supply in the refrigerator in the garage, along with modified tranquilizer guns to deliver the dosage from a safe distance.

The guards will never see us coming. Or going. I grab Draven's arm and look him straight in the eye. "I need to get to my house."

"What?" He looks appalled. "No way! How do I know you won't tell your mom and blow the whole thing?"

It's a good question, and I don't really have a good answer. At least nothing beyond, "I guess you're just going to have to trust me."

CHAPTER 9

"Y ou didn't have to drive," I tell Draven for the third time as he puts his car in gear and backs out of the driveway. He ignores me.

I mean it, but I'm also glad he insisted on coming. I know it's more about the fact that he doesn't quite trust me than from any desire to protect me. Still, now that the reality of the situation is settling in. I'm not sure I would be the best person to be behind the wheel right now.

"Turn right at the light," I say as we leave the neighborhood.

He flicks on the turn signal but otherwise gives no recognition that I'm in the car. Understandable. He's just found out that one of his best friends, his cousin, is being tortured by his archenemies. And that his fate is now in the hands of two girls raised in the superhero world.

It'd be hard for anyone to take. Then again, we're both dealing with world-shattering news...and having to trust people we normally wouldn't.

We drive a few blocks in silence before Draven finally speaks.

"How long—" He clamps his jaw shut like he's fighting the question. He regroups and then asks, "Did he look... strong enough?"

I could pretend I don't know what he means, but I understand exactly what he's asking. I could lie, but I don't think that will help anyone.

"I don't know," I answer. "He was in pretty bad shape."

Really bad. I'm not sure how long he will be able to hold on. I only hope that we'll get to him before it's too late.

Draven white-knuckles the steering wheel and stares blankly at the road.

"Is he... Is he the first?" I ask. "Do you know if other villains have been..."

"Tortured?" Draven's nostrils flare. "Beaten, starved, water-boarded, electrocuted? Experimented on like they were some kind of lab animals instead of human beings?"

I shrink back a little at the venom in his words. And the images they paint.

"No," he says after a minute. "Deacon isn't the first."

The subtext is clear. He might not be the first, but if Draven and Dante have anything to say about it, he will be the last. I never in a million years thought I would stand with villains, never thought I'd feel so desperate to save the life of one. Then again, I never thought I'd see the day when even a single hero would do something as awful as what I saw tonight. Whether this is a small group of rotten heroes or as widespread as Rebel says, I side with villains on this.

The torture has to stop.

Draven surprises me by continuing. "This shit has been going on for decades. Ever since the Collective formed and those assholes decided that some of you were in and the rest of us were out."

That long? The Collective was created more than fifty years ago with the sole purpose of uniting heroes against villains. Fifty years of torture? My stomach lurches.

"I'm not one of them," I say.

"You might as well be." He pulls onto the highway that leads to my side of town. "Your mom is their very own Einstein, Edison, and Josef Mengele, all rolled into one."

"Seriously? You're comparing my mom to a sadistic Nazi freak?"

"If the unethical experiment fits..."

"You're wrong," I argue. "She's not like that. She only wants to help people."

"So she told you about the secret level then?" When I don't answer, he laughs humorlessly. "Didn't think so. Dr. Swift may want to help people, but only if those people are heroes. How many of her magical potions and pills have been used to help villains?"

I open my mouth to answer, but he cuts me off.

"Zip. Zilch. Zero. Every possible word for none at all." He shakes his head. "How many have been used to hurt villains? To *kill* us?"

It's the word "us" that breaks me. No longer are villains some nameless, faceless evil enemy. No, now villains are Draven and Dante. Deacon.

"I-I'm sorry," I say. It's lame, but it's the truth. "I didn't know. I never thought of it that way. If I had—"

"What?" he snaps. "You would have stopped the heroes? You would have given them the Kenna Swift stamp of disapproval?" He shakes his head. "Oh, wait. I know. You would have pulled that fire alarm a lot sooner. Of course, the only one who avoids getting burned in that situation is you."

I get it. He's hurting. He's upset. But just because he's one step from losing it is no excuse to take everything out on me. I'm on his side here.

I have to remind myself that he's still a villain. Just because I feel bad for him doesn't mean I trust him. And it doesn't mean we'll be on the same side once Deacon is free. This is a one-time-only partnership. Because while I may have discovered there are superheroes who can't be trusted, I'm not stupid enough to think that means all villains can be.

But I can't rescue Deacon alone, so it's either trust Draven and Dante or just let him die. I'm not okay with that.

"If I had known superheroes were torturing people, I would have done exactly what I plan to do now," I say.

Draven snorts as he pulls into my driveway. "And what's that?"

I meet his mocking gaze straight on as I reply with the most truthful answer I've got: "Stop them."

Then I climb out of the car and head for my front door without waiting for him to respond.

He catches up to me halfway up the sidewalk. He doesn't say anything, but I feel him at my back.

He wants to see me as his enemy, fine. Just because we have a mutual goal doesn't mean we're on the same team. That suits me fine.

Key in hand, I reach for the door.

Draven grabs my shoulder and yanks me back.

I spin, ready to rail on him for manhandling me—he should know by now I don't stand for that kind of treatment—when he lifts his finger to his mouth. Then he points at the skinny window next to the door. The glass is shattered.

"Mom!" I gasp, panic racing through me.

I shrug out of Draven's grip and push open the door, my only thought to make sure she's okay. But after I step into the glass-strewn front hall, I freeze. The door should have been locked. When I snuck out earlier, I used the back door. And Mom would never leave the front door unsecured. Between her experiments and what happened to my dad, she's way too safety conscious to ever forget to lock up.

"Wait," Draven whispers. But it's too late. I'm already in the kitchen.

"Oh my God."

Every drawer has been dragged out and dumped—on the counter, on the floor, in the sink. Every cabinet is open, as is the refrigerator. The orange juice has been knocked over, and it's dripped down the shelves to puddle on the floor below.

"Mom!" I scream for her again, racing through the living room, where cushions have been sliced open and the TV is lying on the floor. I hit the stairs running, take them three steps at a time, and make it to the second floor in a flash.

"Mom!" I ignore the open doors to my bedroom, the bathroom, and her home office. Her door is the only one that's not either swung wide or hanging off its hinges.

I hear Draven's footsteps in the hall as I reach for the doorknob to her bedroom. My heart tries to beat its way out of my throat. When I left, Mom had been sound asleep. Considering the damage done to the rest of the house, I'm dreading what I'll see inside.

What if she didn't get away?

What if whoever did this got to her?

What if they…hurt her?

I stand there, heart pounding and lungs aching, as my hand squeezes the cool metal, willing myself to twist my wrist. I can't seem to make myself do it.

Draven comes up behind me, his presence a welcome heat at my back. He reaches around, places his hand over mine, and slowly turns the handle. He pushes open the door but doesn't let go of my hand.

Mom's bedroom is just as destroyed as the rest of the house. Her bed has been stripped, her mattress is on the floor, and the contents of her dresser drawers have been thrown everywhere. Her walk-in closet has suffered the same fate.

The bathroom light is on. Draven and I make our way across the room, with me holding my breath. *Please, God. Please, God. Please—*

My breath rushes out in a huge sigh of relief. She's not here. There's no lifeless body in the tub. Though the mirror above the sink is shattered, cracks and fissures radiating out from a single point of impact where it looks like something—or some*one*—hit the glass.

I reach out to touch the web of cracks, but feel pressure on my hand as I do. That's when I remember that our hands are still linked, and I'm squeezing him in a death grip.

"Sorry," I say, releasing him.

I don't miss him shaking the feeling back into his hand, even as he tells me, "Don't worry about it."

"Maybe she went to the police," I say, mostly to myself. "Maybe she wasn't here when it happened."

Draven gives me a skeptical look—like I'm living in a fairy tale—but I ignore it. Instead, I pull out my phone and dial Mom's cell number. A moment later, I hear the muffled sound of "She Blinded Me with Science" coming from back in the bedroom. I follow the music to a pile of bedding in the corner. Tossing sheets and pillows aside, I find the phone at the bottom of the pile.

I hold it up, staring blankly as it continues to ring. And ring. And ring. Then the noise stops as abruptly as it started and my call goes to voice mail.

"That's her phone?" Draven asks.

I nod dumbly.

The house is trashed. Mom's not here. And she doesn't have her phone, the one thing she never goes anywhere without. I punch a button, hoping to find some clue to what happened here. The screen stays black. The battery must be dead.

Where is she?

I slide her phone in my pocket and then use my phone to try her office number. She doesn't pick up there either.

Next, I try the lab itself. Nothing.

I decide to try another lab on our floor. After three rings, someone picks up.

"Neurotoxins," the gentle male voice says, "Dr. Harwood speaking."

"Dr. Harwood, it's Kenna." I turn away from Draven. "Is my mom around?"

"Haven't seen her," he replies. "Did you try her office?"

"No answer."

"Be careful with that bottle," Dr. Harwood says, muffled like he's turned away from the phone. "Do you want to paralyze us all?"

I rub the spot between my eyes.

"If I see Jeanine, I'll tell her to give you a call."

"Thanks," I tell him.

I stare at my phone for several long seconds. Mom lives at the lab. She mostly comes home to sleep and eat—and those only when I remind her. If she's not there...

I keep myself from imagining a worst-case scenario.

Before I give up on reaching her, I try her office one more time. I'm about to hang up when it goes to voice mail again, but then I freeze. Instead of Mom's distracted instruction to leave a message, a male voice says, "You have reached the voice mail of Dr. Jeanine Swift. Dr. Swift is out of the country and unable to check messages. If this is an emergency, please contact the main office at ESH Lab."

I hang up before the beep. Then I dial again and play the message on speakerphone.

My thoughts accelerate from worry to terror.

"They took her," I whisper.

Draven steps into my line of sight. "You don't know that. Maybe she—"

"Someone took her," I repeat. "She wouldn't just take off without saying a word to me. She *especially* wouldn't leave the country."

"But why would the superheroes take her?" he asks. "She's their poster child."

"I-I don't know." I shake my head. This makes no sense. None of this makes any sense.

Everything in my world is tumbling too fast. My mind can't keep up. *Get a grip, Kenna.*

I'd only let my guard down for a second, allowed myself to think about trusting villains because a few heroes are doing bad things, and suddenly my first thought is to blame the good guys? The world doesn't change that fast.

"You're right," I say, "it couldn't have been heroes. It had to be villains."

Draven scowls. "No way."

"Yes way." I advance on him. "Who took her? Where are they keeping her?"

He holds up his hands. "Whoa. Villains did *not* take your mom. We aren't the ones with a proven record of kidnapping here."

"You're the bad guys!" I punch him in the chest.

He doesn't flinch, but it feels good anyway. I hit him again and again. Harder and harder.

He grabs my wrists and holds me back. "Kenna, listen." His voice is steady and, for once, not full of anger and snark. "You asked me to trust you and here I am, trusting you. Now it's your turn. Trust me when I say that villains did not do this. We try to keep a low profile."

My fury deflates a little—even if villains took my mom, that doesn't mean *this* villain had anything to do with it— and I fight the urge to snort at the idea of villains keeping a low profile.

"Besides," he says, "who could have changed her voice mail message? We don't have that kind of access."

All of the tension leaves my body. Everything inside me goes still. He's right. Only someone with the highest security clearance could have overridden Mom's voice recognition access to her voice mail. Not even a gifted technopath could bypass that without authorization. It had to have been the heroes.

Worse, it had to be someone with status. Someone in the Collective.

"But why?"

"I don't know," he answers. "Maybe they just took her in for questioning about the break-in last night. They'll grill her for a while and then let her go when she tells them the truth. She has nothing to lie about."

I want to believe him. I want to believe that Mom's disappearance is routine and that she'll be home in no time. But one look at the destruction around me and I know that's a fantasy. Whoever took her was looking for something and tossed our entire house to find it. And if they took Mom with them, they must not have found it.

Besides, if it means keeping my immunity a secret, she absolutely would lie to them. In a heartbeat.

If they'd do this to the house, what would they do to her?

"We need to get her back as soon as possible," I say. "We need to get both her and Deacon back. Tonight."

We head back downstairs through the chaos. I don't need to see any more. Not when my mind is too full with my new mission: get Deacon and Mom away from the bad heroes—and pray that Rebel and the villains are wrong about the pervasive corruption.

I mentally cross my fingers, toes, and eyes hoping that whoever tossed the place didn't bother with Mom's makeshift home lab in the garage.

But that was a futile hope. Unlike the rest of the house, the garage hasn't been trashed. There are no beakers smashed to pieces on the concrete, no chemical slime oozing across the floor, no cabinets yanked off the walls. No, everything in the garage is just *gone*.

It's like they backed up a moving truck to the door and

loaded it with every last piece of equipment, every last ounce of chemicals. Every last hope of using Mom's secret stash of knockout serum to rescue her and Deacon.

Sick to my stomach and more frightened than I've ever been in my life, I turn to Draven. "We're going to need a new plan."

CHAPTER 10

D raven looks at me, his jaw clenched. "We don't have time for a new plan."

"Time or not, we have no choice." I gesture to the empty garage. "Without the knockout serum, I've got nothing."

He swears under his breath, words so vile and vicious that only a villain would use them. Then he yanks out his phone, hitting speed dial. "We've got a problem, Dante," he barks when his cousin answers the phone, no preliminaries. "Get here, now."

He doesn't say any more than that, doesn't warn Dante or Rebel about what to expect when they get here. Instead, he just disconnects the call, shoves the phone back in his pocket, and starts to pace like a caged tiger.

I try to think what our next steps should be, but it's hard with panic ripping through me. *Mom. Mom. Mom.* She's all I can think about. All I can see when I close my eyes. All I can focus on, even though I know that if I want to save her, I have to concentrate on being smarter, sneakier, better than the bad guys—whichever side they're on.

She's gone. My mother is gone.

There's no way this is anything but a kidnapping—and it has to have been someone on the inside.

The question is, why? Did they find out about one of her secret experiments? The knockout serum? The night-vision pill? Or the projects she was working on that were so dangerous she wouldn't even tell me about them? My immunity shot?

Just the thought swamps me with guilt. I almost blew my immunity secret with Draven tonight. Maybe it wasn't the first time. Maybe I let it slip somehow when I was in Rebel's dad's office or on sublevel two.

Shit. I used my mother's pass last night—to get to her lab, up to Mr. Malone's office, and down to sublevel two. *Her* access card. *Her* RFID chip. *Her* digital trail. What if that's why they came to get her? Not because of her side experiments, but because of me? Because of what *I* did?

And then when they got here to question her, they searched the house and found her unsanctioned experiments. Experiments Mr. Malone might very well consider treasonous. Experiments she was keeping secret because she wanted to protect us. To protect me.

Me. It all comes back to me. My mother is in trouble because of me. The thought makes me sick, makes my knees feel like gelatin and my stomach feel like I swallowed a bowling ball.

My mother was taken because of me.

My mother is being held captive somewhere because of me.

My mother might very well be tortured *because of me.*

Tortured.

They might be torturing my mother right now.

I try to force myself to be rational. Just because they took her, just because they want to question her, doesn't mean they'll hurt her. But the old argument about the heroes being the good guys is gone.

For a second, all I can see or hear is Deacon. Face pale, body tense, his screams echoing through my brain as they tortured him.

For the first time I understand, really *understand* the helpless rage that is written all over Draven's face. The fury and terror and hate that have him wearing a path into the industrial-grade carpet my mother put in the garage when she turned it into her secret lab.

It is the same fury and terror and hate—yes, *hate*—that is suddenly burning inside me.

"We have to go!" I tell him, urgency beating a staccato rhythm through my blood. "We have to go now!"

"That's what I've been saying," he growls. "You're the one who wanted to scheme and think and wait. If you take any longer with that plan of yours, Deacon will be dead!"

Rebel and Dante choose that moment to walk through the door.

That was fast. Rebel looks pale and shaken, and Dante looks only slightly less murderous than Draven.

"What happened in there?" Rebel asks, her voice trembling. "Where's your mom? Where's her lab?"

She's the only other person who knows all of our secrets. She knows about everything that used to be in here. She alone knows how bad things really are.

"Gone," I tell her, my voice breaking on the single syllable. "She's gone, Reb."

Rebel's next to me in a second, pulling me into a hug.

I just stand there, hiding my face in her shoulder as I

struggle with all the emotions ripping through me. Tears burn my eyes and I can feel a sob—of fear and horror—welling up in my chest.

I swallow it down, refusing to give in to it. Not here, not now. Not with Draven, all curled lip and stormy eyes, staring at me like he thinks this whole situation is my fault.

Not thinks, *knows*. Because it is my fault. It is. *I* stopped them from rescuing Deacon last night. *I* did nothing to stop the heroes from torturing him tonight. *I* used my mom's badge and got her caught up in this mess too.

He doesn't need to say any of that out loud. I already know.

I let myself draw strength from my best friend—all our recent differences forgotten in the wake of everything that's happened tonight—and then I pull away. Dry-eyed. Composed.

No way am I going to let two villains see how weak I feel, even if Rebel trusts them. Even if they're in the same position I'm in now. Even if they don't seem all that villainous after all.

"How did you get here so fast?" I ask when I'm sure my voice will be steady.

"We were just around the corner," Rebel says.

"You followed us?" Draven stares at his cousin incredulously. "After we agreed that you were going to stay put?"

Dante shrugs and looks a little sheepish as he glances my way. "I know Rebel trusts you, Kenna, but I don't know you. The heroes already have Deacon. No way was I going to take a chance on them getting Draven too."

He tries to sound tough when he says it, but I can see the terror in his eyes.

Somehow, that thought grounds me. If villains can keep their fear in check, so can I.

"We need a new plan," I tell them, and my voice is steadier, more powerful than it's been since I walked into the house and discovered this disaster. I look at Draven, daring him to make another comment about my *planning*. The right plan is the only thing that's going to get our loved ones back. "They took everything my mom had, so we're going to have to figure out what to do on our own."

"I say we get Quake and Nitro and hit the lab with everything we've got," Dante snarls. "Between the two of them, they can level the place."

"And Deacon along with it," Draven says with a glare. "If he's in as bad shape as Kenna says, there's no way he can hold out against an attack like that."

"Not to mention the fact that tearing apart the lab would be a declaration of war, which would be even worse than getting your uncle involved," I explain. "The lab is one of the most important League facilities. Blasting it will bring every superhero in a thousand-mile radius after us."

Draven tips his head and gestures at me as if to say, *Exactly*.

"Besides," I continue, "my mom might be there too." *As well as all the other people who work there—people who I love and admire and who I know could never be involved in torturing villains.*

Then again, if someone had asked me twenty-four hours ago if *any* heroes would be involved in torturing villains, I would have laughed at the mere idea. Now, not only do I know they're involved, but my own mother's life might be in danger because of it.

"Do you have a better idea?" Dante demands. "Does anyone?"

The fact is, I don't. But I need to come up with an alternate plan quickly, because Dante's clearly not going to wait long before trying to rescue his brother. And I don't blame him. My skin crawls just knowing my mother is in their clutches.

Mom always says that every problem has a solution. You just have to think it through.

I walk over to the whiteboards that line one whole wall of the garage. They've been wiped clean. A red dry-erase marker lies on the floor a few feet away. It's the only thing in the whole room that managed to escape the purge. I pick it up, uncap it, and draw a rough diagram of the lab, labeling all the entrances and exits—including a couple secret ones that no one is supposed to know about.

"We have ten possible points of entry," I tell them. "Eight of them are easily accessible and highly regulated, but two require a little more ingenuity to access. Because those two are hidden, there isn't as much security staff there, so there are fewer people who could get hurt—"

"Believe me," Draven interjects. "The last thing I'm worried about is hurting a goddamn superhero. In fact, I'm dying for a shot at a few of them—"

"Let's focus on the plan," Rebel interrupts, shooting me a worried look. Like she's afraid I'm going to balk.

She doesn't need to worry. Yes, I've been loyal to the superheroes my whole life, and I don't want to see any innocent bystanders get hurt. But as far as I'm concerned, some of them—her father included—have crossed lines that should never be crossed. If they get caught in the crossfire, then I can't help thinking it's exactly what they deserve.

"They've put in a ton of new security protocols since the break-in," I say. "Not just the villain signature detectors. I got around them using my mom's badge yesterday, but obviously, we can't do that tonight. If they took my mom, then her badge is compromised. We have to figure out another way to get inside so no one will know we're there until it's too late to stop us."

"I can swipe my dad's pass," Rebel suggests. "No one would think to question him."

"Yeah, but people notice him whenever he's in the lab. He's always talking to everyone, making sure people see him. The guards will be on high alert, ready to impress the boss when we swipe in."

She groans. "Good point."

"Then what do you suggest?" Draven asks. "Because I'm running out of patience. I'll storm through the front door to get him if I have to."

"Sounds good to me," Dante adds.

"And get both Deacon and my mom killed? Not to mention yourselves?" It's a challenge to fight an eye roll. "You're not going near the lab."

Draven takes a step toward me, his muscles tensing. "Hell, yeah, we are. No way are you going in there without us."

"Yeah, well, no way I'm going in there *with* you, so I don't know what to tell you, bad boy."

We're toe to toe now, nose to nose—or we would be if he wasn't a good six inches taller. Not that his height intimidates me. He can glower and tower all he wants. No freaking way is he going in that lab with us. It would be group suicide.

"You think you're going to stop me?" Draven growls low in his throat, as he gives me his best villain scowl. I have to admit, it's a doozy. Nerves skitter down my spine, and for a second—just a second—I consider backing off. But I'm right about this. The entire lab is now rigged to sense even a hint of a villain power. If we set off the alarms, the guards will shoot to kill and ask questions never. I've already got my mom and Deacon on my conscience. No way am I adding Draven and Dante to the list. Or me and Rebel.

Squaring my shoulders, I glare at him. "I'll stop you if I have to. I won't let you blow this—"

"Blow it? I would have had Deacon yesterday, if it wasn't for your interference—"

"*My* interference? You were bumbling around the wrong floor without a clue."

"We were doing fine until you beaned Nitro with a fire extinguisher."

"At least I have good aim," I spit back, "which is more than I can say for him!"

Draven's jaw drops. We both freeze as the other's words register.

Oh shit.

"You remember what happened last night?" Draven asks, his voice dropping from shout to whisper.

I close my eyes for a five count. I can't believe I just blurted it out like that. I've spent half a lifetime keeping my immunity a secret, but one argument with a villain who makes my blood boil and I'm spilling the truth without a second thought.

There's no turning back now.

"Well, if I didn't," I reply, "you sure as shit just let the cat out of the bag, didn't you?"

"But you remember. How is that possible?" He shakes his head, looking at me like I'm speaking an alien language. "I planted other memories. My powers always work. On *everyone*!"

He turns to Dante and Rebel, both of whom are looking anywhere but at the two of us.

"You knew?" he demands, staring at his cousin. "And you didn't tell me?"

Dante's eyes widen.

"You told him?" I ask Rebel, aghast.

My immunity has always been our secret. Or at least I thought it was. She knows how important it is to keep the heroes from finding out, let alone villains. If they got their hands on the serum—well, it would be bad.

"I didn't know until tonight—"

"I just told him—"

"I wanted to know why you weren't freaked out by us—"

"I only just told Dante. He didn't keep anything from you, Draven."

Their words are a garbled mess, the two of them talking over each other in their need to convince us that neither of them betrayed anyone. After looking back and forth between them like I'm watching an air hockey match, I put two fingers in my mouth and let out an ear-piercing whistle.

"Everyone stop! We get it."

"Really?" Rebel looks totally freaked out. "Because I swear, Kenna, I just told him in the car, right before Draven called. And I only told him because he was close to figuring it out himself—and because I figured the guys should know you're immune if we're going to be working with them."

"Working with them?" I scoff. *Yeah, right. Because that's off to a great start.*

"How are you immune?" Draven asks. "I didn't even know that was possible. Are you immune to all powers or just psy?"

"All powers." Then I quickly add, "I mean, If Quake causes an earthquake, I could die if something falls on me, but not directly from his superpower."

"You let me think——" Draven shakes his head. Yet another bud of guilt unfurls within me when I see the look of betrayal on his face.

But then last night's events rush back at me and the guilt turns to annoyance. "Don't even bother giving me that look," I tell him. "You left me tied to a lab table with alarms blaring, after Nitro tried to set me on fire!"

"Not that he could have anyway, since you're immune!"

"You didn't know that!"

"Exactly my point!" Draven counters. "I got set on fire trying to save you."

"I didn't ask for your help."

"Wow, that's an impressive defense"—he rolls his eyes—"if you're five."

"Okay, okay! That's enough!" Rebel interjects when we both pause for air. "Amusing as it would be to watch the two of you duke it out all night, we have more important things to worry about. Like security protocols. And how the hell we're going to get into the lab."

Draven and I are panting, jacked up on the adrenaline, primed to go another round. But Rebel's right. We don't have time to bicker. I know she's right, and still it takes every ounce of effort I have not to get right back into it. There's just something about Draven that gets under my skin, and I can't stand that—because of Rebel—he got the last word. Especially since his last word was basically calling me a baby.

Jerk.

The only other person I've enjoyed arguing with this much was Jeremy, when he'd spout off nonsense—

Holy shit, Jeremy! Technopath and computer wizard extraordinaire. Why didn't I think of him before?

"I've got an idea!" I yank out my phone and start to dial. If anyone can get us past those new security protocols, it's Jeremy. And while we didn't exactly part on good terms, I'm hoping he won't hold our last fight against me.

CHAPTER 11

I t takes twenty minutes and more than a little groveling to get Jeremy to my place.

I'm in the middle of arguing with Draven (when *aren't* I arguing with him?) about bringing someone else into the group, when a van rumbles into the driveway. Holding up a hand to keep Draven from retorting—I'm getting the last word this time, ha!—I turn to look through the open garage door just in time to see my ex-boyfriend roll to a stop at the top of my driveway.

Jeremy climbs out of the van. He's trying to pull off the badass look as usual—ripped jeans, leather jacket, dark sunglasses. I bite my lip and try not to laugh as, next to me, Draven stiffens and I can feel him bracing for a fight of the hero-villain variety.

Clearly some people are buying the act.

I start to tell Draven not to worry—Jeremy might look the part, but he battles with his keyboard, not his nonexistent brawn—but then Dante whispers incredulously to Rebel, "*That's* Kenna's ex?"

My spine stiffens. There's no reason for him to sound so surprised. Sure Jeremy's hot, and no, I don't look like a runway model, but I do have other redeeming qualities. My brain, for one. My quick wit, for another. And most importantly, my ability to listen to even the most ridiculous of Jeremy's conspiracy theories without laughing out loud, even when I really, really wanted to.

For Jeremy, that's a critical trait in a girl.

Then again, at least one of his theories is proving to be not so ridiculous after all. During the seven months we dated, I spent hours listening to him go on about secret hero experiments, experiments I never in a million years actually believed could be true. And yet, here we are.

He is so going to make me eat it on that one.

Draven steps in front of me, and for a second I can't figure out what's going on. Then it registers: he's trying to *protect* me. From *Jeremy*. As if. I bite back another laugh. I took on Draven, Dante, and Nitro and came out victorious—except for the whole getting-tied-to-the-lab-table thing. I can certainly handle my ex-boyfriend.

I shove past Draven. I am more than capable of taking care of myself. He raises one dark brow at me, like he has no idea what I'm upset about. Which only annoys me more. If he expects me to trust him and Dante, then he needs to trust me. I wouldn't bring someone onto the team who would sabotage our mission.

"Thanks for coming," I tell Jeremy, and mean it.

"Any chance to hear you say that I was right…" He wraps an arm around my shoulders in a loose hug, then squeezes.

I'm a little surprised at the warmth of his greeting. Our breakup was unfriendly, to say the least, his conspiracy-theory rants having finally sent me over the edge. A year ago, our relationship went down in flames when he tried to convince me that the League was melting the polar ice caps so that Boulder could become beachfront property. We were in our favorite restaurant, and I ended up dumping a chocolate cherry milk shake—his least favorite flavor—on his head. It only went south from there.

But if he can put that incident behind us, so can I. Global warming is a problem for another day; I hug him back. We were friends long before we dated. And he did come all the way over here to help me the moment I told him about my mom.

However, as I pull away, I realize there's more at play here than a simple greeting. Jeremy is smirking—actually smirking—at Draven, while Draven stares him down.

For a split second, I wonder what's going on behind Draven's storm-tossed eyes, but he's not giving anything away. And I have more important things to worry about than some juvenile pissing contest.

"You were right. You were right. You were right," I tell Jeremy, repeating the words like a mantra. When it comes to saving my mom and Deacon, I have no pride.

Besides, it turns out he *was* right when he said there was a secret faction of the superheroes doing evil in the name of justice—assuming they actually believe they're doing a good thing. I wish I'd believed him twelve months ago, but since this theory was sandwiched between one about seeds with a latent gene that would trigger the zombie apocalypse and another that suggests Pop-Tarts are actually the government's vehicle for mind-controlling teenagers, it was hard to take him seriously.

And we're all paying the price because I didn't.

"Hey, Reb." Jeremy glances over and gives my best friend a sexy wink. "How you doing, girl?"

Dante growls.

It takes all my restraint not to laugh out loud. Rebel and Jeremy? That's too funny, considering he's actually terrified of her. This over-the-top flirty attitude is just his defense mechanism. He'd had to ask me out ten times before I saw through the smarmy act to the sweet guy below.

Rebel squeezes Dante's arm before flouncing over to give Jeremy a hug. "Thanks for coming, Jeremy. Everything's a mess."

"Don't worry, babe. I'll fix it."

"Don't call her 'babe,'" Dante says, stepping forward.

"Who's going to stop me?" Jeremy asks cockily. "You?"

"Damn straight." Dante lunges, but Rebel steps between them, wrapping her arms around her boyfriend's waist and pulling him in close.

"Jeremy calls everyone 'babe.' It doesn't mean anything." She gives Dante another squeeze to reassure him whose babe she really is. "Besides, we need to stop sniping at each other and figure out what we're going to do."

"If we're going to be working together," Jeremy says, "do you want to introduce me to your new friends?"

"This is Draven." I nod at the scowling villain standing behind me. "And that's Dante."

Jeremy jerks his chin at the guys in what could have been a friendly greeting if they hadn't just snapped at each other.

"Now that everyone's acquainted, can we get down to business, please?" I start to drag him through the garage and into the house.

Jeremy lets me lead him to the threshold, but refuses to go any further. He mouths something to me, but lip-reading has never been my thing.

"What?" I don't get it.

He repeats himself three or four times, with increasingly exaggerated gestures, but I still have no idea what he's trying to say. I throw my hands in the air. A glance at the others shows they're as clueless as I am.

"Hey, dude, are we going to stand here playing charades all night?" Dante finally asks. "Or are you going to—"

Jeremy clamps his hand over Dante's mouth before he can finish the sentence.

Needless to say, Dante doesn't take well to what he perceives as an attack. He shoves Jeremy's hand off his face, twisting his arm into a position that it was never supposed to bend. "Don't touch me."

"Ow, ow, ow!" Jeremy squeals. "Don't hurt the typing fingers!"

"Let him go, Dante." I tug at his arm until he releases Jeremy.

"Jeez, touchy much?" Jeremy shakes out his arm and stalks over to the whiteboard. He grabs the red marker and scrolls in huge letters, *Has anyone checked the house for BUGS?*

It takes a moment for his meaning to sink in, but when it does, my stomach twists. Draven and I were in the house for a good ten minutes, talking and strategizing, trying to figure out what had happened to my mother and my house. The idea that those douche nozzles might have overheard our conversation—my private fears—triggers a whole new set of emotions.

I shake my head, as does Draven.

Jeremy just rolls his eyes, like we're too stupid to live.

Wait here, he scrawls.

Then he strides into the house.

Draven, Dante, Rebel, and I stand frozen in the garage, staring at one another. Then we scramble after him.

I've seen Jeremy at work before, but usually that involves drinking chocolate milk by the gallon and eating sour gummies while he sits at his laptop, his fingers flying over the keyboard. I've never seen him walk around a house, eyes closed and arms extended, like some kind of witch doctor with a divining rod. Technopaths are so weird.

Even weirder is the eerie quiet that follows in his wake. A Jeremy who isn't spouting off how secondary radiation from listening devices causes cancer in cockroaches, who thinks this situation is as serious as we do, is terrifying.

We trail him through the house, Draven behind me, followed by Rebel and Dante, who bring up the rear. I can feel the tension emanating from the villains, their distrust growing by the second. And this time, I don't blame them. This is bizarre, even for Jeremy.

Except we've barely made it into the kitchen before Jeremy is squatting to get a look at the underside of the counter. A moment later, he holds up a miniscule black bug.

Oh God. I try not to freak out, but it's hard. This wasn't a simple break-in. Yeah, I've known this had something to do with the superheroes and what's going on at ESH—but this confirms a whole new level of intent, a new level of danger.

As we walk through the rest of the house, Jeremy finds bugs in the family room, my mom's office, my room, and the bathroom. Ewww. I feel utterly violated.

These bugs have been here for longer than a few hours.

The one in the family room was under a decent layer of dust. Whoever planted them has been listening to us for a while. Who knows how long?

This isn't just about Deacon. This isn't just about my stealing Mom's badge or her work at the lab. What are they listening for? What do they think they heard?

Panic turns the room dark and shadowy around me. I stop, closing my eyes and bracing my hands on my knees as I try to force oxygen into my lungs.

Someone rests a gentle hand on my lower back, their thumb rubbing over the bare skin between the bottom of my tank top and the top of my jeans in a soothing motion. I shiver from the skin-to-skin contact, and I turn, surprised to find Draven staring down at me.

His face is blank, but his eyes are turbulent as he watches me. He doesn't say a word, but then he doesn't need to. The comfort he's offering comes through loud and clear.

I want to melt into him, into his touch, into the reassurance that rolls off him in waves. But sinking into Draven is not an instinct I can give in to right now. Or ever. So I jerk away. Yank my shirt down to meet the waistband of my jeans. Then turn to follow Jeremy out of my bedroom, down the stairs, and into the kitchen.

Back in the kitchen, Jeremy dumps the handful of bugs into the microwave and presses start before wheeling around to face me.

"Jeez, Kenna, what the hell did you do to the superheroes?" he hisses, his eyes wide and haunted. "Your place is trashed! And those bugs? Serious business. Definitely not your typical Internet-ordered surveillance devices. Those babies are top secret, state-of-the-art bugs that can pick up conversations a hundred yards away. They could hear anything and everything that went on in your house."

Behind him, the bugs start to snap and pop like gunfire in the microwave.

"I've been saying it for years," he continues, ignoring the mini-explosions. "The heroes are in bed with the government and breaking every law in the League and in the Constitution. For what? To turn us into mindless zombies who do whatever they command. I wouldn't be surprised if those bugs came equipped with a mind-control signal."

"Really, Jeremy? Again with the mind control?"

The microwave lets out one final blast before the end timer beeps.

Jeremy squints at me. "You're not being controlled right now, are you?"

I punch him in the shoulder. "Of course not!"

He rubs his arm as he glances over my head with suspicion. "How do you know? The Kenna I know would never willingly work with *villains*."

He whispers the last, as if it's a bad word.

"Yeah, well, that Kenna's mother hadn't been kidnapped, and she still had some faith in the system." Was it only yesterday that I was arguing with Rebel about how crazy her antihero rant sounded? It feels like a lifetime. "Now they're both gone. Why wouldn't I stoop to working with villains?"

"So flattering," Draven says to me, sarcasm ripe in his tone.

"It wasn't meant to be flattering," I answer, flipping him off, even as I keep my attention fixed on Jeremy. "Just truthful."

"Well, I'm not too thrilled to be working with a hero girl," he throws back.

"Then you shouldn't have let your cousin start dating one."

"She's *your* best friend." He jerks his head in Rebel's direction. "You didn't even know they were dating."

"Because she knows how much I hate villains."

"Yeah, almost as much as I hate heroes."

"Enough!" Rebel shouts.

Suddenly, my feet lose contact with the floor and I find myself looking down at her. Hands outstretched, Rebel's face is a mask of irritation as she holds Draven and me three feet off the ground.

I glance over at him just in time to see panic flicker across his face. *Looks like someone is afraid of heights.*

Rebel lowers us gently back to the ground. She shakes out her arms, clenching and unclenching her hands in a tell that means she's only a couple small steps from losing it completely. If we thought Dante losing it was bad, wait until someone pushes Rebel to the breaking point. Like during the last big throw-down with her dad. He had to resod the entire lawn behind her house.

"If you two are done fighting, we need to make a plan," she says. "And quickly. We have to get Deacon out and find Kenna's mom."

The reminder shuts down our bickering.

"Is it safe to talk here?" Rebel asks, casting a wary glance at the smoking microwave.

"My sweep caught all the live bugs," Jeremy says. "But there could be dormant devices or voice-activated transmissions or heroes with super hearing trained on this address or—"

"Jeremy…" I warn before he launches into another stream of paranoia—more out of impatience than disbelief because, really, at this point his theories make more sense than not.

He smirks. "I can shield the house."

I look around at the destruction in my kitchen and have to admit, "I don't feel safe here."

"Then we'll go somewhere else." Rebel wraps an arm around my shoulders.

"Somewhere no one expects us to be," Jeremy offers.

The guys' house is out, because if my house is bugged, then surely the home of the head villain is also being watched. And Rebel's house is no good for obvious reasons.

Jeremy adds, "If it's outside, that would be even better."

"There's a park," I suggest. "About a half mile from here."

Dante pulls out his keys, ready to drive.

"We should walk," Jeremy and I say at the same time.

Draven scowls, and Dante shoves his keys back into his pocket. If my house had that many bugs, I don't even want to think about what kind of tracking devices might be in our cars. And we need Jeremy's focus on something other than keeping eavesdroppers out of our business—like figuring out how to break into one of the most secure facilities in the world.

Ten minutes later, we're settling at a picnic table in the park. As far as war rooms go, it's not great, but any port in a storm and all that…

I pass around the six-pack of soda I pulled from the broken fridge and a bag of chocolate-chip cookies from my secret stash. I can't remember the last time I ate.

Jeremy settles his backpack on the table and pulls out his

laptop. He shrugs out of his leather jacket, revealing a T-shirt that says *There's no place like 127.0.0.1.*

Draven and Dante exchange a WTF look.

I don't get it either. Jeremy has an odd sense of humor. But he's a freaking computer wizard. Only a couple of minutes pass before he's got a schematic of the lab, which is a million times more detailed than the one I drew on the whiteboard in my garage.

It's multilayered, like blueprints, including everything from the ductwork to tech and security wiring. We crowd around him, even Dante and Draven forgetting their distrust long enough to pore over the plans.

"This is too complicated to read," I say after a minute. "How do you even know what we're looking at?"

"I've spent a lot of time studying the lab schematics and security systems over the years. I memorized the layers."

"Why?" Dante demands, suspicious again. "Did *you* have a reason to break in?"

Jeremy tsks. "Are you kidding me? Do you know the kind of experiments that go on in that lab? Irradiating rabbits to give them cognitive thought? Weather bombs? Bacteria that can realign the Earth's tectonic plates? With shit like that going down, I want to be ready to act. It pays to know the best ways in—and out."

"So what *is* the best way in?" I demand, cutting a glare at Dante. Are they *trying* to send him off on a rant?

"That depends where you want to go." He spends another minute or so clicking on the screen, and suddenly the multi-layered diagram disappears. In its place is one very detailed schematic, with every entrance, exit, window, and air duct clearly delineated.

"That's what I'm talking about!" Dante crows, clapping Jeremy on the back. I swear, I don't know what it is about guys that makes them ready to beat each other's brains out one minute and be best friends the next.

"We need to get to sublevel three," I tell him.

"Ah, sublevel three: the holy grail of League supersecrecy." He cracks his knuckles. "I've searched everywhere for blue-prints, a diagram, anything that remotely confirms the secret sublevel exists."

"Oh, it exists," I reply.

He turns to me, eyes wide. "How do you know? Where did you get definitive proof?"

"I've been there. Is that enough proof?"

Without answering, Jeremy turns back to his computer and punches a few more keys, calling up a blank schematic in the general shape of the lab. "Tell me everything you can remember."

"Do we really have time for this?" Rebel demands.

"If you want to get into a level so well-protected that there is absolutely no sign of its existence on the freaking Internet *or* League intranet, then yes, it's necessary," Jeremy all but shouts. "I need as many details as you can remember, and then…"

"And then what?"

"Then I'll check it against the new security protocols and try to extrapolate what measures they're using to pro-tect this level."

"Extrapolate?" Draven barks. "You mean, you're going to guess?"

Jeremy smiles at him over his laptop screen. "Pretty much."

"My cousin's life is on the line, and you're going to make *guesses* about how to get him out?" Draven looks like he's ready to kill something.

Not that I blame him. None of us knows how long Deacon can last.

Jeremy shrugs and reaches into his backpack for a bag of sour gummy worms. "Good thing for you I'm a good guesser," he says as he pops a handful in his mouth.

CHAPTER 12

Rebel has absolutely no tolerance for listening to Jeremy spout a stream of nonstop computer tech-speak, interspersed with the occasional conspiracy theory. Neither do I. Which is why when she starts for the paved path that winds a circle through the park, I follow her.

Well, that and I've been waiting to get her alone.

"We need to talk," I say as I catch up with her.

"Can you save the lecture for another night?"

"It's not a lecture," I tell her. "I just… I'm worried about you."

"There's nothing to worry about." She twists her head, cracking her neck.

She doesn't get it. She's my best friend. I'm *always* worried about her.

"Reb, are you sure about Dante?" I ask after a second. "What if he's just using you to gain access to the heroes? To get insider information they can use against us?"

Her spine stiffens. In that moment she looks exactly like her dad. "I'm sure."

"It's just…" I don't know how to say this without totally setting her off. But it's important, so I take my chances. "It seems really…convenient that the son of the villain leader is interested in the daughter of the president of the League."

She lets out a sharp breath, and for the first time I can see the cracks in her strong façade. The stress and strain are wearing on her. I don't want to add to the burden, but I have to be sure.

"Dante doesn't care about any of that," she insists. "He loves me. *Me*," she repeats. "Not what I can do for him, not who my father is, but *me*. Do you know how hard that is to find in the superhero world?"

"But how can you be sure?" I ask. "If heroes are really doing these horrible things—"

She cuts me off with a disbelieving glare. "If?"

"Okay, they are. But if they've been at this for decades like Draven says, don't you think it's possible that Dante looked at you and saw access, not a smart, cool girl he wanted to hang out with?"

She clenches her jaw and increases her speed. I have to double my pace to keep up.

God, I feel like an ass, but someone needs to look out for her. "I'm sorry, Reb, but you have to admit it's a pretty big coincidence."

"He didn't know," she blurts. "When we met, he had no idea I was even a super, let alone a hero."

I want to believe her. Really, I do. I mean, Dante doesn't seem like a bad guy, but he's a villain. And villains always have an ulterior motive.

"You can't know that," I argue. "He could have—"

She stops abruptly, her blue eyes flashing. "I went after him, okay? I covered my hero mark and went to the Lair looking for someone who knew as well as I did that heroes were hypocrites. I didn't want to be alone in this anymore. *I'm the one who wanted access.*"

"The Lair?" I echo.

A notorious villain nightclub, the Lair has a reputation for epic brawls and SHPD raids. The club's surrounded by enough protections—including an invisibility shield—that an ordinary like me couldn't even see it unless they already knew where to look. It's bad news.

The idea that Rebel not only went there, but went looking to hook up with a villain… If I'd known, I'd have had a heart attack.

"You went alone?" I whisper.

She shrugs like it's no big deal. "He assumed I was a villain, and I let him believe it for a few weeks. I didn't tell him the truth until I was sure of him."

I stare at my best friend. She is full of secrets. I'm not sure whether I should be impressed or terrified. I can't even keep the tiniest secrets from her.

"So, no," she says, getting back to my original question, "Dante isn't using me. If anything, I was using him."

Without waiting for me to respond, she strides down the path.

I'm not sure if this revelation makes me trust Dante any more or Rebel any less. Maybe both. Maybe neither. Either way, I'm ashamed to find out that my best friend felt so alone she had to seek out a villain to make her feel whole, and I was clueless. Dante seems like a decent guy, but what if she'd found someone else? Someone dangerous.

Despite all the secrets and deception, she's still my best friend. Whether I believe Dante's innocent or not, for now we're all on the same team. And that means Rebel and I have one more thing to talk about.

I catch up with her, and when we're shielded from view behind a stand of trees, I grab Rebel by the elbow and pull her to a stop. "Listen," I say, "the guys can't go in with us."

Rebel rolls her eyes. "Try telling them that."

"Seriously, Reb. You heard Jeremy. That villain signature sensor is serious business. If they get within fifty yards of the lab, it'll set off every alarm on campus. We'll all be toast. Including Deacon and maybe my mom."

"Then what do you suggest we do?" she asks. "They're not exactly in a reasonable mood. Am I supposed to levitate them onto a roof or something?"

I shake my head. "They'd find a way down."

"You're right." She lets out a little laugh. "Dante loves to use his wind to fly."

It's my turn to roll my eyes. *Boys.*

"We'd almost have to lock them in somewhere," I say, thinking out loud. "Somewhere they couldn't get out of. Somewhere safe."

I run through all the possibilities I can think of. My house, clearly out. So is anyone else's. I would love to see traditional stud-and-siding construction hold Draven and Dante for more than an instant.

"The vault in the lab would be perfect," I muse. "Except for the fact that it's *in the lab* and Nitro blew its hinges to bits last night."

"Right," she says with a snort. Then, "Wait. That's it!"

"That's what? Those are two big reasons why we *can't* use the vault."

"Not the vault," she says, a smug smile spreading across her face. "Nitro."

As if that makes more sense?

"Follow my lead."

I hardly have a choice when she grabs me by the wrist and drags me back to the picnic table.

+ + +

"Are you sure this is going to work?" I whisper as Jeremy pulls his van into the crowded parking lot.

She nods. Then pokes Jeremy in the ribs.

"Yeah," he says too loudly, "six gallons ought to do it."

"Tell me again why we need cranberry juice?" Draven asks.

Jeremy swallows. "The, um, acid will corrode the, um, sensors in the villain signature readers."

Rebel gives him a death glare. He doesn't need me to translate that it means, *Way to sell it, moron.*

"Whatever, man." Dante shakes his head before climbing out of the van. "Let's get this and get going."

Draven jumps out after him.

I exchange a nervous look with Rebel, and then we follow the boys into the Lair.

Inside, it's everything I'd always imagined a villain nightclub would look like in the wee hours of a Saturday morning. Dark, crowded, and full of pounding music and flashing lights. And leather. Lots and lots of black leather.

It's like hero nightclubs, to be honest (sans the leather), but it *feels* more dangerous.

We weave our way through the crowd to the bar, where

Draven and Dante exchange nods with a huge bouncer-looking dude pouring vodka shots. A massive tattoo of a desert-like landscape broken with jagged cracks and steaming fissures covers his shoulder and upper arm. Everyone in the super world knows that tattoo and the badder-than-badass villain it belongs to. Nitro's brother, Quake.

I shiver and grab Rebel's hand.

Then the boys are pushing through a door that leads to a brightly lit back room. Compared to the flashing lights in the club, the fluorescent lighting is like stepping into a sunny day on the beach. This commercial kitchen serves up the bar food for the hungry villains out there dancing the night away.

"Oi, I didn't know you lot were coming around tonight," Nitro calls out when he sees the guys. His gaze flicks to Rebel, not betraying any hint of the hushed phone call she had with him less than an hour ago. When he sees me, his façade almost falters. But instead of asking, "Why is the chick who tossed a fire extinguisher at my skull here?" he simply says, "And you brought a pair of pretty birds with you too."

"We need a few things," Draven says cryptically. "Okay if we raid your fridge?"

Nitro shrugs. "Fine by me."

Draven yanks open the door of the giant walk-in refrigerator. The inside is lined with wire shelves loaded with produce, packages of meat, and giant containers of juices, sauces, and salsas. Rebel and I hang back as the guys head for the giant jugs of cranberry juice.

Rebel hesitates as Draven pulls the scarlet juice from the shelf.

"Do it now," I whisper.

She doesn't move, but Draven does. He whips around, eyes narrowed. Guilt must be written on our faces because he drops the juice, sprinting for the door. It doesn't take a genius to know that Dante will be close behind. I spring to action, swinging the door closed myself.

"Rebel!" Dante yells.

"I'm sorry!" she shouts back as the door clicks shut.

"Now, Nitro!" I throw all of my weight against the door, holding the handle so they can't release the catch from the inside. It won't hold back two furious villains for long, but hopefully it will give the flamethrower enough time to create a seal.

Nitro already has a bright-green fireball burning between his palms. I dodge left as it comes flying toward me. The ball barely misses me and connects with the door handle. There is a sizzling sound of metal melting and then nothing but the soft thud of fists pounding against the door from inside the fridge.

"Hey," I complain, examining my elbow. Nitro's latest got closer than I thought. "You hit me."

His mouth quirks into an angry smirk. "And here I thought my aim was downright heroic. Saved the day, didn't I?"

I'm about ready to snap back, but Rebel's soft voice stops me.

"You can get them out, right?" she asks him. "When we're done?"

Nitro's antagonism melts away. He squeezes Rebel's shoulder. "Without a doubt."

"They're going to be so pissed," she says, looking a little sick at the thought.

I nod. "And cold. The faster we get back here, the better."

"I'll stay with them," Nitro tells Rebel. "Don't you worry."

She pulls him into one of her signature Rebel hugs and I laugh as his eyes bug out. Even villains aren't immune to her suffocating displays of affection.

"Come on," I say, taking her by the hand. "Let's do this."

CHAPTER 13

"This is a terrible plan." Jeremy parks the van about a block from the lab.

Rebel swipes a brush loaded with blush all over her face. "Do you have any better ideas?" She closes her eyes and really rubs the color in around her lids.

"You know me," Jeremy says, twisting in his seat. "I love a good heist as much as the next tech nerd, but this? What if you get caught?"

I hand Rebel the cayenne pepper shaker. "You didn't see Deacon, Jer." I shudder at the memory. "No one can withstand that kind of treatment for long. He'll be dead before the end of the week."

Rebel whimpers, and I'm not sure if it's from the pepper she just dabbed into the corners of her eyes and her nostrils or from the harsh reality that Deacon might die despite our efforts. I won't let myself even consider that possibility. Or that my mother could be—

I cut off the thought. If I go there, I'm going to be a basket case, and we have a job to do. I *know* Deacon is barely holding on. I just have to assume that my mom is okay…for now.

Jeremy nods. He might be all paranoia and rampant

geekery, but he can settle down when he needs to. He also knows I wouldn't do something like this if there were any other option. It's not like we can call in the police. SHPD would never question Mr. Malone or a League directive, and the ordinary police would never even get through the door.

"Let's go." Rebel smacks herself on the cheeks before bounding out of the van. "Before the pepper wears off."

I let her get a few paces ahead before I jump out after her. Jeremy pockets his keys, zips up the front of his black hoodie, and falls into step beside me.

I run my fingers over the fake all-access security pass he made using his phone, a frequent shopper card, and something that looks like a credit card swiper. The bite of the sharp plastic edges pulls my mind into laser focus.

"When you see me give the signal," I tell him, "you get your ass inside and into the security office. I don't know how long we'll be able to keep them distracted."

"What's the signal?"

"Just…a signal," I reply. "You'll know."

We round the corner and the Malone Building comes into view. Despite the fact that it's the middle of the night, the all-glass façade glows, full of light. But all is quiet and still. Any hubbub that my fire alarm caused hours ago is long over. And why wouldn't it be? There was nothing wrong. The building hides its secrets well.

About twenty yards ahead of us, Rebel starts staggering and shouting at the top of her lungs.

"Where is my dad?" she screams. "I need to—*hic*—t-t-talk, uh, see him *right now*!"

I nod at Jeremy, then race after her.

"Rebel!" I try to sound desperate. Concerned. "Wait! We need to get you home!"

She reaches the front doors, which are uncharacteristically locked. Another one of the new security protocols.

While Rebel rattles the doors, pounding the glass and shouting for her father, I catch up and make a big show of trying to drag her away.

I glance inside to see if our little act is having any effect on the guards at the desk.

"It's working," I whisper under my breath. "Now slap me."

Without hesitation, Rebel whirls around and smacks her palm across my cheek. I gasp. I hadn't expected her to hit me so hard.

Grabbing her by the shoulders, I shove her into the door. Within seconds, we have each other by the hair and are screaming like freaking banshees.

If security doesn't step in soon, one of us is going to draw blood.

Plus the cayenne pepper's really done its job. Rebel's eyes are tearing, her nose is running, and she's drooling all over me.

I see a shadow in my peripheral vision a moment before I hear the lock disengage. *Finally.*

The door slides open, and the two regular night guards—Luther and Travis—each grab one of us and drag us apart.

"What's going on here, girls?" Luther asks.

Travis pulls me out of Rebel's reach. "I thought you two were friends."

"We are," I spit. "She's drunk"—I shoot her a look full of loathing—"*again* and acting like a raging bitch."

"Mmmm-mam not drunk," Rebel sputters. "And ya—yor—*you're* the bitch."

On the last word, she swings for me. As Luther struggles to hold her back, he doesn't notice her slip a hand to his belt and disconnect his security badge.

I shake my head, shifting into concerned friend mode. "Rebel, stop." I turn to Travis. "She needs to sleep it off. Let's get her to her dad's office and she can sober up on his couch."

Travis opens his mouth like he wants to argue, but then Rebel makes a horking sound, and in a flash the two guards are escorting us inside.

Before the door closes behind us, Rebel flicks her wrist and levitates the pilfered pass onto the sidewalk outside. Holding my hand behind my back, I form my fingers into the Vulcan salute. I'd like to see Jeremy miss *that* signal.

Now if only the rest of the plan goes as smoothly, maybe we'll all make it out of this alive.

✦ ✦ ✦

"Thank you both so much," I gush as Travis and Luther let us into Mr. Malone's office.

Luther carries a seemingly-passed-out Rebel over to the couch, and I turn to Travis. "I should get her some orange juice."

Rebel times her moan of misery perfectly. "Kenna…" She flings an arm over her forehead. "I'm dying…"

I rush to her side. "I'm here, Reb. I'm here." I give the guards my best no-Mom-please-don't-make-me-a-guinea-pig-again look. "I shouldn't leave her."

Travis looks uncomfortable. "We can't leave the desk unmanned."

I nod, feigning understanding.

"You get back to the desk," Luther tells Travis. "I'll get our girl here some juice from the dining sector."

Wow, I'm a better actress than I thought.

"Thank you," I say as the guards leave the office.

The moment the door glides shut behind them, Rebel is off the couch. I dig Jeremy's tiny USB device out of my pocket and join her at her dad's desk. It only takes her a couple of seconds to find an open port on the back of his computer.

According to Jeremy, that tiny piece of metal and plastic will give him undetectable control of Mr. Malone's system. Which means he'll be able to monitor the entire building.

Between that and using Luther's pass to gain access to the systems in the security office, we pretty much control the entire facility.

My phone beeps with a text from Jeremy.

Lifted signal jammer

Ur good to go

This bldg is pwned

"We're in." I peer into the hallway, making sure the guards are gone.

Quiet as little spy mice, Rebel and I hurry to the elevators. My heart races as we wait for one to arrive. I sincerely hope that Jeremy is already looping footage of an empty elevator car and disguising the location signal to make the guards think it's still at lobby level.

As Rebel and I step inside, I hold my breath, swipe the fake ID card, and punch the button for sublevel two. The elevator moves swiftly, gliding past the lobby without a pause. When it gets to sublevel two, I fling an arm across Rebel's chest before she can take a step forward.

She gives me a curious look, and I take a step back.

Nothing happens.

What? she mouths.

Maybe her weight is confusing the sensor. I pull her back with me.

Still nothing.

I swipe the card. Again. Nothing. Again.

"Shit."

The pained look on her face is unmistakable. "It's not working?"

I pull out my text and shoot Jeremy a message.

Rear doors wont open

Can u force?

I wait for what feels like an eternity, but it is only a few seconds.

Nothing in sec sys

Trying cmd cntrl

Which I interpret to mean he's going to try accessing Mr. Malone's computer to see if there's anything he can do through there.

While we wait, Rebel gets impatient. She stomps to the button panel, triggering the front door to open. She jabs at the sublevel two button over and over again. When the door slides shut, she returns to the back of the car with me.

Nothing.

I have a bad feeling about this.

The rear door looks just as much like a wall as it did earlier tonight. I press my palms against the cool metal surface, trying to use the friction of my skin to force the door open. Without super strength it's pointless.

"Let me try," Rebel says.

She squints, focuses as she throws her whole power into moving the hidden door.

Not even a budge.

It's as if they've welded the door shut from the other side.

For all I know they have.

My phone dings.

No good

Nothing about sekrit lvl anywhere

I groan and smack my forehead against the back wall.

Rebel lets out a growl to rival Dante's and starts beating on every surface in the elevator. It's not going to get us any closer to sublevel three, but Rebel needs to let out some of her frustration.

"Now what?" she snaps as she whirls to face me. "How do we get down to Deacon?"

"I don't know," I answer honestly.

Another text from Jeremy.

Guard on move

Get back upstairs

Our time is up. If we'd found Deacon, then it wouldn't matter if the guards discovered we were missing. But we don't want to raise any alarms. Not when we're going to need access to the building again. The last thing we want is for them to lock the whole place down.

"We have to go." I press the button for the third floor.

I shoot Jeremy a quick text asking him to stall Luther. Hopefully he can hold the other elevator long enough to let us get back to Mr. Malone's office.

"You're giving up?" Rebel throws me a fierce scowl as the elevator rises. "You're just going to let them kill Deacon?"

I ignore the barb. "No, but it took me half the night to find this access. I don't know how to make it work again, and I have no clue where to start looking for another way to get down there." I watch the floor numbers tick by impatiently. "If Luther and Travis get a whiff of what we're doing, neither of us will ever be allowed in the building again. And that will make it virtually impossible to get Deacon out."

She crosses her arms over her chest, but doesn't argue.

I glance at Jeremy's response.

Can't

He's taking stairs

I mutter a foul curse. *Think, Kenna, think.*

"Do you have lip balm?"

"What?" she retorts. "Oh, I'm sorry. Are your lips getting chapped while my boyfriend's twin is downstairs *dying*?"

I roll my eyes in exasperation. "Luther is taking the stairs," I explain. "If we don't have a good reason for not being in your dad's office when he gets back..."

"Red flags and sirens," she finishes. Without another word, Rebel hands over the tube she always keeps in her pocket.

I palm the cap and twist the balm all the way out. Grabbing the contents, I mash it between my palms until it forms a gooey, chunky paste. Without bothering to explain, I slide my palms over Rebel's blond spikes, leaving little translucent blobs of balm throughout.

"Gross," she says, but doesn't stop me.

The display indicates we're passing the second floor, so I grab her around the waist and tug her tight against my side.

"Put your weight on me," I instruct. "And hang your head."

She does, just as the doors open.

I quickly move us across the hall. There is a ladies' room about three doors down. With the disgusting clumps in her hair, it should look like that's where we're coming from, like Rebel's been hugging the porcelain throne.

We start a lopsided trek back to Mr. Malone's office. Hopefully Luther will be too worried to wonder why we didn't just use the private restroom en suite.

"And moaning," I tell her. "Moaning would be good."

Rebel belts out groans that sound like a dying cow.

The sound of the stairwell door slamming shut echoes down the hall.

"Come on, Reb," I say loudly. "We're almost there."

We round the corner, right as Luther is stepping back out of the empty office, a small bottle of orange juice clutched in his hand.

He looks relieved when he sees us.

"Everything okay?" he asks.

"Oh, just peachy." I struggle to hold my best friend on her feet. "We're at the dry-heaving stage."

On cue, Rebel makes a gut-wrenching sound so believable that I almost expect to see chunks.

Luther's face twists into a mix of concern and revulsion. "Maybe she needs to go to the emergency room?"

Another round of fake-heaving.

"No, no," I insist. "I just need to get her home and to bed."

Luther nods enthusiastically.

"Can you help me get her downstairs?"

He rushes to Rebel's other side faster than I can blink. He hands me the juice and takes her weight from me. A minute later, we're in the lobby.

Rebel and I are almost in the clear, but that leaves Jeremy trapped in the security office. He may have forgiven me for our breakup fight, but he won't take so kindly to being left to fend for himself with the SHPD.

I hook my foot around Rebel's ankle, sending her stumbling toward the guards' desk. She lands against the side with a heavy thud and proceeds to dry-heave in Travis's general direction.

He rushes out from behind the desk and takes Rebel's other side. "Here, let me give you a hand."

I clear my throat loudly, and Rebel manages a stumble that sends all three of them to the floor. The guard desk now blocks their view of both the security office and the front door.

I shoot Jeremy a text. **Now.**

In a flash, he's sprinting for the door faster than I've ever seen him move. He unlocks the door, dropping the security pass on the ground as he races into the night.

"Are you okay, Miss Malone?" Luther asks, climbing back to his feet and helping her up.

She groans, sways a little, and then latches herself to my side.

"I think I can take it from here," I say, flashing them a long-suffering smile.

Travis's eyes widen. "If you're sure…"

I nod and start for the door. He hurries ahead of us to unlock it, only to jerk back, confused, when he sees his security pass lying on the ground. Better he thinks he dropped it there than raise a red flag by it going missing.

"Thanks for everything!" I push past him, not waiting for him to ask the inevitable questions forming in his mind. "I'll be sure to tell Mr. Malone how much you helped!"

Travis's frown turns into a proud grin. "Anything for the boss."

Oh yeah, I'll *totally* be telling the evil king of the superheroes how his guards let us sneak into his top secret facility and his office. Mr. Malone would love that.

"The guys are going to be pissed," Rebel whispers as we make our way toward the sidewalk.

"Maybe Jeremy found something," I suggest.

At this point, he's our only hope.

CHAPTER 14

Rebel cries the entire way back to the Lair. It hurts me to
see her in this kind of emotional pain, especially when
I know it's my fault that we didn't get Deacon tonight. It's
my fault they changed the security protocols on the secret
sublevel. It has to be.

I shouldn't beat myself up. Logically, I know that if I
hadn't been down there—hadn't seen Deacon with my own
eyes—there would be no proof that the secret sublevel exists,
let alone what's going on down there.

But that knowledge is cold comfort. I hug Rebel and try to
figure out what to do next. How're we going to save Deacon and
my mother when we can't get back to sublevel three? If that's
even where my mother *is*. She's not a villain. She doesn't belong
there, and she has friends at the lab. Really, she could be anywhere.

And how are we going to face Draven and Dante when
we've failed to get Deacon back? Just the thought of Draven's
reaction makes my stomach hurt—not because I'm afraid of
him, but because I've seen how much this weighs on him. On
both of them. I know how every second feels like a year and
every hour feels like an eternity.

I've felt that way since the moment I saw Deacon. And it

only got worse when I walked into my house and my mother was missing.

The ride to the nightclub from the lab feels excruciatingly long, but when Jeremy pulls up in front of the Lair all I can think is, it's too soon. I don't have an explanation. I don't know how to tell Draven and Dante what happened without causing them more pain. I don't—

Nitro meets us in the parking lot, throwing open the van door before we even come to a complete stop.

"Deacon!" He climbs inside, but his face falls when he sees Rebel's tear-streaked cheeks.

"Oh God. Is he—" Nitro turns white and looks like he's going to pass out.

"We couldn't get to him." My words come out in a rush. "They've sealed off access to that sublevel and we couldn't find another way in. Not without tipping off the guards and blowing our cover."

"Shit." Nitro rubs both hands over his head and climbs out of the van. "How could you screw this up? You promised this plan was airtight. Draven and Dante are going to kill us. You know that, right?"

Rebel whimpers, and I pat her back a couple times, shooting Nitro a warning glare.

"We couldn't have known," I argue.

He ignores me. "I knew it. I knew better than to trust a couple of heroes to handle something this important."

"Is that really how you want to play this?" Jeremy comes to my side and stands over Nitro.

Jeremy may be lean, but he has almost a foot over the angry villain.

Nitro doesn't look impressed. "I'm not playing anything. Just stating the truth, yeah?" His British accent is out in full force. "You wankers failed, didn't you? You talked me into locking up my two best mates, and then you bloody well screwed up. A guy can't be blamed for thinking maybe you did it on purpose."

Rebel starts to sob harder, which makes me see red. I advance on Nitro. "Must be nice. Easy for you to stand there criticizing when you didn't have a better plan. We risked everything tonight!"

"You think you're the only ones?" he scoffs. "I've got two of the most dangerous villains in the bloody world locked in my refrigerator. You obviously don't know what they've spent the last hour and a half threatening to do to me when they finally get out."

Screw it. Dante and Draven already know about my immunity. What's one more villain at this point, especially since he's their best friend? They'll probably tell him anyway, the first chance they get. "At least I *found* the secret sublevel! You couldn't even do that."

"Because of you!" He doesn't look surprised that Draven's brainwashing didn't stick, which proves that Dante and Draven spilled the beans while we were gone.

Typical. Can't trust villains, can't trust heroes... Who the hell *am* I supposed to trust?

"You almost killed me with that fire extinguisher!"

"Yeah, well, almost doesn't count. If it did, Rebel and I would have Deacon right now."

"I'll believe that when I see it. You lousy hero-worshipper—"

"Hey!" Rebel finally pulls herself together and climbs out of the van. "Don't call her that!"

"Or what?" Nitro glows a little, the air above his hands tinged green as he starts to lose his grip on his power. At least I assume he's losing his grip—maybe he's doing it on purpose. At this point, who can tell?

"Or I'll make sure you regret it." Jeremy's joined the fray now, standing shoulder to shoulder with Rebel and me as he stares down Nitro.

"Yeah, right. 'Cuz I'm scared of a nerdy technopath." Flames lick along Nitro's fingers.

"You should be." Jeremy takes a step forward and I know that if I don't stop this right here, right now, the situation's going to get out of control. Testosterone is such a pain in the ass.

But just as I slide myself between the two of them, the door to the club flies open and Draven and Dante sail into the parking lot. They're both bruised and bloody and more than a little frantic. When they see us, they do double takes, then race full tilt toward us.

"What the hell!" Dante roars.

"How did you get out?" Nitro demands. When they turn to glare at him, he shrinks back, half hiding behind Rebel.

Not that I blame him. I've seen Draven go from surly to tortured to furious in the short time I've known him, but never have I seen him this enraged. If his expression—and the way his bruised hands are trembling—is anything to go by, he's about two seconds from ripping us to pieces.

All of us.

Draven doesn't hesitate. He reaches past Rebel to grab the

lapels of Nitro's leather jacket and yanks him off his feet. "Let's just say you and Quake are going to need a new fridge."

"It's not his fault," I insist. "We asked him to help."

"Bloody brilliant idea that was," Nitro snaps.

I glare at him. *Not helping.*

I wrap my hands around Draven's forearms and yank, as if I'm going to have any effect on him in this state.

To my utter amazement, he actually relaxes. He lowers Nitro to the ground.

"Where is my brother?" Dante peers into the van.

The silence is deafening—taut and terrible and terrifying. The next thing I know, Dante's whirling, advancing on Jeremy and me with his hands curled into fists. "Where. Is. *Deacon?*"

"We couldn't get to him!" Rebel says in a rush, throwing herself against his chest and starting to sob all over again.

His arms wrap around her, his hands stroking her back. But *his* back is ramrod straight and his face is dark. "What does that mean?" he demands. "Deacon's still in that hellhole?"

"They've closed off access to the sublevel where they're holding him. We couldn't get down there," I say. But it's not Dante I'm talking to, not really. It's Draven.

He's calm, the calmest person out here in fact. But somehow that doesn't reassure me.

"So you just left him," Draven accuses. "You didn't even try to get him out."

"We couldn't!" Rebel tells him. "We tried but Kenna's access route was blocked off."

"That's it?" Draven sneers. "The way was *blocked off* so you gave up? Wow, you guys really are hero material."

"Back off," I tell him, slapping a hand against his chest

and shoving lightly. "We did the best we could with what we had."

"Of course you did."

"What's that supposed to mean?"

"It's awfully convenient that the three of you trapped us here in a tin can while you went off to save the world." His face is a mask of rage and resentment. "Except you didn't save anyone, did you? Was that the plan all along?"

I gasp. "You think we left Deacon there on purpose?"

"I don't think you tried very hard to get him out."

"In case you've forgotten, moron, they have my mother too!" I know he's upset, but this is nuts. "You think I'd walk away without trying to find her if there was any other way?"'

He takes a step forward, so we're standing inches from each other. His head tilts down and mine tilts up as we face off.

This is totally the wrong place and the wrong time, but I can't stop the thrill that sparks through me at the realization that he's treating me like an equal. He's not pulling his punches, not treating me like some fragile little ordinary. Maybe it's because he thinks immunity is my power, or maybe it's because he doesn't realize I'm not a super. Or maybe, just maybe, it's because he understands that I'm just as strong as he is.

Then he shatters the moment with more of his mistrust. "How do we even know your mother's there? This could all be some elaborate setup—"

"Are you being serious right now?"

"Does it look like I'm being serious?"

"You've got some nerve—"

"Nerve? *I* have nerve? You locked us in a refrigerator and

then screwed up. You're either a liar or you're incompetent, and either way I'm not impressed."

"Dude, you need to back off." Jeremy shoves Draven's shoulder. "Now."

Draven doesn't flinch. He turns those cold, sharp eyes on Jeremy. Except they're not cold anymore. They're fiery, seething, spoiling for a fight.

"You going to make me, geek boy?"

"Okay, wait a minute!" I hold up both arms like a referee. The last thing I want is for Draven to kill Jeremy, and from his stance, that's a distinct possibility.

Jeremy has no sense of self-preservation. "If I have to."

"We did try, Draven!" Rebel says. "Even if you don't trust Kenna and Jeremy, you trust me. You know I'd do *anything* to help Deacon."

Draven looks at her, and for a moment, the rage subsides and I see the fear he's been hiding.

"I'm sorry," I tell him softly.

"Don't apologize to him, Kenna!" Jeremy snaps at me.

"Don't talk to her like that!" Draven snarls at him.

We all kind of freeze at that. Moments ago he'd been ripping me a new one, and now he's getting mad at the way Jeremy—*Jeremy*—talks to me? Could this night get any more upside down?

"Look, maybe if we all calmed down," Nitro says, "we can figure out what went wrong and try to—"

"What went wrong," Dante growls, "is you locked us in a refrigerator. You sided with the heroes and now everything has gone to shit. What kind of villain are you?"

The whole situation is a powder keg waiting to explode. All

it needs is a little spark, and the four guys are going to beat the hell out of each other—or whatever guys with powers do when they lose their tempers.

The mayhem these three villains could unleash with Dante's wind, Nitro's fire, and Draven's psy abilities is catastrophic. We need to diffuse this fast. But how? A quick glance at Rebel tells me she doesn't know what to do either.

"You think I'm on *their* side?" Nitro shouts incredulously.

"You chose them over us," Dante says. "Don't think I'm going to forget that."

Nitro sputters. "Man, not in a million years!"

"We're not lepers, you know," Jeremy spits out.

"I'd like you a hell of a lot more if you were," Dante returns. "Heroes are nothing but a bunch of two-faced hypocrites."

"Dante!" Rebel gasps.

"I'm not talking about you, babe. These two." He looks at Jeremy and me like we're contagious.

"Screw you!" Jeremy seethes. "Kenna doesn't have to help you and neither do I."

He looks to me, waiting for me to speak up, but I don't know what to say. Dante's insult is ringing in my ears, and even knowing that he's got a good reason to say something like that doesn't make it any easier to stomach. Not when I'm trying so hard to make things right.

Not when just yesterday I saw things just as black and white, just as right and wrong. Only I was certain that every last villain was as bad as Dante insists all heroes are. Are we both right? Or both wrong?

"I'm sorry, were you *helping*?" Dante demands. "Because I thought you were making things worse." He jerks his head in my direction. "Kenna stopped us from finding my brother the first time we broke into the lab. *She's* the one who left him there to get tortured. And *she's* the one who couldn't get the job done tonight, even after she said she didn't need our help."

I take a step back.

He's right. He's totally right. This isn't about black and white; it's about saving Deacon's life. It's about finding my mom. And I failed.

I want to run away—somewhere, anywhere. I can't stay here. Not when it's taking every ounce of self-control I have not to cry.

I won't break down though. Not here. Not in front of Dante and Draven. I won't give them that satisfaction. My whole world might be flipped inside out, but I still have my pride.

I stand tall, even as I'm falling apart inside. I deserve every last word of his scorn.

"You make me sick!" Dante continues viciously, jamming a finger at me. "Walking around all proud of being heroes when—

"Dante!" Rebel shouts his name at the same time Draven says, "Enough."

"No! It's not enough. They—" Dante breaks off as Draven shoves him, hard.

"I said that's enough. This isn't Kenna's fault."

Dante shakes his head. "Are you kidding me? You're taking *her* side?"

"You're being an ass," Draven tells him.

"And you're acting hero-whipped," Dante spits. "Just because you think she's a nice piece of—"

Draven's fist connects with Dante's mouth.

And then all hell breaks loose.

CHAPTER 15

D ante crashes shoulder first into Jeremy, who shoves him into Nitro, who falls to the ground from the force of the impact.

"Hey!" Nitro kicks out at Jeremy's ankle, tripping him.

Dante lunges at Draven.

In a matter of moments the four guys are beating the crap out of each other. Fists are flying, knees and elbows are being driven into guts and jaws, and curses permeate the air. At least they seem to be relying on their muscle, not their powers. Jeremy's technopathy wouldn't stand a chance.

For long seconds, Rebel and I just stare in shock. I'd figured it would be the three villains against Jeremy. But it's not that way at all. Jeremy and Nitro are going at it, and Draven and Dante are hitting each other at least as hard. Maybe harder. And every once in a while, they switch, so that at any given moment any one of them is beating on any one of the other three. Like a musical-chairs version of a parking lot brawl. It's every super for himself.

"We should stop them," I say.

Rebel throws out her arm to keep me from interfering. "No, let them fight." She throws me a weary look. "They need to work off some anger."

"But if it looks like they're going to kill each other..."

"Oh yeah," she agrees. "Then we'll definitely step in."

Almost on cue, Jeremy lets out a particularly plaintive screech.

"And that would be now," Rebel says. Hands outstretched, she heads for Dante and Nitro. A half second later, both guys are suspended several feet off the ground. The fact that they're floating doesn't cool their fight; it just forces them to change tactics. Nitro fires up a glowing, pink energy ball while Dante sends a gust of gale-force wind at his face.

Rethinking her strategy, Rebel releases Dante and grabs his shirt—or what's left of it.

"Dante, babe. Come on. Stop. Please."

He shrugs her off, pretty gently considering he's got Nitro wrapped in a small F5 tornado.

I don't have a power that will help me break up the fight, so I wing it and hope I don't die. Between Jeremy and Draven, my ex is more likely to listen to reason. But since Draven is kneeling on top of him, plowing his fist into Jeremy's face, I don't think Jeremy is in any position to help me out here.

A series of high-pitched beeps sound from the vicinity of the van.

With a muttered curse of my own, I wade into the tangle of bodies and grab Draven's arm before he pounds Jeremy again.

"Stop!" I tell him as authoritatively as I can muster. "Stop before you kill each other."

I half expect him to shove me out of the way, but he pauses. He looks wild, his eyes a bright blue that glows under the parking lot lights. Blood trickles from the corner of his mouth, and I can see a bruise forming on his right cheekbone. Looks like Jeremy got in a couple of good hits.

The series of beeps sounds again in a familiar pattern.

"Stop," I tell him again, more softly this time. "Please."

He shakes his head, like he's trying to clear it. Jeremy, of course, takes the opportunity to punch Draven in the stomach.

Draven's breath whooshes out of him.

"Hey!" I yell at Jeremy as he shoves Draven off him and climbs to his feet.

I expect him to kick or hit Draven again. Instead, Jeremy staggers toward the van, weaving drunkenly from all the punches he's taken.

When the beeps start again, Jeremy reaches for something and the sound cuts out mid-pattern.

Without the energy of another battle going on beside them, the fight goes out of Nitro and Dante. Nitro shoots his latest fireball—a crazy swirl of green and blue—off into the trees. Dante lets his tornado twist away into nothingness. Rebel lowers Nitro back down to the pavement, and the two villains stare each other down, breathing heavily.

Rebel throws her hands up in the air, as if to say, *Finally*.

"Where are you going?" I demand when I notice Jeremy climbing into the van.

Seriously? I just saved his butt, and he's going to bail?

He waves me away, but Rebel isn't letting him off that easy. "I know this whole thing was crazy, Jer, but we can't—"

"Shut up!" he snaps.

Draven's eyes narrow and he starts for the van. I have visions of another fight breaking out and move to throw myself between him and Jeremy, but I don't have to. Jeremy presses a finger to his lips. He's holding a device in his other hand that looks like a walkie-talkie, and voices are coming from it. Familiar voices. Familiar *hero* voices.

"Listen," Jeremy whispers harshly. "Someone's in Mr. Malone's office."

The bug. Oh God. The bug Rebel and I planted is actually working. I've been so caught up in our failure that I completely forgot about our success. I don't know whether to be excited or terrified.

Rebel and I crowd around to listen, and seconds later the villains join us. The walkie-talkie has gone silent except for the clicking of keyboard keys. We hold our breath waiting to hear if there's going to be any more talking.

Jeremy opens the passenger door, pulls out his laptop, and sets it on the front seat. I wish I could say it's the first time I've lost shotgun to one of his computers. A few keystrokes later, he opens a remote desktop mirror and his screen shows everything that is happening on Mr. Malone's monitor. All of us watch in shock as Rebel's dad types a memo to the officers of the Collective.

June 21
To: Superhero Collective
From: Rex Malone
Subject: ESH Lab Closure

Recent occurrences have brought to light villain knowledge of the ESH Lab at location Bravo Charlie. Therefore, it is my recommendation that we close the Boulder facility immediately and indefinitely.

This is not a decision I make lightly, as doing so will

inconvenience many of our staff members, as well as disrupt numerous top-priority experiments and projects. However, we have had multiple security breaches during these last few days, and for the sake of our research, as well as the future security of the League, it is necessary.

As of 8 p.m. on June twenty-fourth, the doors of this lab will be shut. All research and activities will be relocated to Lima Whiskey. Every effort will be made to do this with as little disruption to our scientists and their work as possible. We will use all safety precautions to ensure that the secrecy of the new facility remains unaffected by this move.

Thank you for your understanding in this matter. I will make every effort to keep you updated on our plans and progress once the move is complete.

Rex Malone
League President
cc: file, TR, SecLev5

The typing stops and we all watch as Mr. Malone saves the memo and emails it to the ten Collective officers who serve with him. He blind-copies two other addresses that aren't on League domains. Seconds later, he logs out, and the League logo screen saver bounces around on Jeremy's laptop like a shield-shaped ping-pong ball.

"Is it done?" a harsh voice from the speaker asks.

"Yes," Mr. Malone answers. "It's just a precaution, but I think it's wise. It never pays to be careless with villains."

"I agree. Some of our research is…quite delicate in nature. We would hate for it to fall into the wrong hands."

"Exactly."

There are a few unidentifiable sounds, followed by the clatter of ice cubes and the slosh of pouring liquid. A lid is screwed back on. Mr. Malone swallows deeply.

There are a couple of clicks. A door opens and shuts. And then there's nothing. Just silence as the six of us continue to stare at the computer, the knock-down, drag-out fight forgotten in the wake of these much larger, more worrisome problems.

Jeremy sets down the walkie-talkie and begins typing furiously.

"June twenty-fourth," Rebel hisses after a minute. "That's—"

"Three days away," Dante finishes for her.

"Three days and Deacon will be gone," Draven says.

Deacon and my mother. Gone. The entire lab moved to a top secret hero facility. The people—the villains—housed at ESH simply disappearing without a trace.

And that's assuming my mom is being held at the lab. Really, she could be anywhere. Literally anywhere. At least we know where Deacon is—for now. He's still within our reach, and he can't hold on for long. As much as it hurts to say, he has to be our first priority. Mom would agree.

Hopefully we'll find some clue about her whereabouts along the way.

Two days ago, my biggest concern would have been Mom losing her research. Today…my perspective has changed. A lot.

This can't happen. It just can't.

"Don't suppose either of you birds know where this new top secret facility is?" Nitro asks.

Rebel's eyes meet mine, and one look tells me she's as lost as I feel. Neither of us had any idea such a facility existed. The ESH lab was kept a secret so our research wouldn't fall into villain hands, but it was never a secret from other heroes. Up until a couple of days ago, I wouldn't have had a clue why they'd need such a place—or what might go on there. Now, I'm terrified that I know *exactly* what's going on there.

"We have to get Deacon before ESH shuts down," I say, frantic now that the truth is sinking in. "We have to get him and then find my mom. We have to—"

"We have three days." Draven brushes his hand over my lower back. It's a fleeting touch, nothing serious really, considering how close we're all standing to see the computer screen, but it comforts me anyway. It helps me draw my first breath in what feels like forever. And the next one. And the one after that. I'm not alone in this. I'm not the only one hurting. And I'm not the only one desperate to get my loved one back.

Unlike the villains, I can hold out hope that my mom is just being questioned, just being…kept. I can believe that she's not being tortured, or worse. Draven and Dante don't have that luxury.

"I doubt we have that much time," Jeremy says, not taking his eyes off his screen as lines of undecipherable computer code scroll by. "Mr. Malone wants the whole lab shut down in three days. Which means that whatever plans they have for Deacon—" The words hang there as he pauses and clears his throat. I'm imagining the worst now, and I can tell by the way the others tense that they are too. "Whatever they're going to do to Deacon, they won't want to wait until the last day."

"So what does that mean?" Dante demands. "We have less time?"

"If we're lucky," is Jeremy's grim answer.

If we're not already too late. He doesn't say it, but we all feel the unspoken words.

My stomach pitches, but I ignore it. Someone needs to take charge. And since everyone else seems shell-shocked, that someone is going to have to be me. The sooner we save Deacon's life, the sooner we can move on to looking for my mom.

"Jeremy, you have to get us in," I tell him, forcing a steadiness into my voice that is far from what I'm feeling. "Find a way around the villain signature sensors, because we're going in as a team."

Draven looks at me, hot and powerful emotions lurking behind his gaze.

That's right. We are stronger as a team, not fractured like a bunch of kids fighting over who gets to play with the cool toys at recess. And it's time we start acting like it.

"I'm on it," Jeremy says. His fingers fly across the keyboard.

"Let's get started," I tell the rest of the group. "We have two days to figure this out."

"I'm in," Rebel says. "Where do we start?"

"With figuring out how to blow that lab wide open without hurting my cousin or Kenna's mom," Draven answers firmly.

"Exactly." I straighten my spine. "Because one way or another, we're going in."

CHAPTER 16

"Tell me again why we need three containers of chocolate milk to break into the lab?" Draven asks suspiciously. Not that I blame him—the whole cranberry juice debacle is still fresh in all our minds.

"Because Jeremy is hypoglycemic and it helps keep his blood sugar steady if he loads up on chocolate milk when he's stressed out," I tell him.

Draven rolls his eyes as he drops the bottles of Nesquik into our cart. "That's some kind of ex-boyfriend you've got there."

"Yeah, well, he's a genius. Through the years, I've learned not to question his bizarre beverage choices as long as he gets the job done."

Draven nods and adds an extra bottle of chocolate milk to the cart. It makes me smile as I push it to the next aisle and pick up a box of Froot Loops for Rebel and a pack of chocolate-chip cookies for Nitro.

It's been eight hours since Rebel, Jeremy, and I failed to find Deacon at ESH labs, and we've spent most of that time holed up in a hotel room at the Extended Stay a few blocks from my house, trying to come up with a new plan. It's not the optimum situation with six of us crowded into a two-room suite, but it was the safest option we could come up with. Right now, not showing up on hero radar is a lot more important than comfort, especially since we have to go back in to find Deacon.

And this time we're all going. That's nonnegotiable, at least according to the villains. Considering the overwhelming guilt Rebel feels over our failure and the knock-down, drag-out the guys got into in the nightclub parking lot, I'm inclined to agree.

Which means we need a really good plan, one that won't get us killed before we can rescue Deacon…and my mother. Thankfully Jeremy has some ideas on where to start, because I'm pretty much tapped out. I'm so freaked out about my mom and everything else that I can barely think.

In the produce department, Draven and I pick up some apples and oranges. I know the guys think all we need is junk food to survive, but a little nutrition never hurt anyone. I'm reaching for some grapes when I get a weird tingle down my spine. I glance up just in time to catch someone watching me. Watching us.

I don't recognize him and he's too far away for me to see if he has a tattoo beneath one of his ears, but every instinct I have screams that he's a super. I start toward him—but Draven wraps an arm around my waist and pulls me in to his side. Then he ducks his head and starts whispering absolute gibberish to me.

I'm about to shrug him off, but he whispers, "Don't." His arm tightens around my waist. He half smirks, half snarls at the guy watching us and—to my surprise—the guy flushes before walking away.

"What was that about?" I hiss as Draven grabs a couple of bunches of grapes without even looking at them, then tosses them in the basket.

"It's nothing. Don't worry about it."

I dig in my heels, refusing to budge. "This isn't going to work if you don't tell me the truth."

"I told you the truth." He sighs and runs an exasperated hand through his hair. "It was nothing."

"Yeah, well. I don't believe you."

"That's your problem then, isn't it?" He reaches for the cart and steers it down the aisle away from me.

I follow him, grabbing his arm. "Draven, if there's something I need to know—"

"He was looking at you, okay?" The words seem to burst from him. "He was looking at you and I didn't like it."

My mind swirls. He can't be implying what I think he is. "What-I-he—" I stumble for a moment, trying to come up with an appropriate response that won't make me sound like an idiot. Finally, I clear my throat. "You mean, he recognized me or something? Should we be concerned? Who is he?"

"Just a guy I know from school. And he wasn't looking at you like he recognized you, Kenna. He was looking at you like he *wanted* to recognize you. Like he wanted to get to know you. So I took care of it. Sorry." He turns and starts pulling random junk off the shelves.

I'm left staring after him, feeling all strange inside. Because Draven just admitted he didn't like another guy being interested in me. Which means what? That *he's* interested in me? Suddenly, it's hard to breathe. Not because I don't like the idea of him thinking about me in that way. But because I like it too much.

He's a villain and I'm…not. I'm not technically a hero either. I guess that makes me majorly confused. And more than a little attracted to a guy I have no business falling for.

Draven doesn't say anything else about the other guy—or what he's admitted—and neither do I. Partly because I don't know what to say, and partly because this isn't the time or place for that kind of discussion.

Although for a villain and an ordinary, is there really ever going to be a perfect time?

We're pretty quiet as we pick up other supplies—sandwich fixings, carrots, granola bars, a few different bags of chips. As we pass back through the dairy aisle on the way to the checkout counter, I grab a couple more bottles of chocolate milk. It's going to be a long day, and the last thing we need is Jeremy running out of his very particular, very peculiar brand of fuel.

Draven helps me unload at checkout, but when I reach for my wallet, he insists on paying for the groceries. I try to fight him on it. Owing a villain doesn't sit easy with me. But by the time I get my debit card out of my wallet, he's already handed over the money.

A hundred and fifty dollars. In cash. Of course. We're lying low. Under the radar. I stare at my debit card with horror. I almost messed everything up. I don't think our visit to the lab raised any red flags last night, but there's no guarantee the guards won't mention it to Mr. Malone. No guarantee that he won't start putting the pieces together and trace back through our digital trail. After all, my house didn't get ransacked for nothing, and the last thing I need is for the heroes to know where I am or where I've been. Or worse, who I've been with.

Jeremy is adamant about leaving no tracks. Avoid cameras, keep cell phones powered off, and above all else, don't pay with credit. I should know better.

"Thanks," I mutter as we walk to the car.

Draven looks genuinely perplexed. "For what?"

"I almost ruined everything back there. I didn't think about using cash."

That's not like me. I'm the planner, the one who thinks about every detail from every angle. The one who doesn't make mistakes. But ever since Draven broke into the lab, ever since my life turned upside down, I seem to be making blunder after blunder.

It makes me feel like I don't know myself anymore. Like this whole situation is turning me into someone I'm not.

Three days ago, I was an ordinary girl in a superhero world. It wasn't ideal, but it was tolerable. It was normal. It made sense. Black was black, and white was white. Good was good, and bad was…bad. Villains were bad.

Now, everything is topsy-turvy. Nothing makes sense. And as for life being black and white? I feel like I'm drowning in a million shades of gray. Like the suits of the Ray-Ban brigade.

I don't know what's right anymore. How can I when I might be falling for a villain? And he might be falling right back?

But I have more important things to focus on right now. I have to find my mom. Stop them from torturing Deacon. Figure out how to stop what I'm beginning to think is an entire hero agenda—not just one project with one villain, but a massive program that spans decades, has had countless victims, and involves bugging the house of the League's most prominent scientist and then kidnapping her. That's a pretty big freaking agenda.

I don't know how we're going to do what we need to, or what's going to happen after. Who knows. My whole life could fall apart completely. But I can't stress about that now. There are too many other things at stake.

"Don't worry about the debit card," Draven tells me as he transfers the bags from the cart to the van. "You did fine."

"No. I didn't. If you hadn't been here—"

"But I was." He stops and looks me in the eye. "And I'm going to keep being here. I'll save you from mistakes; you'll save me from mistakes. That's how this whole partner thing works."

"Partners?" I repeat, rolling the word around on my tongue, trying to decide if I like the way it feels. Turns out I do—maybe too much.

"Partners," he reiterates. "Unless you lock me in a refrigerator again. Then it's every person for him or herself."

"Are you still stuck on that?" I demand with a roll of my eyes. "I already told you, it was the most logical—"

"No." He leans forward so his face is only inches from mine. His beautiful blue eyes glow with intensity and determination as he stares me down. "It really wasn't."

Eight hours ago—hell, eight minutes ago—I would have argued that point with him. Would have told him I only did what I needed to keep everybody safe.

But after everything that has happened, standing right here, right now, breathing the same air as him, working on the same side as him, it's impossible for me to form any other thought. Impossible for me to do anything but stare at Draven and wonder what it would be like if he leaned forward just a little and—

I cut off the thought. I mean, seriously, what am I even thinking? That I want Draven to kiss me?

I flash back to the intensity when he said he didn't like that guy looking at me. My heart beats faster. It gets harder to breathe.

A part of me is screaming that this is impossible. He's a villain. He's dangerous. He left me tied to a lab table. I can't trust him. I just can't. I shouldn't...

Then again, I locked him in a refrigerator and he still wants to be partners. That has to count for something. Right?

I don't know anymore. I focus on Draven's lips and think about what it would be like to kiss him. He shakes his head as if he's waking from a trance. Then he steps back and slams shut the back door of the van.

"Time to go," he says.

I nod, wiping my suddenly sweaty palms along the legs of my jeans. Right. Go. We need to go. And I need to focus on the job at hand. Things are messed up enough. Adding any additional complications to the mix would be absolutely crazy.

Except, as I climb into the front passenger seat of the van, I can't help thinking about how warm his body felt next to mine. How his eyes had that crazy, sexy look in them. How much I really, really want to know what he tastes like.

"Here." After starting the van, Draven drops a small bag in my lap.

"What is it?" I ask.

"Open it and see."

I stare at him uncertainly before reaching into the bag. I pull out three of my favorite chocolate bars. They're the same kind that I was trying to get out of the vending machine the night we met.

"I don't understand."

"You never got your candy the other night, you know, with the break-in and all. So"—he shrugs—"I figured I owed you."

His voice is steady, but his fingers tap nervously against the steering wheel. He doesn't put the van in gear. Is he waiting for something?

I want to reach over and cover his hand with my own, press a kiss to his darkly stubbled cheek. But neither is a smart move. Not now when everything is such an uncertain mess. So instead, I just say, "Thank you. That was really nice."

"It's a couple candy bars, Kenna," he tells me with a smirk. "Not world peace."

True. But he didn't have to buy them for me. They aren't necessary, not the way Jeremy's chocolate milk is. That he did it anyway, because he was thinking of me, feels...nice. The simple gesture makes me feel special and that's not an emotion I'm usually acquainted with.

"Well, thank you, anyway." I open one of the bars and break off a piece. Then I hold it out to him. Instead of taking it from me, he leans toward me. Opens his mouth a little. My throat goes desert dry as I feed him the chocolate.

His lips brush against my fingers as he closes his mouth around the candy, and suddenly I can't breathe.

To hell with everything I just told myself about villains and complications. I want to kiss him.

I lean forward, nearly falling off the van's bucket seat in the process. But I don't because he's leaning forward too—meeting me, catching me. We're so close that I can feel his warm, sweet breath against my cheek, my lips.

He stops though. He doesn't move any closer, and I know he's waiting for me. Making sure this is what I want. This villain, this self-proclaimed "bad guy" is turning the control over to me, letting me make the decision. It's something no other guy—not even Jeremy—has done.

This sends me over the edge, and I close the last of the distance between us in a rush.

I brush my lips over his, my eyes fluttering closed. And then nearly jump through the roof when his cell phone explodes with the old Guns N' Roses song, "Welcome to the Jungle."

He groans and curses, but pulls away. "Dante," he mutters bitterly before yanking his phone out of his jeans pocket. "What?"

He listens for a second. "Slow down, Rebel. What's going on?"

I sit up at the mention of my best friend's name and give him a quizzical look. He holds up a hand for me to wait.

"They're doing what?" His voice gets louder. "We're on our way."

"What's wrong?" I demand as Draven throws the van into drive and barrels through the parking lot and out onto the street.

"Nitro," he spits out.

All kinds of visions flash through my head. "Did he burn down the hotel?"

"Not yet. But give him ten minutes."

I'm a little afraid to ask what that means, so I keep my mouth shut for the rest of the ride except to ask, "Is Rebel okay?"

"She's fine. Dante won't let anything happen to her."

We squeal into the parking lot, and Draven barely takes time to turn off the van before he's racing through the lobby to our suite. We're in the back corner of the top floor so it's a bit of a run, especially when Draven refuses to wait for the elevator. We asked for that room because there were no close neighbors—a fact I'm grateful for when I follow Draven inside to find Jeremy hanging from the spinning ceiling fan while Nitro lobs small orange fireballs at him.

So far, it doesn't look like any of them have hit Jeremy, but with Nitro's control issues, I'm not sure if that's by accident or design. Then again, his aim could be messed up by the fact that Jeremy keeps trying to fry him. He's using his technopathic powers to send volts of electricity straight at Nitro from every object in the room that is currently plugged in.

The side effect of him using that power is that everyone in the room's hair is standing straight up. It's not a bad look on Draven or Dante, but Nitro's looks even more like a matchstick. And I really don't want to know what I look like.

"What. The. Hell?" Draven demands over the noise of Nitro and Jeremy's yelling.

"Get him down!" I order Dante, who is watching the scene with a huge smile on his face.

"I'd love to, but I'm not the one who put him up there. He jumped up himself."

"Seriously?"

"I had no choice," Jeremy howls.

I look around for my best friend, but she's nowhere to be seen. "Where's Rebel?"

"On the balcony. She got fed up and went outside."

I consider joining her, but since Draven looks like he's on the verge of committing murder, I decide I should probably stay—at least if I want Jeremy and Nitro to stay whole and relatively healthy. Mental health is obviously another issue altogether.

Nitro gets set to lob another fireball, but I step directly in front of him and block his path. "Stop it! You're going to burn down the whole damn hotel!"

"But he—" Nitro starts to argue, but I cut him off with a fierce glare.

"And you!" I whirl on Jeremy. "Get down from there this instant."

"I can't. I'll be in range of the electricity."

"Here's a thought," Draven bites off sarcastically. "Maybe you should stop trying to electrocute people, then."

"That's what I said!" Nitro shouts as he builds another fireball between his hands.

I count it as a small victory that he holds it in his palms instead of throwing it straight at Jeremy's ass.

"Shut up, moron!" Draven snaps at him. "Are you trying to get us caught?"

Nitro pouts. "He started it!"

I look to Jeremy for confirmation, but he shakes his head vehemently. "No way, man! He's the one who turned off my laptop right when I was in the middle of finessing—"

"I tripped, asshole. It was an accident!"

"How do you accidentally turn off a laptop?" I wonder amid the chaos.

"Exactly!" Jeremy crows. "I told you he started it."

"It's hard to take your argument seriously when you're hanging from a ceiling fan," I tell him, as deadpan as I can manage. "It's like you guys are three years old."

"Fine." Jeremy lets go and lands on the floor with a thump that I'm certain our downstairs neighbors don't appreciate. "But tell him to stay away from my stuff."

The zing of electricity in the room dies down. Seconds later, all our hair settles back to normal.

"Like I'd purposely touch your stuff?" Nitro demands. I'm relieved that he's snuffed out the fireball in his hands. "The last thing I want is *zero* cooties."

I scowl at the derogatory hero dig.

"Seriously?" I say again, more forcefully this time. Because, come on. They really are acting like toddlers. "Get it together."

Besides, if Draven and I can put aside our less-than-ideal first meeting, surely these two idiots can try to get along. For Deacon's and my mom's sake, if nothing else.

I leave Dante and Draven to sort out the mess and I join Rebel on the balcony. She's sitting on one of the two chairs out there, her legs folded up so that her chin rests on her knees. And though she's right there in front of me, I can't help thinking that she's really a million miles away. That she's lost deep inside herself, tangled up in the mess our lives have so quickly become.

"Nice show," I tell her, settling into the chair next to her.

After several long moments, she rolls her eyes. "I'm not sure who's the bigger moron."

"Nitro, definitely."

She snorts. "Yeah, probably."

"No 'probably' about it. He just told Jeremy he had cooties."

"Nice."

"Do you ever wonder how we're going to break into the lab with these guys when the group can't get along for more than five minutes at a time?"

"Pretty much every second of the day." She closes her eyes and blows out a long breath.

"I'm glad I'm not the only one."

We sit in silence until—eyes still closed—she asks, "Do you ever wonder what that's like?"

I'm not following. "What do you mean?"

"Nitro knows exactly who he is. So do Dante and Draven and Jeremy. Villain. Hero. They wear their labels proudly. Absolutely." She opens her eyes and gazes off into the distance. "It's the same at home. Dad, Riley, even Mom. They know which side of the line they stand on. They know who they are and never question the fact that they're the good guys. And me"—she breaks off and takes a couple deep breaths—"I'm the black sheep. The *rebel*. Between the pressure to live up to the family name and the fear that I'll never live it down, I don't know if I even have a clue who I am. Hero. Villain. Both. Neither? I don't even know."

"You're a hero," I tell her firmly. "The real kind. More so than your dad or any of the others working with him are. "

"Why? Because I don't buy into the bullshit?"

"Yes." I lean back and stare up at the starry sky. "And because you're willing to do something about it. You've always known the superheroes had a weird agenda. And you've fought it. That's totally heroic behavior."

"Yeah, well, if I'd fought harder, maybe your mom wouldn't be missing. Maybe Deacon wouldn't be half dead in some six-by-six cell none of us can find. Maybe—"

I interrupt her with the most absurd idea I can think of. "And maybe I'd grow a superpower or two. Anything is possible, Reb, but you can't live in a world of what-ifs."

I twist in my chair to face her and make sure she's looking at me before I continue because it feels really important that she understands what I'm about to say.

"I could sit here making up a million scenarios about what might be different. What if I'd bought into Jeremy's conspiracy theories years ago? What if I'd listened when you'd tried to tell me things weren't what they seemed? What if I hadn't left my mom alone, sleeping, totally vulnerable, while I went to the lab to check things out?" I huff out a tight breath, the weight of all those what-ifs crushing my chest.

"If any of that had happened, everything could be different right now. But it's not. There's no going back, no power of time travel. So we just have to work on the problem, you know? We have to deal with what is, not what might have been."

Rebel sits silent for a long time. She's totally withdrawn, totally locked inside of herself, and there's a part of me that wants to break her out, to smash through the walls she's putting up in self-defense. But I don't, because I get what she's going through. With everything I've had to process during the last couple days, I never stopped to think that finally discovering the truth, finally learning that she's been right all along, must be weighing on her.

Feeling alone led her to seek out villains. I won't let her feel alone ever again.

"You're right," she says with a grimace. "Still, sometimes I wish I could be more like you. More like Riley."

"Riley? You want to be more like your brother?" I ask incredulously. "Okay, who are you and what have you done with my best friend?"

"It may sound crazy, but it's true. Yeah, my brother drives

me nuts, but everything is easy for Riley. The world makes sense to him. He sees the superverse in black and white, good and bad. So do you, Kenna."

I think back to the supermarket and how nothing seemed black and white anymore. How complicated everything was and how I didn't know what to think—what to feel—about any of it.

Nothing is easy anymore.

I don't know where this upside-down path we're on is headed, and I sure as hell don't know where it's going to end up. But I'm certain that Rebel is the one person in all of this who shouldn't be beating herself up.

"But you were right," I tell her. "Good isn't always good, and bad isn't always bad. You've always seen the shades of gray."

I think about Draven, about what a good guy he is deep down, under the long hair and villain tats and that ridiculously obnoxious smirk. Under his screw-the-world attitude. He may be a total badass, but that doesn't mean he's bad. How can he be when he spends so much of his time trying to do the right thing?

"Seeing in black and white is highly overrated," I say.

She gapes at me. "I never thought I'd hear you say that."

"Yeah, well, it's a brave new world, isn't it? And what do they say about new worlds? Adapt or die?"

She looks at me strangely as she echoes my earlier question. "Who are you, and where's the real Kenna? What have you done with my best friend?"

"That seems to be the question today, doesn't it?" I reply with a forced laugh.

Too bad I don't have an answer anymore.

CHAPTER 17

D ude, are you *sure* this is going to work?" Dante asks.

"Absolutely," Jeremy answers as we inch forward on our stomachs. "Thanks to the codes on Mr. Malone's computer, I disabled the villain sensors and the perimeter alarm. There should be an entrance to one of the evacuation tunnels a little bit ahead."

"*Should?*" Draven echoes.

"Just how confident are you that there *is* an evacuation tunnel? It wasn't on the blueprints," Rebel hisses at Jeremy.

"Totally confident. There has to be at least one, if not more." Jeremy squints into the shadows. "I'm, like, eighty percent confident—well, maybe seventy-five percent—that we'll find it. But—"

"Seventy-five percent?" Draven whisper-yells. "We're betting my cousin's life on a *seventy-five percent* chance that you're right?"

It's dark so I can't see his face, but I can all but feel the anger radiating off him. Not that I blame him. Seventy-five percent odds just aren't that great, especially when that's just to get *into* the facility. God only knows how difficult things will get once we actually set foot in the lab to rescue Deacon.

Hopefully we'll also find some clue about where my mom is being kept. Despite two straight days of hacking and exploring Mr. Malone's computer, Jeremy didn't find even a hint about her. He's convinced she's not here, and I'm afraid I believe him.

"Do you have a better idea?" Jeremy snaps back. "Besides, I was ninety-five percent confident before you guys started messing with my head." He ups his pace, looking like a cross between an earthworm and a yogi as he scoots across the hard ground.

We're making our way through one of the undeveloped fields that surround the lab, the plants and weeds providing cover as we creep forward, dressed entirely in black. I have to admit, we blend into the night pretty well—certainly better than I thought we would when Jeremy laid out this leg of the plan—but I'm still not confident we won't be discovered. With all the extra precautions Mr. Malone has taken to protect the lab, I can't believe he left this area with nothing but an easily disabled perimeter alarm for protection. Especially if Jeremy's right and there are access tunnels out here.

"I'm giving you ten more minutes," Dante growls. "If we don't find the tunnel by then—"

"What?" answers Jeremy. "What are you going to do? Walk up to the front door and blow the thing wide open?"

"If we have to," Draven tells him grimly.

My mouth goes dry at the determination in his voice. One way or another, Draven is getting into that lab tonight, and I have a feeling he doesn't give a damn whether or not he gets hurt or killed in the process. He's willing to do anything, take any risk, to save someone he loves, and I can totally relate to that. I feel the same way about Mom and Rebel. But while he doesn't seem to care much about his safety, I do. The thought of him getting hurt upsets me more than a little.

Closing my eyes, I send a quiet plea into the universe that we all get out of this alive.

"You won't get two steps into the lab that way and you know it," Jeremy says.

"Ask me if I give a crap."

"Can you all just bloody well shut up and get moving?" Nitro says from his spot at the back of our wiggling, dysfunctional line. "It's only a matter of time before something crawls up my pant leg, and I have to be honest, I'm not okay with that."

"Don't be such a—"

"Yes!" Jeremy crows in a loud whisper, cutting Draven off mid-insult. "Found it! Down there to the left. Do you see it?"

I narrow my eyes, trying to peer through the darkness at where Jeremy's deliberately dim flashlight is pointing. "That round thing in the ground?" I ask, excitement thrumming through my blood.

"Yes! That's an access grate!" Jeremy does a crazy little wriggle that I assume is his version of a victory dance. "I told you it was here. I told you we'd find it! I knew it! I just knew it!" Another wriggle. "Who's the man? Who. Is. The. Man?"

It's a rhetorical question, so nobody answers him. And we don't interrupt his moment of victory either—he's earned it.

"Nice job, nerd king," Rebel says affectionately when Jeremy finally stops congratulating himself and we're congregated around the grate. "Now what?"

"We rip the thing off its hinges and go in," Dante says. He reaches for the grate, when Jeremy yells, "No! Don't!"

We all freeze.

"What's wrong?" Draven demands. "I thought this was what we were looking for."

"It is." Jeremy gets on his knees, pulls off his backpack, and starts rummaging around in it. "Just because it wasn't on any of the security diagrams or property blueprints doesn't mean it's not protected. It's an outside access point. It's probably wired."

"With explosives?" Nitro asks, eyes wide.

Jeremy rolls his eyes. "With security devices that alert the big guys with superpowers."

He pulls a gadget from his backpack and aims it at the grate. The device lights up like fireworks on the Fourth of July. An intricate web of crisscrossing lines shimmers over the entire drain.

Lasers.

"What are we going to do?" asks Rebel. "We can't get past that."

Jeremy snorts. "Speak for yourself."

He retrieves some other handheld machines, presses a sequence of buttons, then waits. He repeats this three times, then reaches for the original gadget and points it at the grate. This time it doesn't so much as beep.

"Excellent!" Jeremy quickly shoves his equipment back into this backpack. "Let's move."

"What did you do?" Draven demands as Jeremy starts prying at the gate with a crowbar.

What doesn't he have in that backpack?

He glances at us and shrugs. "I jammed the signal."

"All *that* to jam a signal?" Nitro asks.

"It was a very complicated signal." He keeps working with the crowbar, but the grate barely moves.

"This is taking too long," Dante says. Suddenly, a huge gust of wind comes out of nowhere, knocking us onto our backs and slamming into the grate.

The metal rattles and moans, but the hinges hold.

"Heads down," Dante warns before an even more power-ful burst of air whooshes back out and past us. The hinges bend under the force, the metal squealing as it slowly gives up the struggle. After a few seconds of Dante's reverse tornado, the grate flies off, narrowly missing Nitro's head.

"Oi! Watch it!" he yells.

"I told you to stay down," Dante answers.

"Let's go," Draven says, jumping to his feet.

He's the first one into the tunnel—no surprise there. "Watch your step. It's slippery in here."

Slippery? I exchange a look of trepidation with Rebel. I don't even want to know what's inside the tunnel that makes it *slippery*. When Jeremy told us that he suspected there had to be hidden access points in these field, far enough out that no one would suspect their association with the lab, he'd been very vague about what kind of tunnels they might lead to. I have a feeling we wouldn't have wanted to know anyway.

I enter the tunnel behind Draven and Dante, and my foot sinks four or five inches into sludge. *Gross.* Never have I been so grateful that Rebel made me borrow a pair of her Doc Martens.

"Eeeew!" Rebel screeches, her voice echoing through the

tunnel and almost—*almost*—drowning out the disgusting suck-ing sound our feet make as we plow forward through the muck. I'm kind of glad it's dark so I can't see what we're walking in.

"Damn," Nitro says. "Is this stuff radioactive?"

Rebel reaches around and smacks him on the shoulder. "Why would you even say that?" Then she starts trying to walk a lot more softly than she was just a minute ago. "It's not, is it, Kenna? We aren't going to turn green, are we?"

"Does it matter?" Draven demands, picking up his pace so that he's all but running. "We're not turning back."

I lean close to Rebel and whisper reassuringly, "It would be glowing if it was."

Dante takes off after Draven and we try to keep up, but it's hard. I feel like I'm running through quicksand and the further we get, the deeper the sludge. Jeremy is struggling more than the rest of us. Probably because he's been up for forty-two hours straight, hacking into the security program so he could disable systems as needed.

And maybe because he's got eighty pounds of extra gear in his backpack.

Fifteen minutes of running, trudging, falling through sludge, and we're all gasping for air and covered in muck. But we've reached the entrance—a round, metal door three feet off the ground that looks barely big enough for me, let alone the guys, to crawl through.

Draven stops before touching anything, waiting for Jeremy to catch up. He and Nitro have fallen so many times that they're a good two minutes back.

"This one wired too?" Draven asks when Jeremy arrives, scooching by Rebel and me.

He waves one of his gadgets over the door and the thing goes nuts. "These aren't standard security sensors."

"What does that mean?" Nitro asks.

"Must be part of the new security," Jeremy says, reaching into his backpack for a pen. He throws it at the door and when it hits, an electromagnetic wave pulses, knocking us into the disgusting sludge. I swear to God, if we get out of this alive, I'm going to kill my ex-boyfriend.

"A little warning next time, asshole," Dante says bitterly as he climbs to his feet. He reaches down to help Rebel up, and Draven gives me a hand.

"Sorry." Jeremy's already rummaging through his backpack. "I didn't realize it would be that powerful."

"How are we going to get through it?" I demand. Staring at that door, knowing we're so close, I've never felt more desperate. Or more powerless.

Jeremy doesn't answer, just pulls out another gadget, waves it at the door, and frowns. Another gadget. Another frown. Another gadget...

The wait is killing me.

I inch closer to the door, my whole body tense. The closer I get, the stranger I feel. There's a weird tingling under my skin. I've never felt like this before, and I can't help wondering if Rebel's right and this sludge we're standing in really is radioactive.

"Can't you just"—I wave my hands at him in a vague, you're-a-superhero, use-your-powers gesture—"take care of it?"

He scowls at me. "Only if I want the equivalent force of twenty nuclear bombs coursing through my body."

"Would it deactivate the security *before* it killed you?" Draven asks hopefully.

Jeremy ignores him, pressing the button on his latest gadget, but nothing happens. Or at least, it doesn't look like anything is happening.

We all wait tensely, and after a minute Jeremy says, "Huh. That's strange."

"What's strange?" Dante demands, his voice stretched taut as a circus high wire.

"It's not picking up any more electromagnetic activity." He shakes the gizmo, aims it again. No lights, no beeps, nothing.

"Did you break it?" Draven demands.

"It worked twenty minutes ago, at the grate." Jeremy pulls out another pen.

"Bloody hell!" Nitro shouts, crouching down. "Not again!"

I brace myself—we all do—and clamp my mouth closed so when I hit the ground this time I won't get any of the disgusting sludge in my mouth.

Jeremy throws the pen.

It strikes the door with a *ping*, then falls to the ground. That's it.

"What the hell?" Nitro and Draven say at the same time.

Jeremy shrugs. "I have no idea." He pulls out a book and repeats the pen test—with the same result.

"Maybe the electromagnetics were defective," he says after a minute. "One pulse could have knocked a weak connection out of commission."

"So much for security," Dante sneers. He raises his hand to summon his wind, but Rebel stops him.

"Let me do it, babe. One blast of your power in here and we'll all be on our asses again."

She extends her hands and the lock and hinges squeal, the steel literally bending to Rebel's will. Moments later, the door floats right toward us and she lowers it next to Nitro.

"Stay behind me," Draven says as he hoists himself up and peers through the opening, looking both ways for danger.

"Is it clear?" Dante asks, shifting restlessly.

"Looks it." Draven climbs through the doorway. Dante follows him. They reach down to help Rebel and me. Normally I'd have no problem lifting myself up, but my hands are slippery and keep sliding as I try to boost myself up. So I just gratefully accept the help.

"Now what?" Nitro asks as he joins us.

"If I'm right—" Jeremy leans in through the door, holding a new device, which is the size of a chocolate bar. He punches a sequence of buttons, and then suddenly the building's blueprints are projected out in front of us in full 3-D. He gestures to a spot on the second sublevel. "We're right here."

Crap. "We're in the most secure part of the main lab," I tell them. I take the device from Jeremy so I can point out details while he hauls himself into the hall. "The physical and chemical labs have the most dangerous materials in the entire facility. They keep them on tight lockdown. There are security doors every hundred feet down here and cameras every fifty."

"Of course there are," Dante mutters under his breath. "Why should any part of this be easy?"

"What are those?" I point at pairs of red dots moving through the rendering.

"Guards," Jeremy says flatly, grunting slightly as he tries

to pull himself up and over. "The system is tracking their RFID chips."

"We need a distraction," Nitro says. "Something to draw their attention."

"Like what?" Rebel asks.

He starts creating a ball of fire in his hands. The glowing green energy creeps me out even as it fascinates me. "Fire's always good."

Jeremy teeters in the opening. Someone should probably pull him through. No one does.

"Already been there, done that. I pulled the fire alarm, remember?" I tell Nitro. "I don't think they'll fall for it again, even if there is a real fire." Besides, his control and aim are not what they could be. I have visions of him burning the whole building to the ground—this time, with all of us inside.

"What do you suggest then?" Nitro pouts a little as he extinguishes the flame.

"Dante and I have this," Rebel says. An evil grin plays across her face. "I've always wanted to tear this place apart. Now's my—"

"Aaaack!" Jeremy whisper-screams as he finally makes it through the door and pitches awkwardly to the ground.

Nitro snorts.

"Are you okay?" I ask.

"No," Jeremy pants. "My ankle."

He tries to put weight on his foot but collapses into me. In an instant, Draven has an arm looped around Jeremy's torso.

"Broken?" Draven asks.

"I don't—ow, ow, ow. Yeah, maybe."

"Shit." Dante runs his hands through his fauxhawk.

The look on Jeremy's face is about more than physical pain. I can tell he feels like he's letting the team down, like he's letting the mission down. We may not have parted on the best of terms, but I still don't want him hurting.

I think quickly. "Rebel, you can get Jer back to the van? That will be command central. Dante can cause the distraction solo. Nitro, guard the door, make sure it's clear when Draven and I come out with Deacon. We might need to make a quick getaway."

Dante nods. "Let's do it." He turns to Draven. "Get my brother out."

"We will," Draven promises. "But be careful. I don't want to have to break you out next."

"Here," Jeremy says, digging in his backpack. "Take these."

He holds out a handful of what look like skin-colored plastic beans.

"Communication earbuds," he explains.

We each take one. I smile at him as I pop mine into my right ear. Always prepared. You would think he'd been a Boy Scout.

"Find Deacon," Rebel says as she uses her power to lift Jeremy off Draven's shoulder. "Then get the hell out."

"And keep your eye on those blueprints so the guards don't sneak up on you," Jeremy warns. "I'll make another stab at finding your mom too."

I give him a grateful smile, and he and Rebel disappear through the tiny access door. Dante turns and walks to the glass doors at the front of the room. The second he hits the hallway, a tornado rips down the corridor in front of him. Tiles fly off the walls and doors start flapping open and closed. We want the guards' attention anywhere but where we're going.

"That's a distraction, all right," Nitro says.

"Let's go." Draven turns to me. "Where does geek boy think we'll find the emergency staircase?"

"At the end of the other hall." I gesture to the place on Jeremy's projected blueprints. "The best bet is to cut through the spontaneous external combustion lab. There are doors on both sides."

"Let's do it," Draven says.

Counting on Dante to draw the guards in the other direction and Nitro to safeguard our escape route, we head out the lab's back doors and slink down the hallway.

It only takes about two minutes to reach the SpEC lab—though it feels like two hours. When we get there, I enter the code, praying Dr. Anthony hasn't changed it. He hasn't. It pays to have been every scientist's backup intern. The door opens smoothly when I push on it.

We walk in, expecting the lab to be empty—the building is usually clear at this time of night except for guards, and Dante's distraction was supposed to draw them away. But we've majorly miscalculated. Standing about thirty-five feet away, backs to us, are two guards I don't recognize. These guards aren't on Jeremy's blueprint. And they're carrying a body bag toward the incinerator room in the corner. Several other body bags lay on tables around the room.

We're frozen.

"This is the last batch," the fat one says.

"Good. I'm ready to shut this place down." The short one readjusts his grip. "It's creepy, all empty like this."

They take a few steps toward the incinerator.

"This kid sure is heavy," the fat one tells him, struggling with his load. "You wouldn't know it to look at him."

"He's a villain," the short one answers. "Who knows what his bones are made of. Those tattoos of his glow like nothing I've ever seen before. Too bad he died before we could—"

Next to me, Draven makes an inhuman, tormented sound.

The guards drop the body bag and whirl toward us, but before they can so much as yell a warning, they crumple to the ground, hands clutching at their heads. They moan with pain—the kind of agony you see in horror movies and true crime documentaries.

What's going on? I can't hear anything. I turn to Draven to see if he has any idea, but he's staring at them so intently that he doesn't even notice me.

And that's when I know. Whatever's happening to the guards right now, Draven is the one doing it.

CHAPTER 18

D raven!" I shout, but he ignores me.

Rebel's voice echoes in my earpiece. "What's going on?"

"I don't know," I tell her. "There are guards. They said something about tattoos, and he just started—"

Dante cuts me off. "I'll be right there."

"Babe?" Rebel asks.

I stare, stunned, as the guards writhe on the ground in agony. One of them lifts a hand from his face. It's covered in blood. Streams of red trickle from his eyes, nose, and ears.

"Stop!" I scream at Draven. Whatever he's doing, he's not in control. His anger has taken over his power.

Unable to just stand by doing nothing, I fling myself at him, knocking him a few feet to the side. I lock my arms around him. He tries to shrug me off.

"Let go," he snarls, still not looking at me. But I don't let go. I can't. Not when whatever is happening here, whatever he's doing in anger, will end up hurting him in the end. Will end leaving him with nothing but regret.

Nitro races into the room, skidding to a stop at my side.

"Draven, what the—"

"Get her off me," Draven snaps.

Nitro doesn't hesitate. He grabs me by the arm and yanks. I wince as a burning pain shoots up my body. It feels like someone pressed a hot poker against my skin. But there's no time to worry about that, not when—

"He's killing them!" I scream as Dante bursts into the room. "They might have information. They might be able to help!"

"They're not going to help us," Draven spits out. For the first time I can see the villain in him. The rule-breaker. The vigilante.

It scares me, not because of who he is and what he's capable of—there's a part of me that's known it all along—but because I don't care. This side of him, anger and strength, doesn't make him any less attractive to me. It should, but it doesn't.

Dante steps into Draven's line of sight. "Talk to me."

"Please. Stop." I jerk against Nitro's grip.

The screaming stops and guards lay limp on the floor, hands no longer clutching their heads.

Draven has regained control now. Oh, he's still furious but at least we've gotten through to him and he's released whatever weird hold he had on the guards. Then again, maybe it's Dante's presence that got through to him. He turns to his cousin, to his best friend, and says, "Deacon."

Draven's voice is choked, his shoulders slumped, his face desolate, as he points at the body bag.

Nitro releases me.

Dante turns white at the implication. He doesn't move. Doesn't breathe. He just stands there, as precious seconds tick by. Then, just when I'm about to start for the body bag myself, he stumbles toward it and yanks back the zipper. His whole body sags.

"It's not him." Dante's eyes fill with tears. "It's not Deacon."

In my ear, Rebel sobs with relief.

Nitro walks over to the other body bags laid out on the lab tables. One by one, he unzips them and shakes his head. Seven in all. Seven bodies. Seven dead villains. None of them Deacon.

Relief fills me, followed by shame. Seven people are dead. Relief is the last emotion I should feel. Shame, horror, rage— but not relief. Never that. And yet, I can't help but feel grateful that Deacon's not in one of those bags. There is still hope.

"We should keep moving," Draven says after a minute, drawing all of our attention back to him. "Keep searching."

"What was that?" I ask, gesturing at the guards who are still writhing on the floor.

"Not now," he says.

I want to argue, but I know that he's right. This isn't the time and it definitely isn't the place. But before I can so much as nod, Nitro whispers, "Vane is in one of those bags."

Dante and Draven freeze.

"Vane?" Dante's voice is strangled. "Shit. Which one?"

Nitro nods to the last one on the right. "What should we do?"

"We shouldn't leave him," Draven says. "He's a friend."

Dante shakes his head. "We can't carry him out of here."

"You would carry Deacon out."

"Yes, but he's my brother. And we might still have to carry him out."

Draven looks sick.

Dante continues, "If Vane was alive, I'd do anything to get him out of here. But he's dead. They can't hurt him anymore. We can't risk it."

Draven nods, and eventually so does Nitro. Tears burn the backs of my eyes.

"So now what?" Nitro asks.

"We need to find Deacon." Dante pushes to his feet. "We'll contact Vane's family after we get out of this hellhole. But for now, we need to figure out where my brother is."

I'm so wrapped up in the horror before me that it takes my mind a few seconds to get back on track. "No," I whisper. "He's gone."

"What do you mean *gone*?" Dante looms over me.

My mouth goes dry, but I force out the words, "The guards said these were the last of them. After this they're closing down the building."

"And you believe them?"

I shrug. "I don't know. Maybe? They were talking to each other, not to us. They said the building is empty."

Which means—my heart sinks further at the realization—that my mom really isn't here. Despair creeps in, but I shove it aside. This isn't the time or place.

"Yeah, well, there's only one way to find out." Draven strides over to the security men, grabs one by the collar of his uniform, and lifts him off the ground. "The other prisoners?" he demands. "Where are they?"

The guard whimpers.

"Where!" Draven roars.

"G-g-g-gone," the guard stammers. "N-n-new lab."

"All of them?"

The guard nods. "All but these last ones."

"Shite." Nitro pounds his fist on the lab table beside him.

I step forward. "What about my mom? Do you know where Dr. Swift is?"

"Kenna?" He frowns at me.

Draven shakes him again. "Answer her."

"I-I-I don't know," the terrified guard replies. "Maybe at the new lab? I haven't seen her in a few days."

"Where is it?" I demand.

"I don't know," the guard wails. When Draven tightens his grip, he says, "I swear, I have no idea. All the guards are being reassigned."

Draven looks like he wants to keep interrogating the man, but then just tosses him aside like a rag doll, not bothering to see where he lands. "We need to find out where the new lab is."

"Guys?" Jeremy says suddenly, his voice in all of our ears.

"How are we going to do that?" I ask, ignoring my ex-boyfriend. "Jeremy couldn't find any information about that on Mr. Malone's computer."

"If we have to tear this entire building to the ground to find a clue," Draven says slowly, "then we will." And I know he means every word.

"Um, guys?" Jeremy says over the earbuds.

"Back off, geek boy." Draven starts for the door at the back of the lab.

But before he takes more than two steps, the world around us erupts in a storm of flashing lights and blaring sirens.

"What the hell?" Dante shouts.

"That's what I was trying to tell you," Jeremy snaps. "Someone triggered the alarm."

We all turn to the guards on the floor. The one Draven questioned is curled into a fetal ball. The other one, the fat one, smirks at us. He holds up his phone.

"Busted," the guard sputters. "How's it feel to be royal screwups?"

Draven squats down next to him, places a hand on either side of his blubbery face, and stares into his eyes. "You think you're home free?" he asks, pulling at the guard's name tag. "Aaron? You think this is over?" He stands up and kicks the guard in the stomach. "It's not. I know who you are. I know what has happened to these people. I'll remember you. And I'll come back for you."

"Damn it!" Jeremy yells, sounding frantic. "The building is going into lockdown."

"What does that mean?" I ask.

"Systems are instituting Tier Red protocols," he replies.

Tier Red ? Is that supposed to mean something? I clench my jaw at his unhelpful response.

"Translate." Draven growls.

"Essentially, every hack I did to get you inside is now code-blocked." Jeremy mumbles something unintelligible. "This building is about to become more impenetrable than NORAD."

It takes a moment for his words to sink in, and then we run, full out, toward the hall and the evacuation tunnel.

If everyone's gone, if the place really has been cleared out, then there's no point in searching the facility. I don't know if we should take the guard's word for it, but staying pretty much guarantees we'll be caught.

"We're on our way," Draven snarls.

I'm panting. "We'll be at the tunnel door in—"

"No!" Jeremy shouts. "It's armed it with some kind of bioelectric explosive. You'll die if you go anywhere near it."

"Can't you deactivate it?" I ask.

Tortuous silence follows as the alarms shriek, then, "No. It's a closed system. I would have to be hardwired in."

"The front door," Dante suggests.

Draven nods. "Go big, or go home."

"Just"—Jeremy gets distracted—"give me a minute."

A computerized voice fills the air around us. "SHPD forces have been dispatched. Estimated time of arrival…" We all hold our breath as the voice calculates. "Four minutes."

Draven mutters a string of curses.

"We don't have a minute," Dante shouts.

"Hold on, baby," Rebel tells him, her voice tight with strain. "Jeremy's working. We'll get you out."

I trust her, trust Jeremy, but standing there waiting for Jeremy's instruction—doing nothing while guards are probably closing in—is the hardest thing I've ever done. My heart is racing, my breath coming in little shallow pants. Not wanting to hyperventilate, I force myself to breathe in through my nose and out through my mouth. But it's hard. So hard. Especially with Dante and Draven pacing the hallway like caged animals.

Nitro isn't much better. He pounds his fist into his palm, sending a spray of amber sparks each time his hands connect. It's only a matter of time before he sets something on fire. But freaking out won't solve anything, I remind myself as I try to calm down. Jeremy will figure it out. Jeremy will get us out of here. He may be a paranoid conspiracy nut, but he's good in an emergency.

I wrap my arms around myself for comfort, but when I grab my right arm with my left hand, I feel that same burning sensation I'd felt earlier when Nitro pulled me off Draven.

"Okay, I've got it!" Jeremy shouts. "Kenna, tell me your exact location."

I look around. "We're in the south hall on sublevel two, between labs B227 and B229."

We listen to the keyboard clicks.

"I need you to get to the freight elevator at the end of the west hall."

I take off at a run. The guys follow close behind. Tonight it pays to know this building like the back of my hand.

"Freeze," Jeremy shouts. "There are guards around that corner. Hold on, I'll set off a sensor in the lobby, so they should be..."

I plaster myself to the wall as his words trail off. Our harsh breathing is masked by the blaring alarm as we wait for Jeremy's next instructions.

"Okay, they're in the stairwell. Go."

It seems like an eternity before we reach the freight elevator. The door is easily three times as large as a normal elevator door, built to fit even the largest scientific equipment.

"We're here," I pant. "Should I press the—"

"No," Jeremy interrupts. "Don't. I'm locking the elevator on the floor above you."

Now what? If he didn't want us to take the elevator, then why are we—

"Okay, the car is locked. The doors are carbon-reinforced steel. Nitro, can you burn through them?"

"*Can* I?" Nitro's face twists into a look of maniacal glee. A bright-green ball of energy, no bigger than a cupcake, floats between his outstretched palms.

"Stand back," he says.

I watch as he slowly runs the ball over the surface of the door in what looks like the supervillain version of Tai Chi.

Then he stands back and admires his work.

Which, as far as I can tell, is nothing more than a big scorch mark.

Nitro tilts his head at Dante. "Would you?"

With a flick of his fingers, Dante sends a gust of wind at the doors. The area inside Nitro's scorch mark sails into the elevator shaft, leaving a door-sized opening in the carbon steel.

"Nice," I tell him with a grin. "Now what, Jer?"

"Now," he replies, "you climb."

Draven steps up to the opening and waves me forward. "Ladies first."

He says it casually, but there's gravity to his words. Under the guise of chivalry, he's making sure I get out first. There's no time to argue about gender politics right now, and besides, going first means I get to lead the way. And fend off trouble, if there is any. I step through the opening and pull myself up the service ladder that runs up the side wall.

"How far?" I ask.

"All the way," Jeremy says. "There is an exhaust vent that opens onto the roof. The building locks down from the bottom up, so I can still disable that alarm."

"Great," I say as I start to climb.

"But you need to hurry," he replies. "They've almost got sublevel two completely locked. You need to get up and out before they get to the top floor."

There is no more talking as the four of us climb as fast as we can. Now I really wish I *had* argued gender politics with Draven. I'm the slowest of the bunch and I'm holding them back. If they get caught because of me, I'll never forgive myself.

The thought of being responsible for us being captured— for them being tortured like Deacon—paralyzes me with fear. But I can't let it. Instead, I use it to motivate me to push my body as hard as I possibly can.

We are exhausted by the time we reach the top floor. My arms and legs are shaking and even Draven looks a little worse for wear.

"We're here," I gasp.

"The vent is above you," Jeremy explains. "In the center of the shaft."

I look up. The elevator shaft is at least twenty feet across, which means the vent is ten feet out in the open. The elevator car is now four stories below us. That's not the kind of fall that someone can survive.

"Can you call up the car, Jer?" I ask. "Then we could stand on the roof to get to the vent."

"Can't," he says. "It's locked on sublevel one."

"I've got this," Dante says.

A powerful wind fills the shaft. I have to struggle to hold on to the ladder.

My apprehension must show. He smiles. "Trust me."

There's a lot of trust going around tonight.

I bite my lips, close my eyes, and exhale. It's easier to let go of the ladder than I thought. I just relax my fingers and then…I'm floating.

I feel myself moving away from the wall. Forcing my eyes open, I look up—not down, never down. The vent is right above me. I reach for the grate, but it's screwed to the frame.

"I can't," I say. "It's—"

"Move her," Nitro says.

The wind shifts, and I float to the other side of the shaft. Nitro shoots a series of flaming red, bullet-sized balls. The grate falls with a clang on the elevator car below.

Before I can say a word, Dante shifts his wind again and I float through the opening into the night, then drop in a squat when the wind leaves me.

Nitro flies through a moment later.

When Draven doesn't immediately follow, I peer into the elevator shaft. He and Dante are at a stand-off.

"Now is not the time, dude," Dante says.

Draven's entire body is rigid. Tense…with fear.

Right. When Rebel suspended us in the air in my kitchen, he'd looked nervous. Now he looks downright freaked out. It's weird, considering he's always been so fearless about everything else.

Everyone has a weakness and I'm not letting him give in to his, not when we're so close to freedom.

"Hey, Draven," I shout, intent on distracting him.

He looks up, his eyes wild.

"You're not chickening out now, are you? I mean, even Jeremy could do this."

"Hey!" Jeremy exclaims. "I heard that. And maybe you've forgotten since it's been a while, but there's a lot I can do, Kenna." His voice is rife with innuendo and Draven growls. He actually growls. Which works for me. This jealousy is exactly what I'm trying to play up right now. If nothing else, it will distract him.

"Shut it, geek boy," Draven snaps.

Dante waves his hand and Draven slowly starts to rise. He's seething at the taunts so he doesn't notice until he's two feet away.

I reach out and grab him before he can look down.

"Come on," I say. "Let's get out of here."

Seconds later, Dante flies through the vent.

"You need to get to the south edge of the roof," Jeremy tells us. "From there you can—oh shit."

"Oh shit, what?" Dante demands.

"Guards," Jeremy barks. "They'll be on you in seconds."

We run full speed to the south end of the roof. From there we can see the van parked on the access road that runs behind the campus.

"How do we get down?" I ask.

Dante holds up his hands. "I can take care of—"

"Freeze!" We turn to face the trio of guards who have appeared less than a football field away. In addition to whatever superpowers they're packing, they have their weapons drawn. Real guns with real bullets.

Dante turns his wind on them. Faced with the force of a hurricane-strength gale, the guards struggle to remain upright. Advancing is out of the question.

"Reb, babe," Dante shouts to be heard above the howl of wind, "I can't hold off the guards and get everyone on the ground at the same time."

"I've never lifted something from this far away." She sounds scared.

"You can do it, Rebel," I insist. "You just have to focus."

"Shit." I can hear her take a deep breath. "Yeah, okay. I'll do my best."

"Take Kenna first," Draven orders.

"No," I say. "That's crazy. It's way more dangerous for you guys to get caught. I've seen what they do to villains."

Draven is firm. "Too bad. You're going—"

"Take the guys first," I tell Rebel. "Don't let them get captured."

"Out of the quest—"

Before Draven can finish his pointless, chauvinistic argument, he's flying up and over the edge of the roof and soaring across the field toward the van. I let out a sigh of relief as I watch Rebel set him down gently as soon as he's cleared the property line.

"Nitro," she says, "you're next."

He doesn't protest as Rebel lifts him.

"Dante—" I begin.

"No way!" he shouts. "I have to be last. I have to hold off the guards."

"There's time," I insist. "Give them one last shove and then go. Rebel will get me before they recover."

"Kenna," her voice wavers and she sounds tired. "That's not a lot of time."

"Forget it," Dante replies. "Babe, take us together in three, two, one."

Before I have time to react, Dante sends one last blast of wind at the guards, then runs at me. He leans down, like he's going to tackle me, but instead lifts me onto his shoulder without losing his momentum. He pushes off from the roof with a leap.

We are going to fall. We *are* falling.

Then Dante throws some wind behind us and I feel the pull of Rebel's telekinesis. We shoot across the field, reaching the others in half the time it took Draven and Nitro.

When we land, I want to collapse with relief, but there's no time. SHPD vehicle sirens blare. Rebel climbs into the driver's seat while Jeremy shouts for us all to get inside. The door shuts behind me, and the van tires spin out.

We're racing away for our lives.

CHAPTER 19

Rebel drives like a highly trained wheelman. She burns rubber on the straightaways and takes the corners like she's on rails, pushing the limits of the coefficient of friction. Which is impressive, considering we're in a minivan.

We weave and squeal down residential streets before we finally lose the SHPD. I'm trying to process everything that happened inside the lab—everything we saw. Body bags. Corrupt guards. Dead villains. The heroes aren't just experimenting on them anymore, aren't just imprisoning them. They're killing them.

And if the seven we saw were just "the last of them," then who knows how many others they'd killed?

I fight the urge to throw up. But if Rebel takes even one more corner the way she's taken the last few, I might not be able to hold it in.

Then there's the confirmation that my mom wasn't at the lab. Which means she could be…pretty much anywhere else on the planet.

On top of everything, I have another thought weighing on my mind. Gingerly, I press my fingers against my arm through the thin sleeve of my tee. I wince when I connect with what feels like a burn.

I've burned myself before on the stove. That's not unusual. But I haven't been near any ordinary heat sources tonight. The only thing that might have burned my arm is Nitro's fireballs. Which can only mean one thing: my immunity is wearing off.

If I'd been paying attention, I would have seen the signs. Rebel levitating me in my kitchen. Dante using his wind power to lift me to the roof vent. Not to mention Rebel's telekinesis carrying me off that roof. If my immunity were intact, none of them would have been able to touch me.

My stress level ratchets up about twelve notches. My immunity is the only thing that protects me against the super-powers in my everyday world. How am I supposed to stay safe without it? Other ordinaries don't even know that superheroes exist, but in my life I can't exactly avoid them.

I've grown so used to hiding my immunity. What am I going to do now that I actually have to protect myself from the powers?

"Damn it." Draven snaps out of the fog first. "I screwed up. I should have wiped their minds."

"You didn't have time, dude," Dante insists.

Nitro shakes his head. "Not a chance."

"They knew we were villains." Draven pounds a fist against the van door. "There will be retribution. We need to warn Uncle Anton."

Dante digs out his phone, punches an access code, and dials. "Come on, come on." He listens impatiently and, when the call presumably goes to voice mail, pounds the screen so hard that I'm surprised it doesn't shatter. Then he starts texting.

"Where should we go?" Rebel asks. "I can't drive around forever."

No one has an answer for her. Dante is trying to reach his dad, and Draven and Nitro are sending out a series of text messages to warn their fellow villains that the superheroes will be looking for payback. Jeremy is typing furiously on his laptop, searching for…I don't know what. And I can't stop thinking about my vanishing immunity.

How can I save my mom when I don't even know if I can save myself?

Rebel turns onto another street and guns it, steering the van up a steep mountain road. I lurch against Draven's side, wincing when my arm smacks into his. I can't believe how much it hurts. It's been so long since I suffered a super-related injury that I forgot what they feel like.

Trying to hide the pain, I regain my balance and put some distance between us. He turns and frowns at me, his gaze darting to my arm.

Suddenly, Rebel slams to a stop. She's driven us to a small mountain park that overlooks the city. It's a beautiful view of the twinkling lights of Boulder and the vast dark of the plains beyond. It's way more peaceful than the reality of what is happening down there behind closed superhero doors.

"We need to regroup," she says, cutting the engine. "No one should be looking for us up here."

Rebel flings open her door, jumps down, and starts pacing off some of her nervous energy. Nitro and Dante pile out too. Jeremy takes one look at Draven's scowl, and then he's struggling to climb down on his injured ankle.

"Hey, a little help," he calls out, and Nitro gives him a hand. They hobble toward the low stone fence at the edge of the overlook.

If he can hobble, then it probably isn't broken. That's one good thing.

I start to follow everyone out—the crisp mountain air will be good for clearing our heads—but Draven puts out a hand to stop me.

"Can we—can we talk for a sec?"

I nod. "Sure."

"I'm sorry," he says.

I frown. What does he have to be sorry for?

"I didn't mean to scare you back at the lab," he continues. "I just—when they mentioned the tattoos, I thought it was Deacon in that bag. I lost it."

"Totally understandable." Knowing how much he loves his cousin I'm surprised he was able to pull back at all.

"No, I mean I really lost it." He lowers his gaze. "I lost control of my power. I *never* lose control of my power."

"So...that thing you did," I venture. "You did that with your psy ability?"

He hesitates. "No."

"No?" I echo. "Then what—oh. *Oh.*"

If his memory-wipe ability didn't take down those guards, that means he has a second power.

Second powers are extremely rare in the super world. Extremely rare. In fact, only children with both a hero and a villain parent are gifted with double powers.

The implications shake me deep inside.

One of Draven's parents is a hero.

Oh my *God.*

"So one of your—"

"Yes." He cuts me off. "My mom was a villain."

Which tells me two things I didn't know. First, that his mom is dead. I place a sympathetic hand on his knee. No matter how long it's been, it's never easy to lose a parent. I would know.

The second thing it tells me is that Draven's dad is—or was—a hero.

Stunned is a ridiculous understatement.

I have a million questions, but I can't ask him. Not when he's looking at me like that. Not when he whispers, "No one knows. Only Dante, Deacon, and Uncle Anton."

"Then why are you telling *me*?"

"I know it scared you, and I needed to explain. I don't want you to be afraid of me."

The silence stretches as I process his revelations. Not just his second power and his mixed parentage, but the fact that it bothers him to think I'm afraid of him. And how much courage it must take for him to trust me with a secret almost no one else knows.

"I would never hurt you, Kenna, even if I could." He stops then and glances away, his hands fisting and unfisting by his sides. I start to answer, but then his gaze returns and my breath catches at the intensity in his icy blue eyes. "I only want to protect you."

"You don't scare me." The words are out before I even know I'm going to say them.

I meant to reassure him with the words, but if possible, he only grows more tense. What did I say wrong? "I…" I want to fix this, but I don't know how. Don't know what to say. I have a brief mental debate and decide to confess a secret of my own. At this point, it's only fair. "My immunity is wearing off."

He scowls. "What do you mean *wearing off*?"

I lift up my sleeve and show him the burn on my arm. It's the first time that I'm getting a look at it myself. It looks as bad as it feels. A patch of skin from above my elbow to halfway to my shoulder is bright red and covered with a web of tiny blisters.

"Nitro," I say with an awkward laugh. "Besides, how do you think Rebel and Dante were able to use their powers on me? If I still had immunity—"

"I thought you could choose to be immune. Like, if you wanted someone to use their powers on you it would be fine, and otherwise you had immunity. Or like, maybe you could block powers at will or something."

"No. That's not how it works. Either I'm immune to everything, or I'm immune to nothing.

"But immunity is your power." He looks from the tender burn on my arm to my face. His eyes are soft and sweet and sorry. "How can it wear off?"

I have to tell him everything. It's only fair after all he's shared with me. Still, it had been nice to have someone think that I had an actual power for a while.

"Not a power," I explain. "Mom developed a serum."

His brows twist with confusion, like what I'm saying doesn't make sense.

"I get weekly shots." Memory intrudes, and I correct, "Well, I *got* weekly shots. Mom keeps the formula top secret. She was making another batch, but..."

I stop, figuring I won't have to spell it out for him. Draven is still. He doesn't seem to be impressed or freaked out, relieved or concerned. He's just...blank.

I close my eyes and my head droops. I've just confessed to the biggest crime in the super world. I've admitted that I'm a useless, powerless ordinary.

I should have expected this response. After all, superheroes turn down their noses at me for not inheriting my father's amazing powers. But I wanted to believe that Draven was different. Wanted to believe he wouldn't care.

I don't know why it matters so much—to him or to me. I'm still the same person I've always been.

But it *does* matter. Another glance at Draven proves that.

Fine. Whatever. I'm not waiting around for his disappointment or—worse—his disgust to surface. I push out of my seat.

A warm hand wraps around my wrist and pulls me back.

Our eyes meet for a split second before his mouth is on mine.

I can't think, can't breathe, can't do anything but feel.

The pressure of his lips.

The sparks along my nerve endings.

The sizzle of his touch.

His right hand cups my cheek, his fingers tangling in my hair as he sweeps his tongue along the seam of my lips. The stress I've been bottling up releases, and I sink into him. All I want is to stay right here with Draven, forever.

I stroke my hands up his arms, over his neck, across the rough stubble along his jaw. Then my fingers tangle in the cool silk of his hair, tugging at him. Closer, closer, closer.

He slips his right arm around my waist and presses his hand on my lower back until we're flush against one another. All I can feel is the heat and strength of his body against my own.

We're chest to chest, hip to hip, skin to skin, and still I want to be closer. Still I want to fall deeper into him—all the way into him.

Draven growls low in his throat and nips at my lower lip. He shifts against me. I hold tight, but he pushes me away, holding me at arm's length when all I want is to burrow into him again. We stare at each other. I can't catch my breath.

I want to lift my fingers to my lips, to see if they are as hot as they feel, but Draven has my arm in his iron grip. When I look down, he's holding the spot that got burned by Nitro's fireball.

Only it's *not* burned. The pale skin looks perfect.

My gaze flies back to Draven. "What—?"

"Biomanipulation." He releases my arm, dropping his hand to his thigh.

I look from him to my miraculously healed arm and back again. "Your second power," I say, pointing out the obvious. "You can heal?"

He nods. "Among other things."

Right. *Other things.* Like whatever he did to the guards in the lab tonight. He was doing something to their bodies from the inside out.

I keep running my hand over my arm, expecting the burn and blisters to return. But they're gone, and I am totally overwhelmed. Who were Draven's parents that he has powers like *this*? Mind control is rare—and one of the most potent powers out there. But biomanipulation? The ability to heal—or destroy—on a cellular level? Maybe even on a genetic level? Only a couple supers in the world have a power like that.

His eyes are guarded, as if he expects me to freak out or

recoil in fear. But he didn't turn away from me when I confessed to being powerless. Nothing in the world could make me turn from him right now.

If I've learned anything from the last few days, it's that the power is *not* what makes someone bad or dangerous— it's the person who wields the power. Draven and I may go toe to toe on pretty much everything, but he's not a bad guy. In fact, he's one of the strongest, fiercest, most genuine people I've ever known.

I lean forward and press a soft kiss to his lips.

"Thank you," I say, and it's for a lot more than healing my arm.

Draven smiles, then nods toward the low rock wall where the rest of the team has assembled. "We'd better get out there."

He sounds cool, in control, but I see the way his hands tremble before he shoves them into his pockets. The knowledge that he's as affected as I am makes me feel okay about my own vulnerabilities. My own shaking knees.

Draven climbs out first, then reaches up to help me down. When I'm on the ground, he doesn't release my hand. Instead, he laces our fingers together, his thumb gently stroking the back of my hand.

Of all the times to start falling for a guy, in the middle of this mess is pretty much the worst possible option. One star-crossed relationship in the team is more than enough. This is only going to make things that much more complicated.

And yet, I can't bring myself to care.

As we approach the group, Jeremy and Nitro are involved in some kind of heated debate, while Rebel and Dante are wrapped so tightly together that I can't tell where one ends and the other begins. My best friend glances at us, takes one look at our joined hands, and raises a curious eyebrow.

I ignore her.

"You're a complete cock-up!" Nitro yells.

"It's not my fault. Once the guard initiated the lockdown protocol, I was shut out of the entire system." Jeremy doesn't even glance at Nitro as he types furiously. "If you would just give me a minute…."

"We've given you more than a minute. What kind of hacker genius gets 'imself locked out of the system he's trying to hack?"

"The kind," Jeremy says, pausing while he finishes typing, "that still has access to Rex Malone's desktop. Which means"—he spins the laptop so we can all see the screen— "we can still read his private communications."

"Hmm," Nitro says, leaning closer. "Maybe you're not a total wanker after all."

"Wanker?" Jeremy repeats, offended. "I'm a bloody genius."

I laugh—Nitro's obviously rubbing off on him. But it doesn't feel like the time to point that out, especially as line after line of text scrolls across the screen. Messages—texts, emails, transcribed calls and voice mails—flying by so fast that I can't read it all. But I do see mentions of the break-ins and three villain escapees.

"If we're lucky," Jeremy says, "we'll get a clue to Lima Whiskey's location."

"And my mom?" I ask.

Jeremy nods.

"How will we even know?" Draven asks. "Can you read that fast?"

Jeremy laughs. "Of course not. I'm running a screen

recorder and a rootkit that is specifically searching for any reference to the secret facility."

Draven tenses and then releases my hand. "And what if we learn the location?" He runs his fingers through his hair. "What then?"

"Then we go save Deacon," Dante says.

"And my mom," I add. "If she's there too."

Draven gives me a sympathetic look. "They're not going to hurt your mom," he says. "She's too important to them. But Deacon…"

Though he doesn't say the words, we can all fill in the blanks. The odds that Deacon is still alive, that he survived the torture and was transported to the new facility, are pretty slim. Just because he wasn't in any of the body bags we saw doesn't mean…. My stomach pitches at the unfinished thought.

Dante obviously believes otherwise. "Deacon is alive."

"You don't know that," Draven argues.

"I do. He's my twin. If he were…" His voice cracks and Rebel gives him a squeeze.

Dante recovers, shaking off his emotion. "I would feel it. In here." He smacks a fist to his chest. "I know he's still alive."

"It doesn't matter if he is," Jeremy says.

"The hell it doesn't!" Draven shouts.

"What I mean," my ex says, "is that what Malone and the hero leadership are doing is tantamount to villain genocide. The six of us are the only ones who know what's going on."

"He's right," I say.

Rebel looks at me like I have gone insane.

"No matter what happens, we can't just walk away. Not from this. Even if it's too late for Mom or Deacon," I explain.

"There are others. And if we don't stop it, there will be a lot more. We can't just pretend we don't know what's happening. We have to do something."

"Damn straight," Nitro says, cheering.

"The seven dead villains we saw tonight are too high a price to pay." My voice breaks. "And if we don't stop this now, there will be another seven. And another seven. And another—"

I shudder at the thought of how many people the heroes might have already killed in the name of research, or whatever their excuse is. There is no way I can live with myself if even more die and I could have done something—anything—to stop it.

"Exactly," Jeremy says. "I won't walk away. I can't."

"None of us can," Rebel agrees. "Not now. Not from this."

They nod, faces solemn and eyes coolly determined. That's when I realize that the villains never planned to just walk away after finding Deacon. He's not their only goal. Even if Rebel, Jeremy, and I never thought beyond rescuing him and my mom, Dante, Draven, and Nitro had always intended to be in this to the end. They'd always intended to end this.

"We need a new plan," I say, fighting a yawn. Far out on the horizon, the first pink of sunrise is beginning to show. "But we've been up for going on forty-eight hours now. We need to go somewhere safe where we can get some rest and regroup."

Nitro jams his hands into his pockets and glances at Draven and Deacon. "I have an idea where we could go."

They exchange a long look, and then Draven nods. "The safe houses."

"What, like in witness protection?" I ask.

"More like villain protection," Nitro tells me.

I start to ask why villains need safe houses, but considering what I've seen, everything I now know, it doesn't seem so far-fetched. The only thing that seems far-fetched is that the heroes have managed to keep this whole program under wraps. That they've managed to torture and kill villains for years—without reason and definitely without trials—and no one has been the wiser. Well, no one but the villains, and nobody was listening to them.

"We have a dozen or so houses scattered throughout town," Draven explains. "The closest one is across from the cemetery on Ninth."

"Then let's go," Jeremy says.

The others nod, and for the first time we really feel like a team. Not like a bunch of strangers with a common goal, but a real team. One that trusts and respects each other.

It's a powerful feeling, which makes me think that maybe, just maybe, we have a chance.

We all pile back into the van, this time with Draven behind the wheel and me in the passenger seat. Two days ago I would have never thought I'd feel so comfortable in a vehicle with three villains, let alone trust them as much as I do. But a lot can change in a couple of days, especially when two days feel like two lifetimes.

As we drive back down the mountain, I start to drift. I'm locked in my thoughts and half asleep when Draven starts cursing, his voice low and calm despite the words pouring out of his mouth. The contrast is terrifying. I look up as he rolls to a stop in front of a house. In front of what used to be a house.

Now it's just a pile of smoking rubble.

CHAPTER 20

H oly shit." Nitro presses his forehead to the van window.
"They leveled it."

"Keep moving," Jeremy instructs. "If they destroyed this
location, it's likely that they'll have surveillance in place."

Draven squeals away. No one says a word as he drives on,
presumably heading for another safe house. This one is razed
too, as are the next six. The entire villain network has been
compromised.

"They're gone," Dante keeps repeating. "They're all gone.
The public records are clean. There was nothing to trace those
properties back to us."

"How could they know?" Nitro demands. "Only villains
knew about the safe houses."

"How many villains have they taken over the last few
weeks? How many have they tortured? Is it such a stretch
to think that some of them broke under the pain?" Draven's
voice is aching. It rips my heart to shreds.

"Was anyone—?" I can't finish the question.

"No," Dante replies. "They should have been empty."

"We only use them as a last resort," Nitro adds.

Draven slams both fists against the van's steering wheel,

lost in his rage and helplessness. I want to help him find his way out, but I don't know how.

Nobody says anything as Draven pulls into the shadowy corner of a grocery store parking lot.

"They've declared war." Draven pulls out his phone and tries calling his uncle again. Dante and Nitro are both texting people like crazy too. Desperate to find out if the empty safe houses are the only places that have been hit.

I wish I could do something, but I have no one to call. There's no one I can trust who isn't already in this van. But what scares me most is that the friends Dante and Nitro are calling and texting aren't answering.

I know it's crazy, but I try calling my house. Maybe if I wish for it enough, Mom will be home and fine. As I pull out my phone to dial, the screen flickers, then goes dark.

Stupid battery. I reach into the center console and pull Mom's cell phone off the charger. There's a notice on her lock screen. Two missed calls and three text messages from Dr. Harwood.

Did Kenna reach you? She sounded worried.

Where are you?

The scarlet phoenix flies at dawn.

What the hell? Dr. Harwood has always been a bit odd, but that last text is beyond weird. I don't have the time or energy to wonder at his cryptic message.

I swipe my finger across the screen so I can call home, but despite the full charge, Mom's phone flickers and goes dead too.

More weird.

Jeremy's computer starts beeping. He enters a few keystrokes and curses.

"What?" I ask nervously.

"They put out an APB." He looks up at Rebel, his face white. "Wait, no, it's more than that. Your father has issued a new directive."

Rebel scowls and grabs the laptop out of his hands. She reads the memo on Jeremy's computer.

"'Tier Red Protocol in Effect: All members of SHPD and ESF are hereby called to active duty. Report to headquarters for assignment. Use highest levels of caution. Villains to be approached with utmost prejudice.'"

"ESF?" Dante asks.

Jeremy explains, "Elite Superhero Force. They're like the Navy SEALs, Army Rangers, and police SWAT team all rolled into one."

Draven's hand clenches into a fist.

That's great. That's just…great.

"'Pursuit of the villains and traitors who compromised the ESH Labs facility tonight must be unrelenting,'" Rebel continues reading. "'They are to be found and apprehended at any cost.'"

A shiver of fear skitters down my spine.

"Among the wanted are three known offenders—villains Dante Cole, Draven Cole, and Nitro Willoughby. Also on the run are villain sympathizers Kenna Swift and Rebel Malone. All are to be treated with extreme prejudice under assumption of deadly intent. All League resources will be dedicated to this manhunt until further notice. "

Rebel chokes on a sob. I reach for her hand and for something to say, but there's nothing I can tell her that will make this better. I mean, it's one thing to know that your dad is a genocidal asshole, but it's another to know he's sending elite forces to apprehend his own daughter.

I'm still searching for the right words when the computer emits an ear-splitting beep in a sequence that sounds like old-school Morse code.

Jeremy grabs for his laptop. "No!" he shouts, typing furiously. "No, no, no."

"What?" At this point I'm afraid to hear the answer.

"Come on, baby," Jeremy says to his computer, "don't do this to me. Don't—*shit*!"

The laptop lets out one last beep, then goes black. Smoke puffs out from the vent in the back.

"That doesn't look good, mate," Nitro says.

"Thanks, Admiral Obvious. They just burned my laptop."

"They can do that?" Dante asks.

"They can if they send enough malicious packets to overwhelm my hard drive while disabling the cooling system at the same time." He slams the lid shut and throws the laptop carelessly into the back of the van. "Irreparable. They must have found my bug. There's no other reason to come after me so hard."

"So where does that leave us?" I ask.

"Screwed," Draven and Rebel say at the same time.

"Not entirely," Jeremy says. "They can't have found my rootkit, not this fast, which means it's still scanning for details about the secret location."

"But can you access the program?" My stomach clenches.

He smiles grimly. "All I need is a secure Internet portal and a computer that doesn't suck."

"We'll find you one," Draven promises.

"First we need to ditch the van," Dante says.

"For sure," Nitro agrees. "They'll be looking for it."

"And they'll be able to access the city closed-circuit cameras to find it," Jeremy adds.

"If they can access cameras," I say, "then can they see us? Wherever we go?"

He nods ominously.

We sit in stunned silence for several moments as we try to assimilate our new identities as public enemies number one. This must be what Draven, Dante, and Nitro feel like all the time. It's a terrifying sensation that will turn me into a whimpering mess if I dwell on it too much.

So I focus on the most immediate problem. The superheroes are searching for us and we need to get to safety. The only problem? How are we supposed to do that when every law enforcement agency in the state has our names and descriptions?

"Okay, here's what we're going to do," I say. "I'm going to run into this store and get whatever I can find to disguise our appearances."

"No," Jeremy interrupts before I can reach for the door handle. "I should go. I wasn't on the APB list, probably because I wasn't caught on camera tonight."

"But your ankle…"

He gives me a cocky smile. "I'll manage." He pulls out his wallet and checks the contents. "I've got twenty-four bucks. Anyone else have cash? No way am I paying with credit."

We all empty our pockets. After two days of living off the radar, it's amazing we have anything left, but Jeremy ends up with close to eighty dollars. We watch nervously as he limps across the parking lot toward the twenty-four-hour entrance. I swear I don't breathe until he limps out several minutes later with a shopping tote in each hand.

When he gets back to the van, Dante and Draven help him inside while Rebel and I grab the totes. Inside are stacks of baseball caps, a few University of Colorado tees and hoodies, and half a dozen pairs of sunglasses.

Nitro holds up the shades. "Seriously?"

"Facial recognition, man," Jeremy retorts. "And it's not like eighty bucks was going to buy you Ray-Bans."

We divide up the goods. The guys pull on the shirts and hoodies, while Rebel and I hide our hair under the caps. When we're as disguised as we're going to get, we look around at each other.

"Now what?" Jeremy asks.

"Where can we go?" Rebel adjusts her cap.

"We could find a motel," I suggest.

"Security cameras," Jeremy says. "Even if we pay with cash, again, facial recognition. The software will flag the five of you in seconds."

We sit in silence. Where *can* we go? We need to rest. We need to get Jeremy back online. And we need to figure out what to do next.

Reb shakes her head, like she doesn't want to say it. "I have an idea."

"We're all ears, babe," Dante tells her as he rubs a hand up and down her spine.

"It's a crazy idea," she explains, "but it would be the last place they would ever look. We should go," she says, wincing as she does, "to my brother Riley's."

To say you could have heard a pin drop in the van would be an understatement. Riley Malone, son and egotistical heir of the Malone family. The guy who takes the job of being a superhero way too literally. The guy who wears a freaking *cape* to the office.

Oh yeah, we should totally stay with him.

CHAPTER 21

That's not going to happen." Draven's tone is flat. He sounds completely immovable.

"My brother is the only one who might know about the lab relocation *and* might actually tell us where it is."

"Who are you kidding? The perfect son of Rex Malone would spill the beans on the top secret hero hideaway?" Draven sounds bitter, angry. "That's so not even in the realm of possibility."

"Well, I didn't mean we should just walk up and ask him," she says. "Jeez." She gestures to Draven, Dante, Jeremy, and Nitro. "Between the five of us, we've got some serious power. He won't be able to hold out against all of us. No matter how much he wants to."

It still hurts a little—okay more than a little—to be counted as powerless, especially by my best friend. Just because I can't move things with my mind or crush skulls with a thought doesn't mean I'm useless. I thought I'd proven that tonight. Thought I'd shown Rebel and the others that I'm just as important as the rest of them. It sucks that she still doesn't think I can contribute.

But now's not exactly the time for self-pity, not when

so much hangs in the balance. Deacon's life. My mother's freedom. Exposing the superheroes for their crimes. Saving the villains.

We don't exactly have room in our schedule for my existential crisis, no matter how overwhelmed I feel. Ignoring my hurt and embarrassment, I force myself to concentrate. To think logically about our next steps since emotions are running high right now. They're not reacting; they're overreacting.

"Don't you think Riley's is the first place they'll look for us?" I ask Rebel. "They know you and I are part of this now. It's not a stretch for your dad to think you'd go to Riley for help or—"

"I'm not going to that kiss-ass for *help*," Rebel says through gritted teeth. "I'm going to him because my dad trusts him. He knows everything that we want to know."

I hold up a placating hand. "I'm not saying he doesn't. But you didn't let me finish. Even though your dad knows you and Riley don't get along, your dad has to know that Riley would be the first one you'd try to break. You've made him cry more than once through the years."

"And I'll do it this time," she tells me determinedly. "If we get in and get Riley under control fast enough, he won't have time to notify anyone that we're there and we'll be gone before Dad can send in the troops."

"And if his security system alerts them first?" I ask.

"That's what I'm here for," Jeremy says. He's trying not to show it, but I'm pretty sure he's as concerned about this idea as I am. "I cracked into the lab's mainframe. You think I can't hack Riley's home security system? I'd be insulted if I knew you weren't just being Kenna—looking at every angle of the situation."

"How many angles are there?" Rebel demands. "We're out of options. Unless we find out where they're holding Deacon, it's game over. He's as good as dead."

Dante sags as if he can't handle the weight on his shoulders for one minute longer.

I know exactly how he feels. That, more than anything else, has me saying, "Maybe you're right. If we can get to Riley—"

"I'm not okay with this," Draven cuts me off.

I don't know why he's turning down what seems like the only solution to our problem. It's not like I don't agree it's a long shot, but it's the only shot we've got.

Nitro must be thinking the same thing because he jumps in with, "Screw it. Does anyone have any better ideas?"

Nobody has anything to offer.

Draven's eyes darken to nearly midnight. It doesn't surprise me when he yanks open the door and jumps to the ground, stalking away from the group with his head bent and shoulders hunched.

"We don't have any more time to argue," Rebel insists, her voice rising with fear and impatience. "We need to go now."

I hold a hand up to her to still her impatience and then go after Draven. He stiffens when my fingers brush against his arm. A part of me wants to pull him close and let him lean on me the way that we've been leaning on him for so much of this journey.

"I know this isn't a great plan," I begin. "But—"

"It's crap," he tells me, scowling at the ground.

"I know." I rub his shoulders. "I think so too. But we're out of options."

I give it a moment to sink in. "We need to get to Deacon.

Before he ends up in one of those body bags. If Riley is our only access, then we have to suck it up."

"Suck it up?" he asks incredulously. "You want me to put the fate of my cousin, my best friend, in the hands of a *hero*?"

I wince at his virulence. "You kind of already have, haven't you?"

He doesn't answer. Then, reluctantly, "I don't trust the Malones."

"Neither do I. Neither do any of us at this point. But you trust Rebel, right?"

Again he doesn't answer.

"Draven, come on. You know Rebel would never do anything to hurt Dante." I've only known for a couple days that they're together, and even I know that much.

"I know."

"You're starting to trust Jeremy," I press. "And I'm not technically a hero, but you trust me too."

He shrugs, not arguing.

"Then maybe we need to give this a shot. We've tried everything else. Besides, if it's a trap…if it's a trap, we can find a way out, right? Between the six of us, we can do a lot."

"I'm not worried about getting caught," Draven says, and I can tell from the slant of his shoulders and the clench of his fists that his comment is not bravado.

Besides, except for that heights thing, he hasn't been afraid once since this whole nightmare started—at least, he hasn't shown it. He's never hesitated. Never backed away from anything we've had to do.

So whatever this is—whatever's going through his head right now—has to do with something else, something inside him that I can't see, can't reach. There's so much about him that I don't know, and never has it been more apparent than right now.

I mean, we may be team members. He may have kissed me. We may have kissed *each other*. But on this, I'm flying blind.

"What are you worried about?" I ask.

He looks me straight in the eye. For a moment, I can see the real Draven, all alone behind the badass, beneath the layers of darkness and angst he wears like a second skin. And then it's gone. In its place is the smirk I'm coming to hate even as it makes me smile.

"I'm worried about busting into Riley's place and being blinded by all his glory and goodness," he tells me. "There's only so much superheroic awesome a villain like me can take at any one time."

He delivers the line well, his voice cocky and his sneer perfect. But there's a tension in him that says it's so much more than what he's letting on. And just like that, all the trust we've been building crumbles.

"When are you going to tell me the truth?" I demand. "I've done everything I could to prove that I'm committed to rescuing Deacon. That I deserve your trust. You don't have to trust Rex Malone, but when are you going to *really* trust me?"

"Trust you?" His look turns incredulous. "You locked me in a *refrigerator*."

I roll my eyes. "Be glad it wasn't the freezer."

"Seriously? That's the best you've got? No apology, no mea culpa? Just 'be glad it wasn't the freezer'?"

"I was trying to save your life! If you got caught—"

"If I got caught, it wouldn't be *your* problem."

I recoil. He's right. I know he's right. We're not together. We're not dating, despite the kiss we shared—well, kiss and a half. We're not even friends. We're barely acquaintances. But we *are* partners in this mission. We're on the same team. And if something happens to him… My stomach lurches violently. If something happens to him, I'm not going to be okay.

Only a few days ago, I despised villains as much as he clearly despises heroes. I've changed, but he obviously hasn't.

It hurts more than I want it to.

But this isn't about me or my messed-up feelings. It never has been. "Yeah, well, if you get caught it's everyone's problem. That's what it means to be part of a team."

He stares at me like I'm speaking Greek. And maybe I am. Because up on that roof, I stopped thinking of Draven as a villain and started thinking of him as a person I care about.

"Come on," I reach out a hand to urge him along. "I'm not sure this Riley thing is a good idea either. But Rebel seems to think it's the only way and I trust her. So let's just *suck it up* and get it over with."

He doesn't move. I expect more arguing, more sarcasm.

But then he does the most extraordinary thing. He grabs my hand. Slides our palms together. Interlaces our fingers.

Sparks race along my spine at the contact, and though I know it's the wrong time—that there are so many other things I should be thinking about right now—I can't help the way my breathing becomes shallow or my heart beats faster.

When he says, "So how far is Riley's place from here anyway?" I know I was right to trust him.

CHAPTER 22

The streets around Riley's condo are quiet, and we walk right up to the wrought-iron front gate before running into a camera.

"Shit," Dante hisses, as he spots the small circle at the corner of the roof.

"I've got it covered," Jeremy says, fingers already flying over his tablet. It takes less than a minute before he's nodding at the gate. "Go, Kenna. The camera's off-line and the gate is unlocked."

I reach out to push to open it, and sparks fly. An electric shock zaps up my arm.

"What the hell?" Draven snaps at Jeremy, pulling me away from the gate. "You said it was safe!"

My ex-boyfriend looks completely baffled. "It is. I mean, it should be."

"Obviously it isn't." He turns to me. "Are you all right?"

"I'm fine." My arm tingles a little and my muscles ache, but telling him that won't change anything, so I keep it to myself.

Jeremy spends a couple minutes working on his tablet as we all wait impatiently. "Try it now."

I reach for the door again. Jeremy's the best technopath I

know, and if he says the gate is safe, I'm going to believe him. Besides, it's not like I want anyone else to get electrocuted.

But Draven's having no part of it. He shoves me behind him and reaches for the gate. It's total he-man behavior and normally it would set me off, but considering how much he's already compromised tonight, it doesn't bother me. Especially when the gate swings smoothly inward under his touch.

He holds it open as we all file into the courtyard.

"Which apartment is Riley's?" Dante asks as we move between the shadows, trying to be as inconspicuous as possible.

Rebel and I point to the second-story, back-corner unit at the same time.

"You've been here before?" Draven asks me. The tone of his voice makes me feel weird, even though I'm not sure what the problem is. Is he...*jealous*?

"Once. With Rebel."

He doesn't say anything else, which just makes things feel weirder. I keep my mouth shut as we stand outside Riley's door and try not to look too nervous as Jeremy works.

This time it takes less than a minute before he's glancing up at us, a surprised frown on his face. "There's *no* security."

"What do you mean there's no security?" Dante pulls Rebel against his side where he can shield her with his body. "Rebel said her brother's security system is state of the art."

"Dad insisted on it when he moved out," she says. "Didn't want to take any chances with the heir to his superhero throne."

There's an unmistakable bitterness in her tone. She and Draven definitely share that sentiment.

"Yeah, well, there's nothing," Jeremy says. "I'm running every type of scan I have, and they're all coming up blank."

"What does that mean?" Draven demands as he once again angles his body in front of me like a shield.

I push at him a little this time. I understand he's being protective, but he needs to know I'm not his damsel in distress.

"It's dangerous," he hisses.

"Everything about this is dangerous," I snap. "And we don't have time to stand around. Either we're going in or we're coming up with another plan. But freaking out won't do us any good."

"She's right," Rebel says, shrugging off Dante. She reaches for the door handle. I remember from the last time I was here—when Rebel's mom made her bring by chicken soup when her brother was sick—that Riley's lock has a biometric keypad that requires a fingerprint for access. It shouldn't open for anyone but him, but when Rebel turns the handle it opens without so much as a whimper.

She's the first one inside. Dante follows behind her, so close that you can't see where he ends and she begins. Nitro goes in after them, then Draven, leaving Jeremy and me to bring up the rear.

I keep waiting for alarms, lights, sirens to go off, or for Riley to jump out of the shadows or for Mr. Malone and the goons in the gray suits to descend on us. But none of that happens. *Nothing* happens as we creep into the dark and silent condo.

"This is weird," Rebel murmurs softly.

Is it a trap?

We're all on alert. We tiptoe down the hall to Riley's bedroom, and there he is, sound asleep. It's not an act either—he's got some drool in the corner of his mouth.

"Wake him up," Draven snaps, as Jeremy scoops Riley's laptop from the floor by his bed and then disappears into the living room to get hacking.

Dante rips off Riley's covers and I can't contain my laughter. Seriously? *Seriously?* Riley's wearing Superman pajamas. Honest-to-goodness Superman pajamas, including a blue shirt with a red *S* in the middle of his chest.

"Are you kidding me with this?" Draven says. Then he shakes Riley awake.

Rebel's brother wakes up slowly...until his eyes focus in the dark and he sees three villains and his sister looming over him. I hang back, trying not to get in the way. Something tells me this is going to be all Rebel and Draven's game.

Riley squeaks when he sees them, jumping out of bed, arms extended in front of himself in a defensive move. "Rebel! What are you doing here? Who are these guys?"

"I need to talk to you."

"Dad says you're in trouble." He darts his gaze over the three villains in the room. He doesn't look happy, but then again, neither do they. Focusing on Rebel, he grabs her shoulders like he's going to shake her. "The Cole boys, Rebel? And *Nitro?* Have you lost your—"

"Don't touch her." Dante is between them in a flash, pressing Riley into the wall.

"She's my sister!" Riley answers indignantly, like it means something. Maybe it does. I don't know. I mean, he looks sincere and sincerely offended that anyone thinks he might hurt Rebel.

"And she's my girlfriend," Dante growls. "You don't get to touch her."

"Rebel!" Riley looks scandalized. "He's a villain. You don't know what he's capable of."

"We're *all* villains," Draven says. "And you're going to find out *exactly* what we're capable of if you don't start talking."

Riley stares at him, a little stupidly in my opinion, but Rebel's brother never has been the brightest bulb in the lantern, so it's not entirely unexpected when he answers, "We *are* talking."

Draven's fingers tangle in Riley's ridiculous pajama shirt as he hauls him to his toes. Riley is tall—almost six feet—but Draven is taller. And stronger. And obviously in control. "The heroes have a secret underground bunker. Code name Lima Whiskey. I want to know where it is."

Riley goggles at him. "I don't know what you're talking about."

Draven growls deep in his throat, and Riley's life flashes before my eyes.

Then Rebel shoves Draven and her boyfriend out of the way. "Come on, Riley. We both know that's not true. Tell us and we'll get out of here."

"What's wrong with you, Rebel? Have you been brainwashed? When Dad said you were with the villains who broke into the lab, I didn't believe him. But now?" He lifts his hands helplessly. "Think about what you're doing. This could ruin all of Dad's plans."

"Maybe your dad's plans need to be ruined," I say, shouldering my way past Draven. "Do you know what's been going on at ESH?"

"Kenna, I never thought I'd hear *you* say that!" Riley's eyes widen. "Aren't you supposed to be the reasonable one?"

"Like torture and murder are reasonable?" Nitro pipes up.

Riley looks at him blankly. "What are you talking about?"

"You know exactly what I'm talking about, mate. Everyone knows you're Daddy's number one pet." Nitro's hands have started to glow. "I bet you know a hell of a lot more than we can even begin to know about."

Nitro's fireball grows.

Riley notices the ball of green flame balanced on Nitro's hands. He shrinks back, looking more like wall art than a human being.

"You're crazy! And you need to leave before I call the SHPD." He looks at Rebel meaningfully. "Leave my sister and Kenna here, and get the hell out."

"We'll leave when you grow a conscience and tell us what we need to know," Draven says. "Until then, we're not going anywhere."

"No way. I'll never talk, no matter how much you torture me."

"Torture?" Draven asks incredulously. "We're not the ones with a history of torture. I think you've got us confused with your hero friends."

Riley narrows his eyes at him. "Heroes don't torture."

"They do," I blurt out. "I saw it at the lab. You don't know how important it is that you tell us where the bunker is. We have to find them or people are going to die. My mom could die, Riley. They took her. Heroes took her."

"Why would heroes take your mom? She works for us." He shakes his head. "We're the good guys."

"Good guys?" Dante tells him, stepping forward. "Good guys? Are you serious right now?" His fist slams into Riley's stomach and Rebel's brother doubles over.

Dante hits him again and again. Riley is no match for his strength or fury.

"Stop!" I shout, grabbing his arm, but Dante's out of control.

"Back off, man," Draven tells his cousin. "This isn't the way to get him to talk."

"Sure it is," Dante says. "Give me five minutes, and I'll get the little pipsqueak to give up everything he knows."

Riley drops to the floor, cowering. Dante pulls back a fist, ready to hit him again.

But Draven pushes his cousin away. "We're not like them. We don't do the things they do."

"Deacon." Dante sounds shattered.

"I swear, we'll find out where he is," Draven promises. "But not like this. Never like this."

He crouches next to Riley, eyes narrowed and hands clenched with restraint.

"Riley, tell him!" I urge. It feels like time is running out. "Please."

Images of Deacon flash before my eyes again. Riley's willful ignorance is killing me, knowing that my own ignorance let the superheroes get away with too much for too long. But I see the truth now, and even one person can make a difference. Right now, that person has to be me.

After all, only a few days ago I was just like Riley.

I try to reason with him. "We know that the lab has been shut down and the most important experiments have been moved to this bunker. We know that the heroes have been torturing the villains for—"

"That's not true!" Riley gasps. "We're not torturing them."

"Liar!" Draven shoves Riley hard enough that his head bangs against the wall.

"I saw it, Riley. I saw what they were doing, and I saw the dead villains—"

"Accidents," he says. "Mistakes. Every great program has them."

"Great program?" Dante repeats. He looks like he's about to lose his tenuous grip on his powers, and I don't blame him. Riley sounds completely insane—not to mention totally heartless. "You think torturing my twin is part of some *great program* like the Peace Corps? Like Doctors without Borders? Yeah, you guys are real humanitarians."

"You. Are. *Killing*. People!" Nitro adds.

"Not on purpose!"

Draven snaps. He doesn't touch Riley, doesn't hurt him, but he leans forward until his face is only inches from the hero's.

Riley's eyes widen as he recognizes Draven's power, sees those blue eyes crystallize with memory control. Rebel's brother squeezes his eyes tight, blocking out the psy access to his mind.

Draven doesn't seem to care. He leans closer, whispers something in Riley's ear. I can only catch a few of the words, but they sound a lot like *pain* and *own medicine* and *death is too easy*.

Riley shakes, trying to curl in on himself.

Clearly Draven doesn't need to use his power to break Riley's brain. And still he keeps talking, whispering new threats.

Riley holds a hand to his nose to staunch the sudden blood flow.

My mind screams at me that there has to be a better way,

but I don't move. I don't intercede. I don't do anything but watch as the darkness washes over Draven.

It's a tangible thing, which fascinates me even as it freaks me out. There's a shift in the way he holds his body, in how he transforms from fighter to predator. A sharpness in his eyes, a clenching in his jaw, a vibe that rolls off him, pumping electricity into the air, into me.

It frightens me, the way I'm responding to him. Not to mention the fact that the whole room seems as spellbound as I am, like we're all just waiting to see what he does next. I know Draven doesn't want to hurt Riley; he just wants to scare him. But I also know that if Draven loses control like he did with the guards, we'll all be sorry.

With that thought in mind, I crouch next to Draven and rest a hand on his lower back. A shudder runs through him.

His eyes are so dark and tormented that my insides twist with fear for him.

"Rebel, you know I can't tell them!" Riley says, eyes closed tight.

"Dad isn't the paragon you think he is, Riley," says Rebel.

"How would you know? You're too busy playing the wannabe villain to know anything about this family anymore."

She shakes her head disgustedly. "For a guy who spends all his free time pretending to be Superman, you sure need to work on your X-ray vision. You can't see shit."

Rebel glances over to the display cabinet in the corner of Riley's room, and a heartbeat later, a very expensive and authentic-looking statue of Superman flies off the shelf.

"Rebel, no!"

It hangs in midair for a moment, then falls to the hardwood floor, shattering into a billion pieces.

Riley gasps. "That was an original piece of artwork from DC Comics!" he screeches, crawling over to the mess and scooping some of the bigger pieces into his hands. "I paid a fortune for it. Why would you do that?"

"Because people's lives are at stake. Lives that are worth a whole hell of a lot more than this ridiculous junk." A collector's plate that has Batman and Robin on it floats off another shelf and wobbles in the air. "You better start talking, Riley."

"Don't you dare, Rebel!" He lunges at her, but Dante holds him back.

"You better make a decision," she taunts. "My power is feeling a little unsteady, and I just don't know how long I can hold it…"

"Darn it, Rebel!"

"Where's the bunker, Riley?"

"There's no way I'm telling a bunch of villains—"

"Whoops!"

The plate crashes to the floor and Riley whimpers. He actually whimpers.

Rebel doesn't give him a chance to say anything else before a three-foot-tall statue of Aquaman and a miniature Iron Man suit go crashing to the ground.

Riley watches in shock, but it's not until she actually grabs his pièce de résistance—original cells from one of the first Superman comic books—that he starts talking.

"Stop! Stop! Just stop. Please, Reb. Just stop."

She narrows her eyes at him, poised to tear the page in half. "Where's the bunker?" she asks again.

"In the mountains." Riley sinks against the wall. He looks sad, defeated. Maybe I should feel sorry for him—he did just rat out his father and everything he believes in. But it's hard for me to be sympathetic when Riley cares more for a bunch of collectibles than he does for the suffering of real, live people.

"Where in the mountains?" Draven demands. "The Rockies are pretty damn big."

"I've got it!" Jeremy crows from the doorway, Riley's laptop in hand. "My rootkit found the coordinates for the bunker."

"Thank God!" Nitro says, and before anyone can say or do anything else, he lets loose a fireball straight at what's left of Riley's extensive—and expensive—collection of comic book memorabilia. It whizzes past me, burns my arm, and then crashes straight into the display case.

Nitro laughs at the horrified look on Riley's face as the whole thing goes up in flames.

CHAPTER 23

For long seconds, we all stare at the burning display case in shock. Then several things happen at once. Riley starts screaming, Rebel dives for the bathroom and comes back with a fire extinguisher, and my shirtsleeve catches fire.

Draven runs for me. He knocks me to the floor and smothers me with blankets.

By the time he lets me up—after patting at every inch of me to make sure there's no latent spark anywhere—Rebel and Dante have the fire under control. Nitro surveys his work, seemingly pleased by the whole proceedings.

Jeremy ducks back into the other room just as Draven finally starts to breathe again.

"Are you all right?" he demands. He drags me into the bathroom and probes at the second-degree burn decorating the bottom of my bicep.

"I'm okay," I tell him. "I mean, it hurts, but I'm a lot better than Riley's comic collection."

Draven's eyes darken at my words. He presses a palm over my burned skin. "This is going to sting."

He's right. My arm erupts in pinpricks, like I can feel the burn on every nerve ending. It takes a little while, but eventually the pain fades. What was a bubbling, red second-degree burn moments ago is now nothing more than a patch of red and a couple of blisters.

Draven releases my arm, his head hung low. "I can't heal it all the way," he says quietly, "or they'll know."

I don't have to ask what he means. He already told me that his second power and his mixed parentage are a secret from everyone except Dante. "It's fine," I say, yanking down the remains of my sleeve. "It feels a lot better."

"Why was it so bad this time?" he asks. "When he hit you before, it wasn't like this."

I shrug. "The serum must be almost out of my system by now."

He moves closer, traces a fingertip over the back of my palm. "So your immunity is gone?"

Considering how much I've always resented those damn shots, I'm surprisingly emotional at the thought that my immunity—the one thing that made me more than ordinary—is gone.

"I guess so."

"When was your last shot?"

I shake my head and look up at the ceiling. "I don't know. Early last week sometime."

He storms out of the bathroom and stalks up to Nitro. He wraps his hand around his friend's throat and lifts him several inches off the ground.

Nitro claws frantically at Draven's fingers.

"Let him go," I say. "We've got more important things to worry about right now."

Draven's grip loosens enough for his friend to breathe.

"What the hell were you thinking, Nitro? It's like you didn't even try to miss her."

"She has immunity. Even if I winged her it wouldn't matter," Nitro gasps.

"She doesn't," Draven snaps. "Not anymore."

Riley looks up from his quest to rescue his prized possessions from the charred and foam-covered mess that was his once proud display case. "Kenna's immune?"

"Not anymore, idiot." Rebel smacks him on the back of the head.

"How was I supposed to know?" Nitro complains, hands in the air as if surrendering.

I'm not happy either—believe me, getting set on fire wasn't in the top one hundred things I wanted to do today—but there's nothing to get angry over. I mean, until we find my mom, there's nothing any of us can do about my immunity, or lack thereof.

"Don't worry. I'll be okay," I say.

"Don't worry?" Draven stares at me incredulously. "How the hell am I supposed to protect you if you can get hurt as easily as any other ordinary?"

"I didn't realize you *had* to protect me," I tell him. "I thought we were all supposed to protect each other."

"You have to admit, you need more protection than the rest of us. So you need to stop getting so offended every time I try to help you. I don't care that you're powerless. I swear, Kenna. But you don't seem to trust me. You want me to trust you, but this is a two-way street. If we're going to get through this, you're going to have to change that. Otherwise, we don't have a chance."

Maybe he's right. Maybe he's not. I don't know. But right now I don't have time to figure it out.

"Seriously," Riley says, oblivious to, oh, apparently everything else that's been said, "Kenna is immune to powers?"

I glare at him.

Rebel answers for me. "No. Her mom cooked up an immunity serum to protect her. It's a huge secret, but now everyone here knows. So she's never gone without the serum before, never tested to see how long it takes to get out of her system."

"That's against League regulations," Riley complains, and starts citing policies and procedures. "All research is supposed to be recorded and approved by the—"

"Yeah, well, torture is against regulations too, Riley," I retort, "and it seems like no one cares about that. As long as the public doesn't know that villains are suffering and dying on your father's watch, those who do know don't give a damn. Including you."

He glares at me. "You keep calling it torture, but it's not. Of course we interrogate villains who have been caught breaking the laws, but torture? We're the good guys. We don't torture anyone."

Before anyone can react to that ridiculousness, Jeremy calls from the living room, "Sorry to interrupt, but can you guys get out here? I want to show you what I've found. And pick your brain for a minute."

The last of Draven's temper mellows at the prospect of good news—or any news. He starts for the door. I grab him by the back of the shirt and tug him back.

"We can't leave Riley alone," I hiss at him. "He'll call Mr. Malone and ruin everything."

"We've got this," Rebel answers.

Sure enough, Dante and Nitro have Riley cornered, and my best friend is armed with a roll of duct tape.

Guess he won't be much of a problem after all. At least not for a while.

In the main room, Jeremy sits in Riley's breakfast nook. He's got Riley's desktop and laptop set up side by side, and there are blueprints on both of them. His phone also displays some kind of schematic I don't recognize. Whatever it is, they all seem to be linked because the pictures change as he works on his tablet.

"What's going on?" I ask, leaning over his shoulder to get a better look. "What did you find?"

"Give me a second," he says, not even glancing up from what he's doing. "Check out the blueprints over there." He gestures vaguely at Riley's laptop. "Breaking into the bunker is going to be ten million times harder than the lab."

That's not exactly a surprise.

"So, any ideas?" I ask.

"Maybe. Take a look at this entrance." He points. "It's the weakest spot. I think I can hack through the security there, and if I can—"

Suddenly, all four of the screens go wonky, blur, and disappear completely.

"What the hell?" Jeremy exclaims, jumping to his feet.

I back away, trying to give him room to work as Draven paces impatiently behind me. Within seconds, the screens are back to normal, the schematics once again prominently displayed.

Jeremy settles back down without another word. As I watch, the graphics on the screen start to move, like the layers are being peeled away.

He points at another spot on the screen. "If I have enough time, I can hack the external system, but they've got all kinds of closed-circuit security that can only be accessed from inside the bunker *and* they have half an army of hero backups. Security guards, check-in stations, locks that actually require keys to get in." He sounds scandalized at the old-school tech. "The good news is they aren't running at full capacity yet. We forced them to move earlier than they planned, so the complete protocol hasn't been implemented yet."

I lean down once more to get a better look, and the screens go nuts. Again. This time the whole array turns to static and the laptop actually shuts down.

"What the hell did you do?" Jeremy snaps at me impatiently.

"Me? I didn't touch anything!" I turn so he can see my hands clasped behind my back, a testament to my innocence.

"Then what is going on?" He goes to restart Riley's desktop, but nothing happens. It doesn't so much as let out a start-up whir.

"I don't know! Why would you think it's my fault?"

"Because everything was working fine until you got close." He sounds completely exasperated. "Unless..." He turns to Draven. "You don't have any tech-based powers, do you?"

"Definitely not." Draven lifts his own hands. "Dante's got wind and Nitro—"

"Trust me," Jeremy interrupts. "We've all seen Nitro's power. What about Riley?"

"He's a flyer," I answer.

Draven lifts his brows in reluctant amusement. "You mean those Superman pajamas actually have some basis in reality?"

"I know. It's ridiculous."

Jeremy checks his plugs and cords. "Then I don't know what the hell is going on."

"Figure it out," I tell him. "We've got to find a way into the bunker, and those blueprints are the only way!"

I'm so frustrated that I start pacing too. I walk from the kitchen into the living room. When I'm on the other side of the room, the computers spring to life again.

"What the hell!" Jeremy yelps. "This isn't normal."

But Draven is looking back and forth between me and the computers, a studious expression on his face. "Come here, Kenna," he says, holding out a hand to me.

I do as he says, and the second I get close to the breakfast nook, the computers freak out again.

"It's you!" Jeremy howls. "You're doing this!"

"How is that possible?" I demand. "I've never had problems with computers before. It must be something with how you linked everything together." I gesture vaguely at the web of cables.

"What? You think I made the mistake?" I've never in my life heard Jeremy sound so insulted.

"I'm not saying that. I'm just saying something is wrong and it can't be me—"

"Let me see your phone," Draven interrupts.

"My phone? It's on the fritz. Why?"

"Just let me see it."

By now, Dante, Rebel and Nitro have joined us and are staring at me like I've grown another head. So, under duress, I pull out my phone and hand it to Draven. He presses a button to turn it on. When he does, the screen goes static-y.

"Told you."

He walks away a few steps, tries again. This time, when he holds up the phone, the display works. Then he takes a few steps back toward me and the whole thing fritzes out again.

"What is going on?" I whine, totally frustrated.

I've worked with some of the world's most sensitive technology in my mom's lab, and nothing like this has ever happened.

"How long have you been taking those immunity shots?" Draven asks me as he hands back my now utterly useless phone.

"Since I was little. Why?"

"And this is the first dose you've missed? Ever?"

"Her mom is obsessive about those shots," Rebel tells him. "What does that have to do with this?"

"I don't know. Maybe nothing. But it's hard to imagine that the same day the immunity wears off, you start making computers go nuts. That's quite a coincidence."

"You think I emit some kind of electromagnetic field and the shots blocked it?"

He shakes his head. "I think the shots blocked some kind of *power* that you have."

"That's not funny, Draven," I snap. "I'm powerless."

"Are you?" he asks. "Or did the immunity shots block your powers the same way they blocked everyone else's?"

His words hit me like a freight train and my knees go weak. I reach out to steady myself and Draven—seeing me falter—starts toward me.

Just in time, it seems, because a second later, a bullet slams through the window and into the wall right where Draven had been standing.

CHAPTER 24

For a second, nobody moves. Then all hell breaks loose.
Draven dives for me. Dante dives for Rebel. Nitro—
God bless him—runs into the bedroom after Riley. And
Jeremy…well, Jeremy dives on top of his electronics. No
surprise there.

Another window shatters as a canister of some sort comes
hurtling through it. Followed by another. And another. Within
seconds, noxious smoke fills the apartment.

"Tear gas," Draven mutters bitterly in my ear. "We've got
to get out of here."

"But that's what they want! They're waiting out there."

"Yeah, well, they'll wait a couple minutes for the tear gas to
do its work and then storm in here. We'll be totally screwed.
We have to go. Now."

He's right. That's exactly what's going to happen. But
that doesn't make it any easier for me to do what needs to
be done. Not when my heart is pounding like a metronome
on high and I can't catch my breath. Not when I know
what the heroes are capable of, what the trouble outside
might bring us.

I can see it so clearly: Draven, captured by the herocs,

bloodied, beaten, destroyed. I want to grab on to him, to beg him to stay here where I might be able protect him.

But it would be a lie. There is no safety here. No safety anywhere, really. Not when Rex Malone is determined to bring us down.

My eyes water as hell rains all around us. It's an impossible situation. Stay until they come in, or run out into their trap. Through the pain I try to wrap my head around what I can do to save Draven and Rebel. Jeremy, Dante, Nitro. And myself. I'd really prefer to make it out of this alive, but there are no guarantees.

"Let's go," Draven yells, pulling me up into a crouch as a spray of bullets comes through the already-broken windows.

Dante uses his wind power to clear the air around us as much as he can, but there's a lot of tear gas in the apartment now and I can barely see.

"Where are we going?" I demand as Rebel and Dante fall in behind us. "How are we supposed to get out of here? Mr. Malone isn't stupid. He'll have people in the hallway as well as on the street. We're trapped."

"The roof?" Jeremy suggests hoarsely between coughing fits. He's crawling along behind us, his and Riley's laptops tucked into the backpack slung over his shoulder.

If we were smart, we'd surrender. Or at least barter Rebel and Riley for our own escape. Except that's not how this team works. Corny as it sounds, we're not leaving anyone behind, not even Riley. Once we're on the street, he can go his own way. But for now, we're all in this together.

"Not the roof," Draven says, his voice just as rough as Jeremy's. "They'll be waiting."

"Well, then, what the hell are we supposed to do?" Dante asks. He's got his hands up, creating a light wind tunnel around us in an effort to keep the tear gas at bay. It's helping a little bit, but the sound of boot steps in the hall tells us we're out of time.

"We've got to get the hell out of this apartment," Nitro says as he starts building a fireball.

I can see where this is going—he's going to end up accidentally burning down the whole damn building in his efforts to save us. It's late; people are sleeping. No way am I going to let Nitro set the place on fire and kill everyone who lives here.

"Draven, our only chance is the hallway!" I shout.

"You just said there will be guards out there!" Rebel gasps between coughs.

"There will be," I reply. "But it's our best shot. We've got this."

"How?" Jeremy demands.

"Rebel can move them with her mind. Dante can use his wind. I'll apparently make their electronics go nuts so hopefully they can't radio our position to anyone."

I'll do my best, anyway. Whatever it takes.

"They're hero SWAT, Kenna," Jeremy tells me. "They've got special suits that neutralize powers coming at them."

"How do you know that?" I demand.

"How do you not?" Jeremy replies. "I mean, come on. Your mom helped design them!"

"So what are we going to do then?" Rebel asks.

"I don't know." I'm out of ideas.

There's a loud crash in the hallway, and seconds later, something heavy slams against Riley's reinforced door. *Battering ram.*

"Screw this," Nitro says, walking over to the common wall between Riley's condo and his neighbor's. The slamming against the door gets worse. Nitro lets loose a fireball that blows a hole straight through the drywall.

"Come on!" he yells, stepping through. We all follow, though I grab the extinguisher and put out the smoldering fire on our way through.

The people who live in this apartment start screaming, but Draven gets them under control, fast, erasing their memories and sending them back to the safety of their locked bedrooms as I put out the last spark. I can't imagine what they're going to think when they wake up to disaster in the morning.

The battering ram pounds against the door while Nitro rips a hole in the far wall of this apartment and we follow him into the next. I do the fire-extinguisher thing; Draven does the mind-erase thing. Nitro gears up for one more hole—to the corner apartment—but just then, the pounding stops as Riley's door gives with a tremendous screech of hinges.

"Move!" Draven yells, and Nitro lets loose his fireball. This time, neither Draven nor I pause to mitigate the damage. Instead, we hightail it through the apartment.

We're aiming for the fire escape, when Riley says, "Corner apartments have attics. We can get up there—"

We don't have time to be shocked by his helpfulness.

Draven's already pulling at the cord hanging from the ceiling. And then we're climbing up the rickety ladder, Dante all but carrying Rebel up the stairs and Riley doing the same for Nitro in their haste to get ahead of our pursuers.

I can hear the SWAT team storming after us as I start to climb. Draven pretty much throws me up the ladder and into

Dante's waiting hands, and then he's there beside me, yanking up the ladder and wedging something against the door to keep it from being opened.

"We need to move," he barks. "They could start shooting at the ceiling—"

He breaks off as gunfire sounds below us, bullets slamming into the floor where we'd been standing only seconds before.

"Bugger it!" Nitro yells. "We're trapped!"

"We're not!" Jeremy says, pointing to a small skylight in the middle of the attic. "That leads to the roof."

"What if they're on the roof?" Rebel demands.

More bullets come plowing through the floor. "You really want to debate what-ifs right now?" Jeremy says.

"Not even a little bit." Dante reaches out and slams his wind into the small skylight. It shatters on the first blow.

"Give me a boost!" I shout.

God only knows what's on that roof, and I want to be the first one through the window. It's the most vulnerable position, the one most likely to get hurt, and I feel like it's my responsibility. I'm the one who convinced Draven that coming here was a good idea, which means it's my job to figure out how to get us out of it alive.

Draven doesn't agree. "*I'm* going up first," he tells me.

"No way. I am."

"Don't fight me on this, Kenna. You're not equipped to go up there on your own."

"Not equipped?" This isn't the time, but my blood begins to boil.

"Yes. You're—" He stops.

"I'm what? Powerless? Didn't we just decide I'm not?"

"An electromagnetic power will do you no good in this situation!" he whisper-shouts, his voice echoing in the narrow chute. "You don't even know how it works yet!"

"Seriously?" Jeremy says. "We're fighting about this? Now?"

"No," Draven, sounding dangerous. "We're not going to fight about this. Kenna, you have no immunity. You can't control your power yet. You need to just go with me on this. You need to let me protect you."

I know what Draven says makes perfect sense. Yet the idea of sending him out there like a sacrificial lamb... It makes me sick.

"You know it's the only way this is going to work," Rebel tells me softly.

I turn to look at her, and Draven takes advantage of my momentary distraction to climb through the skylight.

I brace myself for the sound of gunfire. It doesn't come. At least not from up above. From down below, it's still going strong and getting closer.

"Come on," Draven snaps a second later, reaching back through the skylight to help me up. "They're positioned at the stairwell, expecting us to come up that way. If we move, we can be gone before they learn otherwise."

Taking a deep breath, I jump and grab his hands. He pulls me up. Then Riley flies through the hole dragging Nitro behind him, with the others on their heels. Rebel wavers a bit, tapped out from using her powers so much. Until she gets some rest, she won't be able to reach full strength for a while.

We huddle behind some kind of large, rooftop air conditioner. It's the only reason the guards on the other side of the roof haven't seen us yet.

But as their radios start to crackle, I know it's only a matter of time before they figure out that they're watching the wrong spot.

"We need to split up," I whisper. "There's no way they're going to let seven of us waltz across the roof."

"You guys need to make your way over there," Draven says pointing to the edge of the roof where a fire escape ladder peeks up over the top. "Dante and I will distract them."

"I can fly someone down," Riley volunteers. "I can only carry one person at a time, but—"

"Like we're going to trust you," Dante sneers.

"Do you have a choice?" Riley counters. "They firebombed my apartment. They shot at us even though we're unarmed. It's like the heroes have gone crazy!"

Talk about an understatement, but this isn't the time for an I-told-you-so.

I turn to Draven. "You're not going to sacrifice yourselves for us."

"Damn right we're not," he agrees. "But we are going to give you guys a chance to get away."

"No—"

He places a hand on either side of my face. "Jeremy is Deacon's only chance." His mouth kicks up in that cocky half-grin. "We've got this. We'll rendezvous at the pedestrian bridge in Fine Park. You know where that is?"

His lips brush against mine, and then he's darting across the roof, Dante hot on his heels.

"Shit," Jeremy gawks. "Who ever heard of villains with a hero complex?"

"You have to go," Nitro says, shoving me and Rebel toward the fire escape. "You too," he tells Jeremy.

"What about you?" I demand.

"I'm going to cover your boys. Make sure they get out of here with that fearless skin of theirs intact. Besides, Riley's got my back, don't you, mate?"

"Yeah, I do."

Jeremy chokes a little. "Now I'm terrified for everyone."

"As you should be," Riley says, totally serious.

"Go!" Nitro says again. "And keep nerd boy safe at all costs. He's got the only way into that bunker!"

That's what finally gets us moving. Well, that and the gunfire. As we slither toward the edge, I turn to look over my shoulder as Nitro lobs fireballs at three attacking SHPD officers. Across the roof, Dante is using his power to kick up all kinds of debris in an effort to give Draven and him some cover.

I fight the instinct to turn back and help, but Nitro's words are playing in my head. Deacon and my mom are counting on us. Jeremy's the only one who has a chance of saving them, and Draven is trusting me to make sure he can.

A flash of superhero lightning whizzes over my head and crashes into a pole a few feet away from us. It's the catalyst we need. We dash to the roof's edge, heading for the fire escape.

"Let's go!" I jump over the edge and onto the top platform, then scramble down as fast as I can as a spray of bullets showers the parapet above me.

Seconds later, the whole thing shakes as Jeremy starts down after me. Rebel brings up the rear. We're moving fast, and then suddenly the fire escape ends a few feet from the ground. I climb onto the ladder at the end, which slides down under my weight and finally hits the ground hard enough that my teeth snap together. Then wait for Jeremy and Rebel to follow.

Another spray of bullets hits the side of the building right below Rebel's position.

"Go, Kenna, get moving!" she shouts.

But I'm not going without them. "Hurry, hurry, hurry," I chant.

The heroes are closing in.

As soon as my friends hit the ground, we start to run down the alley. But we don't get very far before we're swarmed by SHPD officers with guns and riot shields and weapons I can't even begin to recognize. We're surrounded.

"Shit!" Jeremy turns in a circle, looking for an opening.

Energy tingles under my skin as my fear and rage grow. Even without ever having felt it before, I know this is my power. Almost like it's itching to get out.

I let it.

I draw in a deep breath and then release the invisible hold. Almost immediately, the helmet of the officer closest to me crackles and starts to smoke. He drops his shield and yanks the helmet off his head, quickly melting back into the sea of officers.

I did that. *I* did that. For the first time, I know what power really feels like. And it feels amazing. I feel like I can take on the world. Like I can take on this whole SHPD squad.

Jeremy gapes. "Whoa."

"Get him out of here!" I shout to Rebel. "Use your telekinesis and get as far away as you can." I know she's tapped out, and asking her to move even one person is a lot right now, but she has to try. It's Jeremy's only chance.

"No. Not without you, Kenna!" he shouts, grabbing my arm. "I think I can use your power to get into the bunker."

Jeremy and Rebel exchange a look. His gaze is desperate. Hers is determined.

"Stay alive," she says, holding out her hands. She gives a telekinetic push, and then Jeremy and I are flying through the air on the last of her power.

"Rebel, no!"

I grab for her, but it's too late. We soar down the alley, high above the reach of the heroes, the pull of Rebel's power jerky and uncontrolled—like the last sputters of a car running out of gas. I'm screaming, crying, desperate to get back to Rebel, but I can't break her hold on me.

The SHPD closes in on her and then she screams, collapsing to the ground. They're tasing her. They're *tasing* her!

Desperate to help, I reach out with my power, hoping to disrupt the Tasers. But nothing happens. We're too far away.

Still she keeps us up in the air for one more second, two, three. One final push takes us higher, faster, and then we crash hard to the roof of a three-story building out of range of her power—and the heroes.

I leap to my feet. "We have to go back for her! We can't leave—"

"Damn it, Kenna, we have to go." Jeremy drags me away with more strength than I ever gave him credit for.

"No," I argue, wrenching at my arm. "We can't just—"

He whips me around. "We can't save Deacon and your mom without you. We can't stop any of this without *you*. Rebel understood. That's why she gave herself up."

I blink at him, tears welling.

"Don't let her sacrifice be in vain."

It takes several shallow, shaky breaths before his words hit home. If I am willing to put my life on the line, then should it surprise me that Rebel feels the same?

Jeremy opens the rooftop access door and waits for me to make my decision. But there's really nothing to decide.

And then we're running. So fast and so hard that my tears mingle with my sweat and I can't tell where one stops and the other begins.

CHAPTER 25

Jeremy and I don't speak as we run through the streets. We keep our path erratic, circling back a couple times. For once I am grateful for his obsessive paranoia. There's no way anyone could be following us.

The guys are waiting on the bridge when we arrive. Draven is pacing. Dante and Nitro stand over Riley, who is sitting on a bench, rocking back and forth like he's in shock.

Draven notices us first. His eyes widen as he realizes we're a group of two.

Dante turns, smiling and expectant...until he also sees that Rebel isn't with us. I expect rage. Fury. A wind storm of hurricane proportion. But instead, he looks oddly calm.

"Where is she?" he demands as we reach them.

I'm exhausted and out of breath, but I force out the words. "They have her. We were trapped, surrounded, and—"

"And you *left* her?" His fists clench.

Riley whimpers. "Rebel?"

A gentle wind whirls around me, so soft I can't tell if it's Dante or just the weather.

Draven moves to my side and places a hand at the small of my back.

"No," I tell Dante, fighting another round of tears. "She gave us no choice. She levitated us away and turned herself in," I explain. "She saved us so that we could save the others."

"I figured out how to get into the bunker," Jeremy explains. "And we need Kenna's power to do it."

"When exactly did you have time to figure that out?" Nitro asks.

Jeremy rolls his eyes. "Apparently being shot at is a powerful motivator."

Dante looks from me to Jeremy and back again. His lips press together as he processes Rebel's sacrifice.

"I'm sorry," I say, knowing it's not enough. "I'm so sorry."

He doesn't say anything at first, then shakes his head. "No. No, there's nothing to be sorry for. We made an agreement going into this that we'd do whatever it took. My girl was courageous. I won't take that away from her by blaming you for her decision."

His words are quiet, his tone resolved. But neither disguises the shattered look in his eyes.

Nitro claps him on the shoulder. Standing here, surrounded by my ragtag team, I know that Dante is right. Rebel knew exactly what needed to be done, and she put our mission above her own safety. I would have done the same thing. Any of us would have. Blaming myself for her act of heroism won't do us any good—and tarnishes her bravery.

I try to tell myself that she'll be fine, that her dad won't hurt her. But it's cold comfort. It's our job to see this through. We have to rescue Deacon and find my mom. And when they're both safe, we'll rescue Rebel too.

My fear and sadness transform into rage. Pure, unadulterated fury. At Mr. Malone for caring more about an agenda than his own daughter. At the heroes for their nauseating hypocrisy. At myself for blindly trusting them my entire life.

First my mom, and now Rebel. I understand how Draven, Dante, and Nitro felt that night when they broke into the lab: desperate to get a loved one back. Terrified of failing. I'd risk anything to see them safe again.

"Now," I say. "We go get them now. Before they have time to regroup, before they have time to prepare for an assault. We go in so hard and fast they won't know what hit them."

Dante nods.

Nitro rubs his hands together. "Now that's my girl."

Draven's arm tightens around my waist.

"I think we're all on the same page," Jeremy says.

We all turn to Riley. He looks small and scared, practically curled into a little ball on the bench. "They really took her?" he whispers. "*Heroes* took my sister?"

Nitro rolls his eyes with impatience, but I understand what Riley is going through. It's a lot to process. I went through the same thing just a few days ago.

"They did," I tell him. "Heroes took Rebel. On your dad's orders. Just like he ordered the torture and murder of countless villains. Just like I think he ordered the kidnapping of my mom."

Riley flinches. He looks at me like I'm the last life preserver on a sinking ship. His voice is barely a whisper as he asks, "It's all true? That wasn't just a rumor about a rogue group?"

I give him a sad half-smile.

His face breaks, just for a moment, and then he's pulling it all back under control. For once, maybe all that hero training will do him some good. Do *us* some good.

"Okay," he says, nodding, like he's building up steam with the movement. "How do we get her back?"

"First, we rescue Deacon. Rebel sacrificed herself so we could get to him, so that is our primary mission," I explain. "Then we find her and my mom and get them back."

"But to get to Deacon," Jeremy says, "we need wheels."

"How far are we talking?" Draven asks.

"Yeah, mate," Nitro says, cracking his knuckles, "where precisely is this bunker?"

Riley and Jeremy answer at the same time.

"Wyoming."

+ + +

Riley offers us the use of his car, but none of the guys except Nitro trust that it's clean. Jeremy insists that our powers—his and mine—would block any kind of tracking equipment, but there's another problem. Riley drives a Porsche. So while his car might get us to the bunker *fast*, it will only fit two of us. Three, if we put Riley in the trunk like Dante suggests.

Instead, Draven "borrows" an SUV from a mall parking lot. It seats all six of us with room for Deacon and a few more rescued villains. If there are more than can fit in a single car, we'll figure something out when we get there.

Nitro is at the wheel, which doesn't exactly make me super comfortable because he's never been the best at control and his idea of road-trip music is some kind of twangy electronica that makes my skin crawl. But since Draven and Dante are making plans for phase two, after we get inside, and Jeremy and I are hunched over his laptop in the third-row bench seat working on phase one, that left us with either Nitro or Riley. And with speed-limit-observing, law-abiding Riley at the wheel, it would take us at least twice as long to get there. Nitro has no problem keeping the pedal to the metal.

Jeremy insists we spend the drive studying the schematics for the bunker security system so that I understand exactly how he wants me to use my power.

My power. It blows my mind to think that I have a power. And not one I manufactured in a lab. One I was *born* with.

I have so many questions for Mom. Did she know I had a power? Did she know the immunity serum would mask it? What about *before* she developed the serum? Had she found another way to hide it even before that? She must have. But why did she keep it a secret all of these years? And that's on top of the questions about the heroes, the secret experiments. Did she know those were going on? Did she participate in them? But first we have to find her. That won't be easy.

Thanks to his rootkit and Riley's insights, Jeremy has pinpointed where in the bunker the heroes are keeping the villain prisoners. But nothing has turned up any clue about where my mom might be. Not a hint, not an intercepted email. Nothing.

Jeremy thinks that he might be able to get greater access from within the facility, penetrate deeper into the secure communications. Which makes getting inside all the more important.

"This relay box here," Jeremy says, pointing at a square on the screen, "powers the force field that shields the entrance."

I start to point to a similar square on the screen but pull back. I spent the first hour of the trip learning how to do meditative breathing to control my power just to be in the same space as Jeremy's electronics without sending them kaflooey. But touching them is another matter.

Jeremy had to modify one of his communications earbuds so that there'd be a layer of foam between it and my skin.

As part of my training, every few minutes I focus on the car's satellite radio and change it to a country station. The funny part is, Nitro has no clue that it's me.

"So if I focus my energy, my *power* on the relay," I say to Jeremy, "then we'll be able to get in?"

Jeremy gives me an almost condescending look. "Hardly." He zooms in on another section of the drawing. "We'll still have to make it through the fence, the guards, and the six-foot-thick titanium door."

"The fence is no worry," Nitro calls out. He lifts his right hand off the steering wheel, casually forming a bright-yellow ball of energy while he bobs his head in time to the music.

I scrunch lower in my seat. I'm not eager to meet up with another Nitro special.

I change the station again.

"And between the two of us," Dante says to him, "we can get the door out of the way."

Nitro grins into the rearview mirror. "Right on."

"Exactly," Jeremy says. "And if Draven can use his woo-woo memory power on the guards, *then* we'll be in."

I look at Draven, who is now on the phone, facing the window and completely absorbed in his conversation.

Honestly, I'm not worried about everyone else following through on their roles. I'm worried about using this power that, until a few hours ago, I didn't even know that I had.

They've had their entire lives to learn how to control and manipulate their powers. I've had an hour.

Fiddling with a radio is one thing. Anything to do with the most advanced security system in the world is another, way more terrifying thing.

"How do I shut down the force field?" I ask. "What if I accidentally send the entire facility into lockdown?"

"Yeah, don't do that," Jeremy says, but he hurries to explain before I can punch him in the arm. "We'll do it together, merging our powers."

I shake my head in a mix of awe and confusion. Rebel tried to explain once what merging powers feels like, but it didn't seem like anything I'd ever understand. Now, I'm about to experience it myself.

"My power," Jeremy explains, "will guide yours."

I nod. I close my eyes, trying to make myself believe.

I can do this, right? I'm a smart girl. I'm focused, and I have serious motivation to get this right.

I'm not sure I believe it though. Panic sets in. So many people are depending on me. Without my power to take out the force field, we're done before we even get in. I don't want to mess this up.

A warm, strong hand closes over mine. Draven. I open my eyes, and he's twisted around in his seat to face me.

"You can do this," he says with no hint of doubt.

"How do you know?" I whisper. "What if I can't?"

He gestures at Jeremy. "Switch with me."

Jeremy opens his mouth like he wants to argue, but he takes one look at my face and shoves everything but the laptop into his backpack. He climbs forward while Draven climbs back.

When Draven is settled into the seat next to me, he tugs me close against his side.

"You are the bravest person I've ever known," he tells me, quiet enough that no one else in the car can hear him over Nitro's beats, but forceful enough that I have no choice but to believe him. "You've never hesitated to take on each and every one of us when you thought we were in the wrong, even when you had no power."

I give him a wry smile. "I was immune," I remind him. "You couldn't hurt me."

"Our powers couldn't," he agrees. "But we could have. You thought we were villains who wouldn't hesitate to kill an innocent like you, and still you stood up to us."

I shrug and shake my head. Now he's making me blush.

"You don't let anything get in your way, Kenna," he says. "Powerless or powerful, there is no one I would rather have coming to my rescue."

"I—" I flick a glance at the rest of the team, but everyone is absorbed in their own preparations. "I'm scared."

"Good." He squeezes my hand. "You should be. We all should be. Are you going to let the fear stop you?"

As if that's even a possibility. "No."

"Then you'll do whatever has to be done. And so will I."

I rest my head on his shoulder. As the SUV eats up the miles between us and the bunker, my nerves gradually fade. Draven is right. He has been since this thing began. He's one of the smartest guys I know—also one of the best. The mark under his ear may claim him as a villain, yet from the moment I met him, he's been nothing but a good guy. Dark, broody, and a little dangerous, but still a good guy. No matter what happens, I know I can count on him.

I want him to be able to say the same thing about me. Especially now that the tables are turned. I reach into my pocket and pull out an elastic band. The last thing I need is my hair getting in the way while we're in battle.

Because as much as I don't want to think of it that way, we really are going to war. It's us against an enemy that outnumbers us both in manpower and technology. If ever there was a day to root for the underdog…. And the whole plan depends on me.

I have to succeed. There is no other option. I have to, and so I will.

We all will.

CHAPTER 26

From the hill overlooking the entrance to the bunker, you'd think it's an overprotected root cellar with a really big door. There isn't even a paved road in. Just the door, the fence, and a small team of guards.

Gaining access looks easy, but I know it won't be.

And once we get inside, it will only get worse.

"Guys, come on," Riley whines. "I can help. I can fly, you know."

He starts to float, and Nitro grabs him by the ankles and yanks him back to the ground.

"No way, golden boy," Draven says. "Just because you say you've had a change of heart doesn't mean you've earned any trust."

Riley turns to me. "Kenna?"

"Sorry, Riley," I say. "The team voted."

I don't tell him it was unanimous. Whether or not I believe his good intentions, I can't take the chance that I'm wrong. Too much is at stake. All it would take is one call, one signal. One mistake. Deacon's and maybe my mother's lives hang in the balance.

Dante walks toward Riley with the roll of duct tape in his hand and a satisfied grin on his face.

Riley blanches. "Come on, is that really—"

His words are cut off as Dante smacks a strip of tape across Riley's mouth. Draven yanks a pair of zip ties tight around Riley's wrists, and they heft him into the back of the SUV, securing him to one of the tie-down points in the floor.

Riley isn't going anywhere.

He looks like a prized pig, trussed up for dinner…in Superman pajamas.

Before he shuts the door, Draven snaps a quick pic on his phone. "This one's going on my wall."

"That's the relay box," Jeremy says, gazing through a pair of high-tech binoculars, which obscure half his face.

He really does have one of everything in his backpack.

I follow his pointed finger. Just inside the fence that protects the entrance is a big, gray metal box in the side of the mountain. It looks like the fuse box in my garage, only about fifty times bigger.

"We all clear on the plan?" Draven asks, pocketing his phone.

Dante cracks his neck. "Let's show these heroes what a team of villains can do."

"Villains *and* heroes," Jeremy corrects.

Dante rolls his eyes but nods in agreement. Sometimes it's easy to forget that this cooperation is new to all of us.

Draven moves in front of me. His face is dark and haunted. It's the same look I've caught glimpses of numerous times in the past few days. It's the real him. The guy beneath the cocky, badass façade.

The girl inside me, the one who is falling for him despite all the reasons she knows she shouldn't, melts.

"Kenna, if anything goes wrong in there—"

"It won't," I interrupt. My spine stiffens. "We're going to get Deacon back and find my mom."

His gaze doesn't waver. "But if we don't, if something goes wrong—"

"Don't." I press a finger to his lips. My best friend already threw herself on her sword for me today. I can't take the self-sacrificing thing from him too. Not when we're so close to rescuing Deacon and my mom. We need to stay positive.

He kisses my palm and gently pulls my hand away. Then he steps closer. There is barely any space between us now, his mouth a bare inch from mine.

He cups my face in his hands and pulls me even closer as his thumb strokes along my jaw. And then he kisses me. It's dark and sweet, edgy and soft, desperate and soothing. It's filled with secrets...and promises. And I want it to go on forever.

I tilt my head, open my lips on a gasp. Wait for him to take the kiss—to take us—deeper. Instead, he pulls away. He's so close that I can still feel his heart beating fast and frantic against my own. Can still feel his breath mingling, harsh and broken, with my own.

I move to kiss him again, but he stops me before I can do much more than slide my lips across his. "I'll do whatever I have to do to protect you," he murmurs.

"That's good." I force my voice to stay steady when every part of me is shaky. Shaking. "Because I'll do the same to protect you."

He reaches out to tuck a strand of hair behind my ear. "Kenna, that's not what I want. I—" Whatever he was going to say falls away when his gaze shifts to below my ear.

"What?" I put my hand to my neck, certain it must be bleeding or worse.

He pulls my fingers out of the way. "Kenna…" He looks at me and hesitates. "Your mark. It's…"

The realization hits me hard. My mark. The symbol that brands me as someone with powers has finally appeared. Not beneath the right ear, where a hero mark manifests, but beneath the left.

"H-how is that possible?" I ask.

My dad is a hero—*was* a hero. One of the most powerful of his generation. A *hero*. So how can I have the mark of a villain?

"Okay, guys," Jeremy calls out. "I'm ready."

I bite my lip, trying to hold in all of my questions, and shake my head. "Not now," I whisper to Draven. He nods. He looks almost as freaked out as I feel. But there will be time for that when everyone is safe. I can scream and shout and destroy everything around me later. Right now we have a job to do. We have villains to save and my mom to find.

Answers can wait.

Now, we attack.

I take a deep breath. "Let's go."

✦ ✦ ✦

Jeremy and I climb around to get as close to the relay box as we can without setting off alarms.

"What if I can't do it?" I whisper, hoping the soft confession won't carry over the earbuds. This brand-new power thrumming under my skin is like a long-caged beast ready to escape. Just because I can mess with a radio and make electronics go fritzy doesn't mean I have any real control.

Jeremy pulls me to a stop and gives me a look that says he knows exactly what I'm thinking.

"You will." Jeremy takes my hand in preparation for melding our powers. "*We* will."

I believe him. We might not have made the best couple, but we've always made a good team. Better even now, with romance off the table.

"I know you're scared, but you have to trust me." He squeezes our palms more tightly together. "I won't let you lose control."

I give myself a mental shake. Everyone else believes in me. Now it's my turn. "Okay," I say. "Let's go."

"Close your eyes," Jeremy tells me, and I comply. "You're going to feel my power tugging at yours."

Almost immediately there is an indescribable pressure. It feels like I'm on a starship in one of Jeremy's favorite sci-fi movies, speeding through the universe faster than the speed of light. Bright colors streak across my mind. Like I'm inside a computer, a video game.

"Where are you?" Jeremy muses, and I know he's not talking to me.

We fly past a rectangular object. "Ah yes," he says with a smile. "There you are, my pretty."

Jeremy pulls our joined energy back to the rectangle.

"This is it, Kenna." His grip on my hand tightens. "Just focus your energy like we practiced."

I take in a deep breath and let it out slowly. With every

ounce of concentration I've got, I try to send a pulse of power at the rectangle. Nothing happens.

"You can do it," he encourages.

"You've got this, Kenna," Draven's voice says in my ear. "Just imagine it's Rex Malone's face."

I laugh a little and try to conjure up that picture. Then I imagine blowing him to bits with every last drop of newfound power I've got.

The rectangle explodes in a shower of sparks.

"That's it!" Jeremy shouts. "Okay, V team, we are go for entry."

I open my eyes. "V team?"

He shrugs. "I'm still working on it."

We run for the gate. By the time we get there, the guards are unconscious on the ground. Dante and Nitro's combined powers send the massive, supposedly impenetrable—but not to a pair of powerful and powerfully motivated villains—door flying off into the mountains.

It's now a race against time. We may have blown our way into the building, but the alarms are already squealing.

Jeremy takes my hand and I feel his power guide mine to another hidden security system within the bunker. When he gives me a squeeze, I pulse my power and the alarm goes silent. I'm getting the hang of this.

"That won't last for long," he says. "This system has redundancy after redundancy."

As we pass the unconscious guards on our way through the blown-off door, I snatch bright-white ID badges from two of the guards' belts. Then we're inside. We sprint through the entrance hall to the first fork.

"Here's where we split up," Jeremy says.

"Take this." I shove a security badge into his hand. "And don't forget to find out where they have my mom."

"Left turns all the way," he reminds me, and then takes off for the security office as the rest of us head into the labyrinth that we hope will lead to Deacon.

Until Jeremy takes control of the internal security system, it's up to me to keep us off the heroes' radar. It takes all of my concentration to create an electromagnetic bubble around us so we're invisible to the cameras and motion sensors.

We wind through corridor after corridor, moving ever deeper into the mountain. I'm not a huge fan of caves. I don't even want to think about how much rock and stone is above and around us right now.

We pass door after door, hallway after hallway. Around every corner I expect to run into guards, the Ray-Ban brigade, or maybe even Mr. Malone himself. But there's no one here.

I can't help feeling relieved. My power must actually be keeping us off the sensors.

Then we round one more corner and I crash dead on into another body. Like a cartoon pile-up, no one behind me can stop in time, sending me tumbling forward into the other person.

Draven grabs me by the shoulders, yanking me back to my feet.

He leans down, like he's ready to do his mind trick on the person on the floor. Before he does, I get a look at our crash victim.

"Dr. Harwood?"

"You know this guy?" Draven asks.

I feel the villains at my back, like a shield of protection. As if the balding, old scientist is a threat.

"I do." I reach down to help Dr. Harwood to his feet. I ask him, "Are you okay?"

His eyes are a little wild as he dusts off his lab coat. "You shouldn't be here."

"I—" I open my mouth, start to explain. Dr. Harwood is one of the good guys, one of the *real* good guys. If he knew what was going on here, he would help us. Would try to stop it. I know he would.

But before I can get out another word, he interrupts. "I've been trying to reach you." He glances around nervously, then whispers, "I know where your mother is."

"You do?" I feel Draven's hand on my back.

Dr. Harwood turns around, startled. "There isn't time now. I will email you what I know."

"You have no idea how much I—"

Before I can thank him, he grabs my hands in his. "And when you find her, tell her—" He leans in close. "This is important. You must remember exactly."

I nod, totally confused, but he seems to need the confirmation.

"Tell her," he whispers, "*the scarlet phoenix flies at dawn.*"

I blink. That's the same weird message he'd texted to my mom's phone.

"What does that—?"

Dr. Harwood backs away. "I must go. Tell her," he says, then turns and rushes down the hall. He calls back over his shoulder, "Tell her."

I look from Draven to Dante to Nitro. Each of them seems just as confused as I am. What the hell did that mean?

"That guy is bonkers," Nitro says.

"Ya think?" Dante replies.

"What do you think—?" Draven starts to ask.

I shake my head. Now isn't the time. My mom isn't here, but Deacon is. We'll get him out, and then we can worry about Dr. Harwood's cryptic message.

We start running again.

"Hey there, Team Hillain," Jeremy's voice echoes in our ears. "The security system is mine."

"Hillain?" Nitro snorts.

"Yeah, it's a mash-up of hero and villain," Jeremy explains.

"We get it," Dante says. "It sucks."

"Team Vero?"

I laugh despite myself. "Vero?"

"Well, what would you call us, smarty-pants?"

"Team Stop-screwing-around-and-tell-us-if-we're-close," Draven snaps as we speed around another corner.

Jeremy clears his throat nervously. "Yeah, you're—oh shit!"

My relief goes up in smoke.

"What?" I demand.

"Nothing, they're just—hold on." A strange scraping sound screeches through the earbuds and then Jeremy is back. "Okay, that should hold them off. You're three turns from the holding area. There's a secure door in the way." He hums for a second. "Well, there *was*. You can thank me later."

Sure enough, we race around the third turn and find ourselves face-to-face with a reinforced glass door. Looks like the indestructible plastic Dr. Valik developed a couple years ago. It really is a masterpiece. And if it wasn't the only thing between us and rescuing Deacon, I would love to take a moment to admire its practical application.

There is a keypad on the wall next to the door.

"The light is red, Jer," I say.

I know before I try the door that it's going to be locked. Without the access code, the security badge won't help. I try it anyway. No luck.

I send a pulse of power at it, but nothing happens. I close my eyes, start to send a second pulse, but before I can, Jeremy squawks, "Don't, Kenna! Whatever you're doing just made you visible to the sensors. Focus on holding the electro-shield."

"No worries." Nitro holds out his hands. "I can take care of this."

"No!" I dive for him an instant too late.

His dark-orange fireball hits the door and ricochets. We both slam into the wall. The fireball barely misses us as it bounces down the hall.

Nitro grins at me sheepishly. "Thanks."

"Thank me later."

"Come on, geek boy," Draven teases. "I thought you *owned* the system."

"I do. I just—oh wait, I see." The sound of rapid clicks transmits over the earbuds. The keypad light turns green. We're already piling through the door when Jeremy says, "Try it now."

"We're in," I tell him, and then words escape me.

We'd been too focused on the door itself to look inside, but now that we're here, the holding area is not at all what I expected. I'd pictured something like a city jail, cells with steel bars and stainless toilets.

This is more like a hospital ward. The room is the size of a football field, with several rows of metal beds, tables really, running down the middle. The wall on one side is decorated with an array of hand and ankle cuffs hanging from the wall. The handcuffs are positioned about six feet off the ground and the ankle cuffs at least three feet apart. Anyone chained to the wall would be spread-eagle and helpless.

I don't let myself imagine what this space would look like if it were at full capacity. Thankfully, today, the tables and the cuffs are all empty.

The other wall is a series of cells, like something out of a futuristic quarantine area. The doors are made of the same indestructible plastic as the one that deflected Nitro's best weapon.

The guys take off, looking for prisoners. The first few cells are vacant, and as clean and sterile as the rest of the room. The fifth cell down is occupied. Not by Deacon, but by an older woman, probably my mom's age, with fiery red hair.

She jumps to her feet and pounds on the door. It looks like she's shouting at the top of her lungs, but the door is soundproof. I try to tell her that we'll be back. From the frantic look she's giving me, I'm not sure she understands.

I pass more unoccupied cells, then reach one that contains a young boy, no more than seven or eight, who is huddled in the corner, "Jeremy, we need to get these cells open now."

"I can't," he replies.

"Not good enough," Draven growls. "Try harder."

"It's not a matter of trying harder," Jeremy explains. "There's no external access. It's a completely closed system. The release mechanism must be somewhere down there."

"What am I looking for?" I ask.

"It could be any kind of panel," he begins. "Keypad, card reader, biometric—oh shit. They're in. I'll meet you guys down there."

I wince at the sound of an explosion and shouting, followed by Jeremy panting as he presumably flees the security room.

Dante has pulled ahead of Draven and Nitro. About half-way down the room he yells.

"Deacon!" He pounds against the glass.

The guys are at his side in a flash. I force myself to remain calm, to think clearly. *Work the problem, Kenna.*

I start looking for the access panel. Something, anything that looks like it might make these doors open. As I loop back to the first occupied cell, the redheaded woman gestures wildly. She's pointing between her cell and the next. I move closer to examine the wall. There is an area, about four inches square, that has a more iridescent quality than the rest of the plastic.

I glance at the woman and she nods vigorously. She forms a rectangle with her fingers. A rectangle the size of a security badge.

I fumble in my pocket to pull out the stolen badge and then swipe it over the iridescent area. The whole front wall of her cell slides up.

"I've got it!" I shout. I turn to the woman. "Are you okay?"

"I'll be fine," she insists, waving me away. "Go. Open the rest."

I run, flicking the badge over the scanners on each cell, the woman following fast on my heels. When I pass a cell with a small, limp body collapsed on the floor, the woman steps inside. I keep going.

Seven occupied cells in all, and Deacon's is the last. The guys are still beating on the door when I swipe the card. I'm overcome with emotion—pride, relief, joy—as Dante drops to his knees and cradles the moaning Deacon in his arms. Draven gives me a tight nod. No matter what happens from here on out, at least the twins have been reunited. At least we've done that much.

The rest of the cells are empty, and we've all congregated around Deacon when Jeremy bursts into the room.

"Half the hero army is on my ass!" he yells, waving a tablet he swiped from the security office. "They were hiding themselves, just like we were, so I wouldn't know they were here. They must have known we were coming. We've got maybe sixty seconds before we're trapped."

I look wildly around the room. There is no other way out. If they catch us in here, we're never leaving.

CHAPTER 27

I turn from Jeremy to face the rest of the team. Dante has Deacon cradled in his arms. He's as close to lifeless as a living person can be. Draven is holding the young boy, Nitro is struggling to keep a massive villain upright, and the red-haired woman is carrying another unconscious prisoner—a girl about my age, with dark hair and ivory skin. The other two villains look pretty rough, but they're upright.

We don't have many options. This little parade won't be able to move quickly. Certainly not fast enough to stay ahead of an entire hero army.

"Here's what we're going to do," I say, forcing confidence into my voice. "Jeremy is going to lead everyone out in the most direct path possible."

"That's crazy," he says to me, pointing at the diagram on his stolen tablet. "There are dozens of soldiers between us and the exit."

"I'll take care of them."

"No." Draven closes the distance between us.

"It's the only way," I insist. "I'll draw the heroes away so you can get everyone to safety."

He shakes his head.

"They won't hurt me." At least I hope they won't. "I'll be fine. And you'll be free to rescue Rebel and keep looking for my mom."

Without a word, Draven walks over to Jeremy and hands him the terrified child. While Jeremy struggles to hold on to both the tablet and the kid, Draven exchanges a look with Nitro. Nitro nods in return.

"I can't let you do that, Kenna," Draven says, turning back to me. "If they're going to have a chance at finding Rebel and your mom, at taking down the whole corrupt system, you and your power will be way more useful than mine."

My eyes sting, both with fear and pride. I've never been so important before, so valued. And I've never been put first. Ever.

"It's the only thing that makes sense." He steps close again and presses his palms to my cheeks. "There isn't time to argue. I'm going to create the biggest distraction they've ever seen. And you're going to scramble the cameras and walk this crew right out the front door."

I shake my head, wanting to find some other way to get us *all* out safely. But I've got nothing.

His lips brush against mine for the briefest second and then he races for the hall. We crowd into the doorway, listening to the echo of his voice as he sings at the top of his lungs.

"We've got to go," Jeremy says, holding the tablet up where he can see the screen. "They're heading for Draven, but as soon as they realize he's alone—"

"They'll come for us," I finish. I take the boy from Jeremy's arms. Then I draw in a deep breath and focus a sphere of electromagnetic energy around us that will deflect the sensors but still allow Jeremy to access the plans on the tablet. It's amazing how quickly I'm getting used to this power. How… *natural* it feels. "Let's move."

Jeremy takes the lead. I nudge Dante and Deacon out behind him, followed by the other villain prisoners. Nitro's next and I bring up the rear. We've worked hard to get this far. I'm not leaving anyone behind.

Draven's voice, still transmitting over Jeremy's communications system, echoes in my ear. He's singing, shouting really. Banging on walls. Anything that will draw hero attention onto him.

Then, all of a sudden, he stops.

My heart stutters.

The sounds of soldiers shouting and some kind of scuffle carries though my earpiece. Then Draven's voice again, this time full of mockery and loathing.

"Well, well, well," he taunts, "if it isn't the king of the superheroes himself."

I gasp. This won't end well.

"Have you located the others?" Mr. Malone booms.

"No, sir," a young man's voice responds. "They aren't showing up on any of our scans."

Because of me. I'm keeping us off the radar. As much as I want to help Draven, he would never forgive me if we *all* ended up prisoners.

"Silly villain," Mr. Malone says so clearly it's almost as if he's speaking directly into my ear. "Did you really think it would be that easy?"

"Did you really think we would just blindly walk into your trap?" Draven throws back.

I can practically see the arrogant smile on Mr. Malone's face. "It looks like you did."

"We're almost there," Jeremy says. "Just a few more turns."

I'm not sure if he says it for us or for Draven.

"If I inherited one thing from my father," Draven says, his voice taking on a cryptic tone, "it's the art of misdirection. Make a big fuss over here, and no one will notice what's going on right under their own noses."

Mr. Malone scoffs. "Is your father a magician?"

"No," Draven replies with such sickly sweetness that it makes my stomach lurch, "he's the President of the Superhero League."

I stumble and nearly face-plant into the concrete floor. Only a supreme feat of recovery keeps me from squishing the boy in my arms between me and the concrete.

Mr. Malone? Mr. Malone is Draven's father?

My mind races as I think back over the past few days, trying to put the pieces together. They fit amazingly well. Draven's icy-blue eyes that look so much like Rebel's. Like Riley's. Like Mr. Malone's. His second power that had to come from a hero parent. His seething resentment when we were interrogating the "golden heir," Riley.

The affection he has for Rebel. I thought it was only because she was Dante's girlfriend, but maybe it's more than that. Maybe it's because she's his half sister.

If Mr. Malone's stuttering reaction is any indication, he is just as stunned to learn that Draven—a villain—is his son. Well, *half* villain.

Wow. Just wow.

Once again, Draven is right. This is pretty much the

biggest distraction ever. There's no time to process all of this as we round the corner, racing the last stretch of hall to the main door.

A line of guards is stationed at the entrance, weapons drawn and pointed at us. Before they can even take aim, Nitro sends a wall of fire at them so fast that they scramble to get out of the way.

Despite having his arms full, Dante somehow manages to whip up some wind to push the line of fire away, keeping the guards at bay while we run through.

We race past the fence and up the hill to where our stolen ride is waiting.

"We're out!" Nitro shouts as he pushes the big villain up the hill in front of him. "We're clear."

The way he says it, Nitro sounds as if he's giving a signal. I turn to ask what's going on, when Draven shouts, "Now, Quake! Now!"

The ground starts to rumble. It feels like we're standing on the edge of an erupting volcano. With the small villain boy clutched in my arms, I look around wildly. Quake, Nitro's bigger, badder brother, stands at the cliff overlooking the bunker about a hundred yards from the SUV. With his hands spread wide and his massive muscles bulging. He looks like The Incredible Hulk trying to levitate a building. Except what he's doing is much harder. He's actually leveling a mountain.

"No!" I set the boy down and start to race back to Draven.

I don't get more than five steps before I collide with a solid wall of wind.

"Let me go!" I scream at Dante.

But he doesn't let up. And it's too late. I stare, helpless—more powerless than I have ever felt in my life—as the mountain crumbles. A geyser of dust and rubble shoots out through the opening to the bunker. Then everything is quiet.

There is nothing left but a pile of boulders.

"Nooooo!" I wail helplessly.

I drop to my knees, put my head in my hands. My mind can't form coherent thoughts. *Draven. Trapped. Crushed. Dead?*

This was his plan all along. His hushed phone call was to Quake; the look he exchanged with Nitro was a promise. He knew it would come to this, and he was willing to give himself up so we could escape.

I'm caught between sobbing and shouting. *How could he do this? How could he do this?*

A moment later, a *lifetime* later, I feel hands on my shoulders.

"Kenna," Dante says, his voice just sympathetic enough to piss me off, "we need to go."

"Don't." I shrug off his hands. "You knew."

He doesn't deny it. "Hero reinforcements will be here soon," he says, half pushing, half carrying me to the car. "We can't be here when they arrive."

This must be what shock feels like. I'm numb. In the SUV, someone buckles my seat belt. Someone else starts the engine.

We speed away, leaving behind the one person who made me feel powerful. Leaving behind a piece of my heart, crushed beneath a mountain.

CHAPTER 28

TWO DAYS LATER

At this altitude, even in the heart of summer, I have to bundle up to go outside and gather wood for the fireplace. The abandoned cabin we found high in the mountains between Boulder and the Wyoming border isn't just off the grid, it's practically nonexistent. No power, no heat, and only icy well water running in the plumbing.

I thought Jeremy was going to have a heart attack when he found out there was no Internet. But with a few mini solar panels—what *doesn't* he have in that damn backpack?—and something he calls a signal replicator, he's connected enough to keep tabs on the situation.

I dump my armful of wood at the base of the porch steps to chop later, carrying a few pieces inside.

When I walk back into the cabin, everyone is gathered around Jeremy at the dining table. He's holding the tablet he swiped from the security office at the bunker.

"Kenna, you need to see this." He attaches something to the tablet and points it at the wall, and then the wall lights up with the projection of a newscast by XSHN, the superhero news network.

The newscaster is on location at the entrance to the bunker, or as the caption at the bottom calls it, ESH Lab Beta Campus. Though large boulders are strewn around, a hole has been dug out of the rubble. And standing there on top of the pile, like a miner rescued from a cave-in, is Mr. Malone. He looks as perfectly pressed as always. As if nothing had happened. As if a mountain hadn't literally crumbled around him.

Draven stands at his right. My heart practically leaps out of my chest to see him there, alive. Unhurt. But definitely not safe.

His head is encased in a powers-neutralizing helmet— technology I didn't realize they'd actually perfected. Titanium manacles encircle his wrists and ankles. The crawl at the bottom of the screen announces the capture of one of the most dangerous villains in the super world.

I brace myself on the table to remain upright as the newscaster's voice echoes in the small cabin.

"The villain infiltrator was brought in by none other than Rebel Malone, daughter of League President Rex Malone."

"What?" I gasp.

Beside me, Riley's jaw drops. "Rebel did that?"

The camera pans to Mr. Malone's left. Standing there in a floral sundress and minimal makeup is Rebel. Only she doesn't look like the Rebel I know. She looks like the daughter Mr. Malone always wanted. A robot. Her eyes are blank, her face carefully neutral, and her spiky blond hair has been washed and styled like she's trying for a beauty pageant. It is all kinds of messed up.

"We all have my daughter to thank," Mr. Malone says, clapping a hand on Rebel's shoulder, the model of a proud father.

The fact that she doesn't flinch is proof enough that something is way, way wrong.

"What happened to her?" Riley asks.

Dante slides him an angry glare. "Your father happened."

Mr. Malone continues, "Rebel single-handedly infiltrated the band of traitors, led by this monster here. Those traitors are responsible for the deaths of heroes and villains alike, as well as numerous terrorist acts that have been kept secret for reasons of superhero security."

Dante slams his hand on the table. "Bullshit."

"That's crazy," I agree. "No way Rebel was working for her dad."

Mr. Malone looks so grossly proud. "Due to the heinous nature of this villain's crimes, I am personally calling for a speedy trial and execution."

I clap a hand over my mouth to hold back the nausea that washes through me. *Execution? He wants to execute Draven? Even knowing he's his son?*

The broadcast cuts back to the newscaster and Jeremy turns down the volume. For several minutes, we all just sit there, staring at the projection of the pretty, dark-haired newscaster.

After everything I've been through in the past week, Mr. Malone spouting lies about Draven and Rebel is too much.

My blood boils at the thought of him distorting the truth about two people who acted so selflessly to free villains from the heroes' vile and illegal experiments. The. Last. Straw.

Over the last week, I've learned a lot about myself. I've learned a lot about the world I thought I knew so well. Heroes can be evil. Villains can be good. Draven has shown me that more than anything else. And if that's true, that bad guys can do good things, then it's time to show the hypocritical heroes that the opposite is also true. With the right motivation, a good girl can do a bad thing. A lot of bad things. Especially if she has a little villain blood in her veins.

I stare at the video projection, focusing all my fury and disgust on the pixelated version of Mr. Malone. "We're going to take them down," I say. I turn back to the group gathered around the table. "We're going to find my mom. Free Draven. Get Rebel. And bring the heroes to their knees. Every last one of them."

ACKNOWLEDGMENTS

A powerful thank you to…

…our agents, Jenny Bent and Emily Sylvan Kim, for the tireless and dogged support for this project from the very beginning, and for all the emails, phone calls, and text messages that remind us that we're not in this alone. We love you and are grateful for you every day of our lives!!!!!

…our editor, Annette Pollert-Morgan, for loving this world and these characters as much as we do, for tightening the boat into racing shape, and, most importantly, for the stick figures, doodles, and swoony hearts. Your enthusiasm is so, so appreciated.

…the entire team at Sourcebooks Fire for giving us a chance to tell our story the way we needed to tell it. Our baby is in excellent hands.

…our friends, Shana Galen, Andy Hertzenberg, Sophie Jordan, Emily McKay, Alison Packard, Crystal Perkins, Shellee Roberts, and Sherry Thomas, because you make this writing thing so much more fun than if we were doing it alone.

…and our many inspirations: Jacob Appelbaum, Suzanne Collins, Cory Doctorow, Neil Gaiman, Glenn Greenwald, Stan Lee, Laura Poitras, Aaron Sorkin, Rob Thomas, Edward Snowden, and Joss Whedon, for telling amazing and important stories…and inspiring us to try to do the same.

READ ON FOR A SNEAK PEEK OF

RELENTLESS

CHAPTER 1

This is Jeremy Abernathy, reporting for Superhero News live from the SHN Power Chopper high above the super-villain trial of the century. Today, Rex Yes-I'm-a-Sadistic-Tool Malone and the entire Yeah-We're-Even-Bigger-Tools Collective are opening the trial of obvious-threat-to-humanity Draven Can't-Operate-a-Computer-to-Save-His-Life Cole—"

"Jeremy…"

"Ah, and there's our intrepid on-the-ground reporter now," he continues, his voice coming loud and clear through my earbud. "The situation is probably pretty tense down there in the courtroom. Let's check in with Draven's lady-love, the incomparable Kenna Who's-the-Ordinary-Now Swift. Kenna?"

Someone else on our system snickers. Probably Nitro.

I clench my teeth and fight the urge to respond.

"Radio silence," Riley reminds the group. "Before a big event like this, my dad always scans radio frequencies for chatter in case—"

Riley's feed cuts out abruptly.

Nobody says anything else, not even Jeremy, and I have to admit I kind of miss his annoying banter. Especially since I know he's just trying to keep me from freaking out. Not that it's working—but that's more me than him.

I've never been more freaked out in my life. And after growing up as an ordinary in a world of people with super-powers, that's saying a lot.

Of course, that was back when I still thought the heroes were the good guys. Back when my life still made some kind of sense.

Back before my mother went missing, my best friend gave herself up to the heroes, and my boyfriend got captured and put on trial for crimes he would never commit.

All of which have led me here to League Headquarters.

Into the lion's den.

My fake SHN credentials got me into the courtroom where Draven is to be tried, a courtroom currently filled with superheroes who are loyal to the League. Which means I'm surrounded by them, fenced in on all sides as I sit here waiting for the trial to start, terrified with each moment that passes that one of them will recognize me beneath my disguise.

I'm channeling my inner Rebel, taking a page out of my best friend's book with a platinum-blond wig, hot-pink lipstick, and a blouse unbuttoned just enough to keep secu-rity from looking too closely at my face. A face that's been plastered on wanted posters throughout the superhero and ordinary worlds in the twelve days since we destroyed the secret superhero bunker—which means if anyone recognizes me, I'll be on trial right next to Draven.

Mr. Malone doesn't think too highly of villain sympathiz-ers, as he calls us.

And if that isn't bad enough, me getting caught would be

the least of our problems. Because we all know that Draven isn't about to get a fair trial. No villain would, but especially not Draven. He's about to become an example. He's Mr. Malone's greatest capture to date, and he knows secrets Rex would kill to keep quiet. He *is* a secret Rex would kill to keep quiet. Which means once this farce of a trial is over, Draven's a dead man.

Unless we break him out of hero custody today. Now. Before this mockery of a trial can even begin.

Which is exactly what we plan to do—as long as I don't get identified before they bring him into the courtroom.

Just the thought has me slouching in my seat as Rex walks through the door in full superhero regalia—a crisp white jacket with red epaulets, decorated by an array of red, blue, and yellow ribbons over his left pec and a big, gold League badge over his right. As president of the League, he also wears a waist-length royal-blue cape.

It's the first time I've seen him dressed like this in years, and if things weren't so serious right now, I'd probably laugh. Riley's Superman pajamas make so much more sense now. Is it any wonder he grew up with a serious hero complex? Or that Rebel has an antihero one?

Shoulders back and head held high, Rex climbs the steps to the raised stage at the front of the room, walking between the long, curved table and the wall of floor-to-ceiling windows. He knows everyone in the room is looking at him, and he is totally eating it all up.

The rest of the Collective follows behind him, all ten of them walking single file, wearing matching white uniforms and smug expressions. I can almost smell the arrogance rolling off them.

Anger wells within me when I think that these are the men and women who've been holding Draven and Rebel for a dozen days, probably the same men and women who've been holding my mother for even longer. When I think about what happened to Draven's cousin Deacon in their hands, when I think about how he still wakes up at night screaming even though he's safe and free and has begun to heal, it both terrifies me and makes my blood boil with rage.

I'm going to make every single one of them pay. For what they've done to my friends. For what I'm afraid they've done to my mother. For what they've done to too many people. I'm going to make them suffer like they've made so many villains suffer in the decades since the Collective came to power.

That's not something I ever thought I'd say, but I'm not the same Kenna Swift I was three weeks ago. I'm done playing their game, done following the rules that the supposed good guys wrote.

If I have anything to say about it, Rex Malone is *never* going to hurt anyone I care about ever again. And he sure as hell isn't going to kill Draven. Not today.

Not ever.

Suddenly, the lights in the courtroom flicker.

"Hey, something's interfering with my feed," the SHN camera guy next to me complains. He fiddles with his wires like there might be a loose connection.

"Steady," Jeremy warns softly, and I force myself to take a calming breath to tamp down my power and keep it from leaking out before we need it. Wouldn't want the superhero world to miss a single second of the coming spectacle.

It took a few days to get past the brain-freezing shock at

the very idea of having a power. After a lifetime of feeling powerless, that was hard enough to process. But the realization that followed was even worse. The mark on my neck declares me not only a super, but a *villain*. Mom is an ordinary. Which means my dad, one of the most famous and revered heroes of his time, was actually a villain.

I have so many questions and no one to ask.

Rex stops at the middle of the stage, behind the long, curved table, and pulls out the centermost chair. After he sits, his minions do the same, filling in the seats on either side of him.

I slouch deeper as he braces his hands on the table in front of him and surveys the courtroom. I'm sitting in the very back row, with dozens of spectators between us, so he would need supervision to be able to identify me in this crowd, but I'm not taking any chances. The self-satisfied smirk on his face—an expression that says he is king of this domain and that he likes it that way—sends chills down my spine.

When he's done looking over all of the reporters, security guards, and special guests, he nods to the back of the courtroom and makes a come-forward gesture.

For a second I think he's seen me. *Recognized* me.

My heart stutters and I can't breathe. I feel the walls closing in. My mind starts racing, desperate to figure out how I might get out of this alive, how we can still make the plan work.

Then I sense movement at my side.

Everyone in the courtroom turns to look as Rebel Malone, my best friend and Rex's black sheep daughter, walks slowly, timidly, toward the front. And if I'm channeling Rebel today, then she's channeling Lilly Pulitzer. Dressed in a pale-pink floral dress that skims her knees and a white cardigan, with her usually spiky bleached hair dyed brown and swept back from her face by a matching pink headband, she's as far from the girl I know as Rex is from the hero I once thought he was.

She walks right by me without noticing me. Not that I'm surprised, considering she'd have to look around to see me. And she isn't. At all. She's staring straight ahead, almost like she's hypnotized, following her father's every direction as she finally makes it to the front of the courtroom and sits down in the empty, reserved first row.

Rex nods in satisfaction, then clears his throat before leaning down to the microphone that sits on the table in front of him.

"First of all, I would like to thank the members of the press corps for being here today," he says, nodding toward my section.

I pretend to scratch my forehead.

"The Collective and I have always prided ourselves on our openness and transparency, which is why you have all been invited here to report on this very important trial."

It takes all my self-control not to laugh out loud—or to scream my outrage. Because a month ago I would have been just like everyone else in this courtroom. I would have believed him without a second thought.

But now I know better. Despite Mr. Malone's insistence that secrets are for villains and that everything he and the hero squad do is aboveboard, the truth is that the superheroes keep deeper, darker secrets than I ever imagined possible.

Their supposed openness and transparency is a joke. Or, more accurately, a travesty.

I wait for him to give his usual song and dance about how

evil villains are. But he must be as anxious for this trial to start as I am—though for totally different reasons—because he doesn't say anything else. Instead, he gestures to the door on the opposite side from where he and the Collective entered.

I turn to look just as two massive hero guards enter, then turn back and level nasty-looking weapons at the doorway. From this distance I can't tell if they're ordinary guns or special weapons from the hero armory. Freeze rays, maybe, or even disintegration guns.

I wouldn't put it past them, wouldn't put *anything* past Mr. Malone.

Then Draven appears and I huff out a relieved sob-laugh. I can't help myself.

He looks exactly like the last time I saw him, streaming live on an SHN broadcast. He'd already been captured by Mr. Malone, was already a prisoner of the war we'd just begun to fight. He was standing with Rex and this new and unimproved version of Rebel that I don't recognize, the three of them in front of the mountain Draven's pal Quake had turned to rubble at his behest while Draven was still inside. All part of a plan the villain boys had cooked up to make sure that Jeremy and I got out safely with the rescued prisoners.

Draven's wrists and ankles are cuffed and connected by shackles that only a super with laser vision could cut through. He's wearing a baggy prisoner's jumpsuit—only instead of bright orange it's solid black, with the word *VILLAIN* painted in white across the chest. And on his head sits the powers-neutralizing helmet.

The helmet isn't one of my mom's inventions, but her research helped them develop the technology that can block a super's powers by creating some kind of Faraday cage for the brain. It may look like a giant fishbowl with a metal collar, but that's no ordinary glass. Tempered, shatterproof, bulletproof, and laced with invisible wires that carry a high-frequency signal that inhibits all powers, it's the perfect villain containment unit.

Draven won't be messing with anyone's memories or manipulating anyone at a genetic level—not that anyone in this room knows about his second power—as long as that helmet sits on his head.

But other than that, he looks surprisingly okay. The heroes had Deacon for only a few days, and they nearly destroyed him. In the twelve days since I last saw Draven, my imagination has drummed up all kinds of worst-case scenarios for the state he would be in when he finally got to stand trial.

I let out a tiny sigh of relief that he appears to be unharmed. We're not any closer to home free, but just seeing him looking...like *him* makes me feel better. Then again, just seeing him makes me feel better. Knowing that it's only a matter of minutes before I get to hold him, talk to him, make sure he really is all right.

Two more guards trail him into the courtroom and prod him across the room as the first two keep their guns aimed at him. I can't tear my eyes away. I need to see every move he makes, need to count every breath he takes to reassure myself that he's really okay.

"Though Draven Cole is only eighteen years old, he is a grave danger to superheroes everywhere," Mr. Malone proclaims to the rapt audience. "He is the nephew of the notorious Anton Cole, the most dangerous supervillain of our times, whose very existence is a threat to our way of life."

Ugh. Cue the fear-mongering propaganda. Everyone gasps appropriately.

"And more than that," Rex continues, "he is responsible for massive destruction at two top secret hero facilities, as well as assaulting numerous SHPD officers and security guards and kidnapping both Rachel and Riley Malone." Another gasp fills the courtroom at this revelation. "Today he must answer for his crimes."

I want to stand up and shout that Draven's only crimes are being born a villain—and having the misfortune of being Rex Malone's bastard son. Something I'm sure the head of the Superhero Collective doesn't want the rest of the hero world to know. But doing so would ruin everything, so I force myself to stay silent.

The quartet of guards push Draven up the steps to the raised box at one end of the table. As he climbs the stairs, he looks out over the crowd. He might be Rex's son, but instead of having the smug look his father wore when he surveyed the room, Draven looks defiant. Scornful. Like he's daring them to judge him.

His gaze skims over me, past me, and then darts back, the mask he wears faltering for just a moment.

I bite my hot-pink lips to keep from grinning. I want him to know that we have a plan, that we're getting him out of here, but I can't risk drawing any attention.

Even from this distance, I can see Draven's icy blue eyes narrow behind the glass helmet. He shakes his head, a small, barely perceptible movement that only someone who was desperate for any kind of communication would even notice. Still, I get his meaning, loud and clear.

Don't. Try. Anything.

Too bad. We're getting him out whether he likes it or not. I give him a solid nod.

He's scowling when he looks away, but he does nothing else that might alert the heroes to my presence. Exactly as I expected. He may not approve of the fact that I'm here to rescue him, but he won't risk doing anything that might get me hurt.

"Today we make history," Mr. Malone drones on as the four armed guards take up offensive positions behind and next to Draven. "Today we bring to justice not one but *two* supervillains. Draven Cole and—"

He points again at the still-open side door, and like viewers at a tennis match, we all turn to see who will walk through next.

"A supervillain even more treacherous, even more duplicitous." He makes another gesture, and two more guards enter, repeating the turn-and-aim procedure we just saw used on Draven. "A supervillain who lived among us as one of our own, even as she worked to destroy us."

The second villain walks through the door.

"No!" I whisper-shout. Then slap my hands over my mouth to keep from blowing my cover. Not that I should worry. Every hero in the room had a similar reaction to seeing a familiar face wearing villain blacks.

"Kenna, who is it?" Jeremy asks in my earbud.

I shake my head, unable to speak. Unable to process what I'm seeing.

Two more guards follow, prodding the second villain to another raised stand at the near end of the table. I watch, in shock as my mind struggles to make sense of this. I might be having a stroke.

"A woman we all believed to be fighting for the right, a woman in whose hands we placed the lives of every super-hero, recently revealed as a filthy villain mole." Mr. Malone gestures at the second villain as she defiantly refuses to sit. "Dr. Jeanine Swift."

My earbud explodes with shocked protests from every member of my team.

"Dr. Swift?" Riley whispers.

"Your mom?" Jeremy asks. "No way."

No way. My thoughts exactly. No freaking way my *mom* is a *villain*. Not when she's the most respected—and decorated—scientist the heroes have ever had.

This has to be a setup. They must have found out about her ultrasecret projects—like the immunity serum she made me take for years—or that I used her ID to find the secret sublevel at ESH Labs where they were torturing villains. Mr. Malone is setting her up as a villain so he can get rid of her. That's the only explanation that even remotely makes sense.

Mom is an ordinary like me. Well, like I used to be. Or like I thought I was before I found out the truth.

But there she stands, hands and feet shackled, head encased in a helmet identical to the one Draven is wearing. A helmet she helped design.

The villain label stamped across her chest stands out like a neon sign.

When Mr. Malone orders her to sit, she turns to spear him with the most venomous glare I've ever seen her give. And when she turns back around, I see the mark beneath her ear. A *villain* mark.

A mark I know never used to be there.

Oh God, I've been so stupid.

The truth overwhelms me—as does the betrayal.

All those years she was dosing me with immunity serum, supposedly to protect little, helpless me from superpowers, when in reality she was trying to hide my villain power from everyone, including myself. I thought she was protecting my dad, hiding the power that would reveal his villainous truth. But she wasn't hiding only my powers. She was hiding hers too.

Mom is a villain. Which means…what? That I got my villain mark from her? Was Dad really a hero, or was he hiding his villain identity too?

My hands shake with the enormity of the revelation. And the enormity of the hurt welling inside me. How could she do this? Why would she do it when it meant crippling both of us for so long?

"Our plan is screwed," Nitro says.

"Not necessarily," Jeremy argues. "We just have to adjust."

"How do you expect us to get Draven *and* the doctor?" Nitro asks. "Riley isn't actually Superman, you know. And neither are you."

"We're getting my sister too," Riley adds.

"Yes," Dante says, for once agreeing with Riley. "There's no way we're leaving here without Rebel."

"Did you miss the part where there is an entire *room full of heroes* who are going to try to stop us?" Jeremy scoffs. "It will be hard to grab two people, but three is practically impossible."

"You better figure out how to make it possible," Dante tells him.

"We don't even know if robot girl wants to be rescued," Nitro argues.

"Don't call her that," Dante growls.

"Forget getting out of the courtroom. I calculated our escape plan based on a six-person payload," Jeremy continues. "I can't guarantee it'll work with eight."

"Well, it has to," Dante replies. "We're not leaving any of them in hero hands."

Jeremy doesn't let it go. "But once Kenna does her thing, I won't even be able to—"

"Enough," I snarl through clenched teeth. "We're getting them all, and we're going to do it as planned."

"Are you sure?" Riley asks. "What if we—"

His voice gets muffled, like someone clamped a hand over his mouth. That's my team.

"Ready when you are, Kenna," Dante says.

I allow myself one more minute to think. To breathe. To convince myself that things are about to get very, very awesome. I ignore the voice in the back of my head that tells me the other option is that things could get very, very bad. But it doesn't matter. We have to try. Like Dante said, we're not leaving them behind. None of them.

"In one of the most extensive investigations in League history," Mr. Malone explains to the rapt courtroom audience, "we discovered that all recent security leaks can be traced back to the efforts of the woman who was, for so many years, our most trusted scientist."

That's total bullshit. At least some of the leaks are thanks to his own daughter, and he knows it.

But as I look at Rebel, I see her smiling blandly and applauding this revelation. Who *is* this girl? What have they done to my best friend?

"In fact, Jeanine Swift has been working with Draven Cole for months now, giving him access to the Elite Superhero Labs—access that led to extensive damage to property and personnel. Because this case is so unusual," Mr. Malone continues, "I will be presiding over the trial. We will first present the case against the villains and then will open the floor to opposing testimony from sympathizers."

Right. As if anyone under Rex's command would be willing to risk his wrath by testifying on behalf of my mom, let alone Draven. No one speaks out against Mr. Malone. Ever. Probably because when they do, they end up here. In the middle of a farce of a trial. Nothing else makes sense. How else could otherwise decent people let him get away with what he does?

And despite a lot of evidence to the contrary, I have to believe that some heroes are good. Jeremy is a hero. So is Rebel. And maybe my dad too—one of the best, or so they say. I can't believe they're the only ones.

"I will begin," he continues, "by reading the full charges against the defendants."

"On my count," I whisper.

I give myself an extra couple of seconds to commit the layout of the courtroom and location of our targets to memory. Rebel is a dozen rows in front of me, across the aisle. Draven is at the right end of the judicial table. Mom is at the left end.

Mr. Malone is dead center.

There are ten members of the Collective.

Sixteen armed hero guards.

More than fifty heroes who are either here to present in the case or to witness the trial of the century firsthand.

Plus the real SHN camera crew that is capturing the entire spectacle for the rest of the hero world to see.

Our goal is to get our people out with as little collateral damage as possible. I mean, if Rex and the rest of the Collective get caught in the crossfire, none of us are going to shed a tear. Well, Riley might. But the rest of us think they can all go to hell. The spectators and the camera crew are mostly innocent bystanders, and the last thing we want is for them to get hurt.

Mr. Malone begins reading the trumped-up charges. "Draven Cole, you are hereby charged with the following offenses—"

"Five," I whisper.

"—conspiring against the Superhero League—"

"Four."

"—destroying the manipulation lab at the original ESH Lab facility—"

"Three."

"—destroying the underground facility at the Lima Whiskey location—"

"Two."

"—using your psy powers to turn Rachel Malone to your side—"

"One."

"—and participating in the genocidal plans of your uncle, Anton Cole."

"Go," I whisper as I flick the switch in my earbud that Jeremy says will keep it functional through what's about to happen.

I stare straight at Rex as I concentrate my power with my mind. In the days since I discovered I have the power to affect electromagnetic forces, I've been working hard to learn how to control it. And the first thing I learned is that emotion makes it stronger.

So I keep my gaze trained on Rex and let all of my anger and rage toward him build. It isn't hard when I think of everything he's done. I let it build, bottling up inside me like a bubble ready to burst.

Then, in one breath, I release it all.

My very own electromagnetic pulse, strong enough to fry every electrical circuit in the building.

The lights in the courtroom flicker and then go out.

"Hey, my camera just died," the SHN camera guy next to me says.

"So did my phone," responds the reporter he's with.

At the front of the courtroom, Rex scowls and rubs at his ear, like he's trying to make it pop.

I place my hands over my own ears to protect them from the coming pressure change. Rex pushes to his feet, like he knows something is up, but it's too late.

The windows behind the judicial table explode into a million tiny shards.

And the courtroom erupts in chaos.

ABOUT THE AUTHORS

One fateful summer, Tera Lynn Childs and Tracy Deebs embarked on a nine hour (each way!) road trip to Santa Fe that ended with a flaming samurai, an enduring friendship, and the kernel of an idea that would eventually become *Powerless*. On their own, they have written YA tales about mermaids (*Forgive My Fins*, *Tempest Rising*), mythology (*Doomed*, *Oh. My. Gods.*, *Sweet Venom*), smooching (*International Kissing Club*), and fae princes (*When Magic Sleeps*). Between them, they have three boys (all Tracy), three dogs (mostly TLC), and almost fifty published books. Find TLC and the #TeamHillain headquarters at teralynnchilds.com. Check out Tracy and the #TeamVero lair at tracydeebs.com. Hang out with all the heroes, villains, ordinaries, and none-of-the-aboves at heroagenda.com.